WAITING FOR NOTHING

AND OTHER WRITINGS

TOM KROMER

WAITING
FOR NOTHING
AND OTHER WRITINGS

EDITED BY ARTHUR D. CASCIATO
AND JAMES L. W. WEST III

THE UNIVERSITY OF GEORGIA PRESS
ATHENS AND LONDON

© 1986 by the University of Georgia Press,
Athens, Georgia 30602
Waiting for Nothing © 1935 by Emogene Kromer
and Katherine Kromer Judy
Waiting for Nothing was originally published
by Alfred A. Knopf in 1935
and was reissued by Hill and Wang in 1968.
Rights to Kromer's works are held by Emogene Kromer
and Katherine Kromer Judy.

Designed by Sandra Strother Hudson
Set in Linotron 202 ten on thirteen Trump Medieval
The paper in this book meets the guidelines for
permanence and durability of the Committee on
Production Guidelines for Book Longevity of the
Council on Library Resources.

Printed in the United States of America

95 96 97 98 99 P 8 7 6 5 4

Library of Congress Cataloging in Publication Data

Kromer, Tom.
Waiting for nothing, and other writings.

Bibliography: p.
I. Casciato, Arthur D.   II. West, James L. W.
III. Title.
PS3521.R57A115 1986 813'.52 85–8610
ISBN 0-8203-2368-3

Illustrations on the title and part-title pages are
from issues of the *Pacific Weekly* published in 1936.

CONTENTS

v

CONTENTS

PREFACE

THIS VOLUME brings together for the first time the known
writings of Tom Kromer (1906–1969), a Depression-era author whose one book, *Waiting for Nothing*, is a classic account of vagrant life during the thirties. *Waiting for Nothing*
was published by Alfred A. Knopf in 1935; it was favorably
reviewed but did not sell through its first printing. Though
severely ill with pulmonary tuberculosis, Kromer continued
to write for two years after publication of his book. He produced several short stories, three book reviews, and some mis-
cellaneous pieces, and he began a novel with the working title
"Michael Kohler." After 1937, he ceased writing and disappeared from the literary scene.

For many years Kromer has been one of the mystery men of
the American thirties. Students of the period have known little about his life, either before or after publication of *Waiting
for Nothing*. That book was reissued by Hill and Wang in 1968
in its American Century Series but went out of print in 1977.
The present collection is meant to make Kromer's work available in relatively permanent form. The biographical/critical
Afterword and the other scholarly matter at the rear of this
volume present most of what is known about Kromer's life
and literary career. We suggest that the collection be read in
the order in which it is arranged—Kromer's writings first,
then the ancillary materials.

WAITING
FOR NOTHING

TO
JOLENE
WHO TURNED OFF THE GAS

CHAPTER ONE

IT IS NIGHT. I am walking along this dark street, when my foot hits a stick. I reach down and pick it up. I finger it. It is a good stick, a heavy stick. One sock from it would lay a man out. It wouldn't kill him, but it would lay him out. I plan. Hit him where the crease is in his hat, hard, I tell myself, but not too hard. I do not want his head to hit the concrete. It might kill him. I do not want to kill him. I will catch him as he falls. I can frisk him in a minute. I will pull him over in the shadows and walk off. I will not run. I will walk.

I turn down a side street. This is a better street. There are fewer houses along this street. There are large trees on both sides of it. I crouch behind one of these. It is dark here. The shadows hide me. I wait. Five, ten minutes, I wait. Then under an arc light a block away a man comes walking. He is a well-dressed man. I can tell even from that distance. I have good eyes. This guy will be in the dough. He walks with his head up and a jaunty step. A stiff does not walk like that. A stiff shuffles with tired feet, his head huddled in his coat collar. This guy is in the dough. I can tell that. I clutch my stick tighter. I notice that I am calm. I am not scared. I am calm. In the crease of his hat, I tell myself. Not too hard. Just hard enough. On he comes. I slink farther back in the shadows. I press closer against this tree. I hear his footsteps thud on the concrete walk. I raise my arm high. I must swing hard. I poise myself. He crosses in front of me. Now is my chance. Bring it down hard, I tell myself, but not too hard. He is under my arm. He is right under my arm, but my stick does not come

5

down. Something has happened to me. I am sick in the stomach. I have lost my nerve. Christ, I have lost my nerve. I am shaking all over. Sweat stands out on my forehead. I can feel the clamminess of it in the cold, damp night. This will not do. This will not do. I've got to get me something to eat. I am starved.

I stagger from the shadows and follow behind this guy. He had a pretty good face. I could tell as he passed beneath my arm. This guy ought to be good for two bits. Maybe he will be good for four bits. I quicken my steps. I will wait until he is under an arc light before I give him my story. I do not have long to wait. He stops under an arc light and fumbles in his pocket for a cigarette. I catch up with him.

"Pardon me, mister, but could you help a hungry man get—"

"You goddam bums give me a pain in the neck. Get the hell away from me before I call a cop."

He jerks his hand into his overcoat pocket. He wants me to think he has a gun. He has not got a gun. He is bluffing.

I hurry down the street. The bastard. The dirty bastard. I could have laid him out cold with the stick. I could have laid him out cold with the stick, and he calls me a goddam bum. I had the stick over his head, and I could not bring it down. I am yellow. I can see that I am yellow. If I am not yellow, why am I shaking like a leaf? I am starved, too, and I ought to starve. A guy without enough guts to get himself a feed ought to starve.

I walk on up the street. I pass people, but I let them pass. I do not ding them. I have lost my nerve. I walk until I am on the main stem. Never have I been so hungry. I have got to get me something to eat. I pass a restaurant. In the window is a roast chicken. It is brown and fat. It squats in a silver platter. The platter is filled with gravy. The gravy is thick and brown. It drips over the side, slow. I stand there and watch it drip. Underneath it the sign says: "All you can eat for fifty cents." I lick my lips. My mouth waters. I sure would like to sit down with that before me. I look inside. It is a classy joint. I can see waitresses in blue and white uniforms. They hurry back and forth. They carry heavy trays. The dishes stick over the edge of the trays. There are good meals still left in these trays. They will throw them in the garbage cans. In the center of the floor a water fountain bubbles. It is made of pink marble. The chairs are red leather, bordered in black. The counter is full of men eating. They are eating, and I am hungry. There are long rows of tables. The cloths on them are whiter than white. The glassware sparkles like diamonds on its whiteness. The knives and forks on the table are silver. I can tell that they are pure silver from where I am standing on the street. They shine so bright. I cannot go in there. It is too classy, and besides there are too many people. They will laugh at my seedy clothes, and my shoes without soles.

I stare in at this couple that eat by the window. I pull my coat collar up around my neck. A man will look hungrier with his coat collar up around his neck. These people are in the dough. They are in evening clothes. This woman is sporting a satin dress. The blackness of it shimmers and glows in the light that comes from the chandelier that hangs from the dome. Her fingers are covered with diamonds. There are diamond bracelets on her wrists. She is beautiful. Never have I seen a more beautiful woman. Her lips are red. They are even redder against the whiteness of her teeth when she laughs. She laughs a lot.

I stare in at the window. Maybe they will know a hungry man when they see him. Maybe this guy will be willing to shell out a couple of nickels to a hungry stiff. It is chicken they are eating. A chicken like the one in the window. Brown and fat. They do not eat. They only nibble. They are nibbling at chicken, and they are not even hungry. I am starved. That chicken was meant for a hungry man. I watch them as they cut it into tiny bits. I watch their forks as they carry them to their mouths. The man is facing me. Twice he glances out of the window. I meet his eyes with mine. I wonder if he can tell

7

the eyes of a hungry man. He has never been hungry himself. I can tell that. This one has always nibbled at chicken. I see him speak to the woman. She turns her head and looks at me through the window. I do not look at her. I look at the chicken on the plate. They can see that I am a hungry man. I will stand here until they come out. When they come out, they will maybe slip me a four-bit piece.

A hand slaps down on my shoulder. It is a heavy hand. It spins me around in my tracks.

"What the hell are you doin' here?" It is a cop.

"Me? Nothing," I say. "Nothing, only watching a guy eat chicken. Can't a guy watch another guy eat chicken?"

"Wise guy," he says. "Well, I know what to do with wise guys."

He slaps me across the face with his hand, hard. I fall back against the building. His hands are on the holster by his side. What can I do? Take it is all I can do. He will plug me if I do anything.

"Put up your hands," he says.

I put up my hands.

"Where's your gat?" he says.

"I have no gat," I say. "I never had a gat in my life."

"That's what they all say," he says.

He pats my pockets. He don't find anything. There is a crowd around here now. Everybody wants to see what is going on. They watch him go through my pockets. They think I am a stick-up guy. A hungry stiff stands and watches a guy eat chicken, and they think he is a stick-up guy. That is a hell of a note.

"All right," he says, "get down the street before I run you in. If I ever catch you stemming this beat, I will sap the living hell out of you. Beat it."

I hurry down the street. I know better than not to hurry. The lousy son of a bitch. I had a feed right in my lap, and he makes me beat it. That guy was all right in there. He was a good guy. That guy could see I was a hungry man. He would have fixed me up right when he came out.

I pass a small café. There are no customers in here. There is only a guy sitting by the cash register. This is my place. I go in and walk up to him. He is a fat guy with a double chin. I can see very well that he hasn't missed many meals in his life.

"Mister," I say, "have you got some kind of work like washing dishes I can do for something to eat? I am damn near starved. I'll do anything."

He looks hard at me. I can see right away that this guy is no good.

"Tell me," he says, "in God's name, why do you stiffs always come in here? You're the fourth guy in the last half-hour. I can't even pay my rent. There ain't been a customer in here for an hour. Go to some of the big joints where they do all the business."

"Could you maybe give me a cup of coffee?" I say. "That would hold me over. I've been turned down at about twenty places already."

"I can't give you nothing. Coffee costs money," he says. "Go to one of the chain stores and bum your coffee. When you've got any money, where do you go to spend it? You go to the chains. I can't do nothing for you."

I walk out. Wouldn't even give a hungry man a cup of coffee. Can you imagine a guy like that? The bastard. I'd like to catch him on a dark street. I'd give him a cup of coffee, and a sock on the snout he wouldn't soon forget. I walk. When I pass a place where there are no customers, I go in. They turn me down flat. No business, they say. Why don't I go to the big places? I am getting sick in the stomach. I feel like vomiting. I have to get me something to eat. What the hell? I will hit me one of these classy joints. Pride! What do I care about pride? Who cares about me? Nobody. The bastards don't care if I live or die.

I pass a joint. A ritzy place. It is all white inside. The tables are full. The counters are full. They are eating, and I am hungry. These guys pay good dough for a feed, and they are not even hungry. When they are through, they will maybe tip the waitress four bits. It is going to be cold tonight. Four bits will buy me a flop that will be warm, and not cold.

I go into this joint and walk up to the middle of the counter. I flop down in a seat. These cash customers gape at me. I am clean, but my front is seedy. They know I don't belong in here. I know I don't belong in here, too. But I am hungry. A hungry man belongs where there is food. Let them gape.

This waiter sticks the menu out to me. I do not take it. What do I want with a menu?

"Buddy," I say, "I am broke and hungry. Could you maybe give me something to eat?"

He shakes his head no, he cannot give me anything to eat.

"Busy. Manager's not in. Sorry."

I can feel my face getting red. They are all gaping at me. They crane their necks to gape at me. I get up out of this seat and walk towards the door. I can't get anything to eat anywhere. God damn them, if I could get my fingers on a gat.

"Say, buddy."

I turn around. A guy in a gray suit is motioning to me. He sits at the middle of the counter. I go back.

"You hungry?"

"I'm damn near starved. I have not eat in two days, and that is the God's truth."

"Down on your luck?" he says.

"Down so far I don't know how far," I say.

"Sit down. I've been down on my luck myself. I know how it is."

I sit down beside him.

"What'll it be?" he says.

"You order it," I say. "Anything you say."

"Order up anything you want. Fill up."

"A ham sandwich and a cup of coffee," I tell this waiter.

He is all smiles now, damn him. He sees where he can make a dime. I bet he owns this joint. He said the manager wasn't in, and I bet he's the manager himself.

"Give him a beef-steak dinner with everything that goes with it," says this guy in the gray suit. "This man is hungry."

This is a good guy. He orders my steak dinner in a loud voice so everyone can see how big-hearted he is, but he is a good guy anyway. Any guy is a good guy when he is going to buy me a steak dinner. Let him show off a little bit. He deserves to show off a little bit. I sit here at this counter, and I feel like pinching myself. This is a funny world. Five minutes ago I was down in the dumps. Here I am now waiting on a steak dinner in a classy joint. Let them gape. What do I care? Didn't they ever see a hungry man before?

This waiter shoves my dinner in front of me. Christ, I've never seen anything look so good. This steak with all the trimmings is a picture for sore eyes. Big and thick and brown, it sits there. Around it, all around it, are tomatoes, sliced. I start in. I do not look up from my plate. They are all gaping at me. Fill up and get out of here, I tell myself.

The guy three seats down gets up and calls for his check. He is a little guy with horn-rimmed glasses. The check is thirty cents. I see it before the waiter turns it upside down. Why do they always have to turn a man's check upside down? Afraid the price will turn his stomach? This guy pulls a dollar out of his pocket and walks over to the cashier. I wonder how it feels to have a buck in your jeans. Four bits will set me on top of the world right now. A good warm flop tonight and breakfast in the morning. That's the way to live. Pay for what you get, and look every copper you pass on the street straight in the eye, and say: "You bastard, I don't owe you a cent."

The cashier hands this guy his change. He walks back and lays it down by my plate.

"Flop for tonight," he says.

He speaks low. He is not trying to show off like this guy in the gray suit. Not that I don't think that this guy in the gray suit is not all right. He is a good guy. He bought me a steak dinner when I was damn near starved. No, he is a good guy, but he likes to show off a little bit. I look up at this guy. He is walking out of the door. I do not thank him. He is too far away, and besides, what can I say? I can't believe it. Thirty cents, the check said. Thirty cents from a dollar. That makes seventy cents. I got seventy cents. A good warm flop tonight, breakfast in the morning, and enough left over for cigarettes. No fishing around in the gutters for snipes for me. I will have me a package of tailor-made cigarettes. I pick up this change and stick it in my pocket. That guy is a mind-reader. I was sitting here wishing I had four bits, and before I know it, I got seventy cents. That guy is all right. I bet that guy has had troubles of his own some time. I bet he knows how it is to be hungry. I hurry up with my dinner. In here I am only a hungry stiff. Outside with seventy cents in my kick, I am as good as the next one. Say, I'd like to meet that guy, and I had a million dollars.

"Do you remember the time you give me seventy cents in a restaurant? You don't? Well, you give me seventy cents in a restaurant one time. I was damn near starved. I was just about ready to bump myself off, and you give me seventy cents."

I hand him a roll of bills. It is a big roll of bills. I walk off. That guy won't have to worry any more about dough. There was plenty in that roll to keep him in wheatcakes the rest of his life.

I finish my pie and get up.

"Thank you, Jack," I say to this guy in the gray suit. "I certainly appreciate what you done for me. I was damn near starved."

"That's all right, buddy," he says. "Glad to help a hungry man."

He speaks loud. They can hear him to the other end of the

counter. He is a good guy, though. He bought me a steak dinner.

I walk outside. I put my hand in my pocket and jingle my money. It feels good to have money to jingle. I am not broke or hungry now. I cannot imagine I was broke and hungry an hour ago. No park for me tonight. No lousy mission flop.

I go down the street and walk through the park. I look at these benches with their iron legs and their wooden slats.

"To hell with you," I say. "I have nothing to do with you. I do not know you. You will leave no grooves in my back tonight. Tonight I will have me a good warm flop. I will have me a flop that will be warm, and not cold."

I look at these stiffs sprawled out on the benches. I like to walk to the time of the jingle in my pocket and think how miserable I was last night.

It is getting late, and I am tired. I head down the skid road and stop in front of my four-bit flop. There is no marquee in front to keep the guests from getting wet. There is no doorman dressed like a major in the Imperial Guards. They do not need these things, because all the suites are on the fourth floor. I am puffing when I get to the top of the rickety stairs. At the landing a guy squats on a stool in a wire cage.

"I want a four-bit flop," I say, "a four-bit flop with a clean bed."

This guy is hunched over a desk with his belly sticking out of a dirty green sweater. He rubs his hands together and shows his yellow teeth in a grin. He winks one of his puffy eyes.

"For a little extra, just a little extra," he says, "I can give you a nice room, a very nice room. But it is too big a room for one. You will be lonely. A little company will not go bad, eh? Especially if the company is very young and very pretty?" He licks his puffy lips. "We have a girl, a new girl. Only tonight she came. Because it is you, and she must learn, only a dollar extra, yes?"

13

I look at him, and I think of the fish-eyed, pot-bellied frogs I used to gig when I was a kid. I imagine myself sticking a sharp gig into his belly and watching him kick and croak.

"A four-bit flop is what I want," I say. "I do not wish to play nursemaid to your virgins. I am broke, and besides, I am sleepy."

"But you should see her," he says, "so tiny, so beautiful. I will get her. You will change your mind when you see her."

"I do not want to see her," I say.

"So high," he says. "Only so high she is, and so beautiful. I will get her. You will see how beautiful she is."

He climbs off his stool.

"Do I get me a flop or do I have to bury my foot in your dirty belly?" I say.

"Some other time, then," he says, "some other time when you have more money. You will see how very beautiful."

He waddles through the dirty hall. I follow him. His legs are swollen with dropsy. His ankles overflow his ragged house-slippers and hang down in folds over the sides. I can imagine I hear the water gurgling as he walks. He opens the door and holds out his hand for the money.

"How many beds in this room?" I say.

"Forty," he says, "but they are good, clean beds."

I walk into this room. It is a big room. It is filled with these beds. They do not look so hot to me. They are only cots. They look lousy. I bet they are lousy, but a stiff has got to sleep, lousy or not. Most of these beds are already full. I can hear the snores of the stiffs as they sleep. I pick me out a flop at the other end of the room. There is no mattress. Only two dirty blankets. They are smelly. Plenty of stiffs have slept under these blankets.

Four or five stiffs are gathered in a bunch over next to the wall. I watch them. I know very well what they are going to do. They are gas hounds, and they are going to get soused on derail.

"Give me that handkerchief," says this red-headed guy with the wens on his face. "I will squeeze more alky out of a can of heat than any stiff I know."

This little guy with the dirty winged collar examines this can of heat.

"The bastards," he says. "You know what? They're makin' the cans smaller and smaller. This can right here is smaller than they was yestiddy. The dirty crooks. They'd take the bread right out of your mouths, the bastards would."

He jumps up and down as he talks. His red eyes flash. The sweat stands in beads on his forehead. How can a guy get so mad about the size of a can of heat? Well, it does not take much to make you mad when you have been swigging heat for a year.

This red-headed guy takes this can of heat and empties it out in a handkerchief. The handkerchief is filthy, but that don't worry them none. What's a little filth to a gas hound? Pretty soon they will be high and nothing will worry them. Pretty soon they won't have any more troubles. This derail will see to that. They squeeze this stuff out of the hand-kerchief and let it drip into the glass. They pour water into the glass. The smell of this stuff will turn your stomach, but it don't turn their stomach. They are going to drink it. They take turns about taking a swig. They elbow each other out of the way to get at the glass. When it is all gone, they squeeze out some more. They choke and gag when this stuff goes down, but they drink it. Pretty soon they have guzzled all the heat they have. In a little while they are singing. I do not blame these guys for getting soused on derail. A guy can't always be thinking. If a guy is thinking all the time, pretty soon he will go crazy. A man is bound to land up in the booby-hatch if he stays on the fritz. So these guys make derail and drink it.

This stiff in the bed next to mine turns up his nose at these guys who are soused up on derail.

"I got my opinion of a guy who will drink derail," he says. "A guy who will drink derail is lower down than a skunk."

He pulls a bottle out from under his pillow. It is marked: "Bay Rum." There are directions on the label. It says it will grow new hair. It says it will stop the old from falling out. But this guy does not need this stuff to keep his hair from falling out. This stiff has not had a haircut for a year.

"This is the stuff," he says. "I have been drinkin' this old stuff for a year, and I don't even get a headache afterwards."

He sticks this bottle up to his trap, and he does not take it down until he has emptied it.

"This is good stuff," he says. "It has got derail beat all to a frazzle."

I do not see how it can be such good stuff when he has to gag so much when he downs it. But that is his business. If a guy has been drinking this stuff for a year, he ought to know if it is good stuff or not. Pretty soon this guy is dead to the world. He sprawls out on his bunk and sleeps. He sleeps with his eyes wide open. Christ, he gives me the willies with his eyes wide open like that. He looks like a dead man, but I never see a dead man with his face covered with sweat like his is. It is plenty chilly in this room, but his face is covered with sweat. That is the bay rum coming out of him. A guy that has been drinking this stuff for a year must have plenty inside him. I bet the inside of his gut is covered with hair. That would be a good way to find out if this bay rum is a fake or not. When this stiff croaks from swigging too much bay rum, just cut him open. If his gut is not covered with hair, then this bay rum is a fake.

I watch him. I cannot keep my eyes off him. His legs twitch. He quivers and jerks. He is having a spasm. He almost jumps off the bed. All the time his eyes are wide open, and the sweat pours out of him. But he does not know what it is all about. He is dead to the world. If this is the good stuff, I will take the bad stuff. I will not even put this stuff on my hair. I would be afraid it would sink down into my gut and give me the spasms like this guy has got. The rest of these stiffs do not pay any attention to him. These bay horse fiends are old stuff to them. But they are not old stuff to me. It gets on my nerves. If this guy is going to act like this all night, I am going to walk the streets. It will be cold as hell walking the streets all night, but it will not be as bad as watching this guy jump up and down with his eyes wide open, and him dead to the world.

I cover up my head with this dirty blanket and try not to think about him.

CHAPTER TWO

IT RAINS. It will rain all night, but I cannot stand here in the wet all night. I shiver in this doorway and watch this peroxide blonde in the red hat hurrying down the street. She jumps from awning to awning, and eyes the cars that plow through the water in the street. She is on the make, and soaked to the skin. The wind drives against her and through her and plasters her dress to her legs. She ducks into this doorway I am in.

"Think it'll rain, sweetheart?" she says.

"If it don't rain tonight, it will tomorrow," I say. "You can't never tell about rain."

"Got another cigarette, deary?" she says. "I'm dyin' for a cigarette."

I give her a cigarette. She pulls out a vanity case and looks at her face.

"Holy God," she says, "look at me. How's a girl goin' to keep her complexion in weather like this?"

"What are you kicking about?" I say. "You're alive, ain't you? It ain't wet. It only looks wet. The sun'll be up tomorrow, beautiful like."

She takes a swipe at her face with her handkerchief. It leaves a streak from her eyes to her chin. The water runs down the streak and drips off her chin in pink drops. She pulls her red hat off her head. It leaves a red smudge across her forehead.

"Tra, la la," she says. "How sweet the blue birdies sing! You flopped in a mission last night. I can tell by the way you talk you flopped in a mission. Look at this goddam hat. Just look at it. Limp as a rag. The goddam kike said it wouldn't fade. Now look at it. I oughta take it back and stuff it down his throat."

She wads it up in her hand and squeezes the water out of it. It makes a red pool at her feet.

"I see you once or twice in Grumpy's hashhouse," I say. "I eat in Grumpy's when I'm lucky on the stem."

"Pleased to meet you socially," she says. "Call me Myrtle. I only eat in Grumpy's for the change. Most of the time I am up on the Avenoo with the swells."

"My name is Tom," I say. "I am expecting a registered letter, myself."

She wipes her face off with her handkerchief and puts on a new coat of paint.

"My hair ain't naturally blond," she says; "I dyed it."

"Yeah?" I say. "You'd never know it."

"Yeah," she says, "I dyed it, and the goddam stuff cost me my job. 'Six blondes is enough for one house,' the madam says. 'Dye 'er black or get out.' 'Like hell I'll dye 'er black,' I says. 'Me spend five bucks for a dye, and then spend five more to ruin it? Not on your fanny,' I says."

"Fire you?"

"Right out on the street. Throws my clothes out on the street and pushes me out on top of them, the old whore."

"How is the street?" I say. "Tough?"

"Tough?" she says. "Say, I ain't seen a live one all day. I jumped in and out of so many doorways I got the jitters."

She peels her eyes across the street. There is a guy standing over there in a doorway. He is a young guy with a sporty front. There are gray spats on his kicks, and white kid gloves on his hands.

"Do you see what I see?" she says.

"Has he give you a tumble?" I say.

"Watch me land him," she says. "This is the first live one I seen all day. I'll let you ding him before I reel him in."

"Thanks," I say. "I could use a few nickels till my registered letter gets in."

"Watch my technic," she says.

I keep my eyes peeled on this guy across the street. He is falling for the bait, all right. He shifts his eyes from her to me. He does not know what to think of me. He makes up his mind. He crosses the street and stops beneath this awning. He whistles low under his breath and keeps time with the drum of his fingers on the window. This is my chance to make a flop.

"Buddy," I say, "could you spare me a few dimes to get a flop? I'm down on my luck with no place to flop."

He looks at me and smiles. I can see that this guy is all right.

"Buddy," he says, "do you know what I would do if I was down on my luck with no place to get in out of the rain?"

"No, what would you do?" I say.

"I would get me a job and go to work," he says.

He turns his back on me and walks over to the girl.

"Hello, good-looking," he says.

"Hello, yourself," she says.

The lousy bastard. And I thought this guy was all right. Go to work, would he? Does he think I would be standing here in the rain and the cold if there was work to be had? There is no work. They laugh at you for asking for work. I give this smart guy a look and walk on down the street. When I hit the skid road, I stop under another awning. I can see that I am not the only one in the wet and the cold. Old Bacon Butts hobbles up the street and stops by my side. I met him in the mission. When he is not gassed up on bay rum, he talks of blowing up the banks.

"Well, well, my little spewm of the system," he says, "where do you flop tonight?"

"On the street," I say. "I am not holding a jitney."

"Say not so," he cackles. His bloodshot eyes sparkle. He is gassed up plenty. "For the meek in spirit, the International House."

We walk through the rain, Bacon Butts and me. It beats down on his matted hair and drizzles through his beard. The drops sparkle like diamonds as the street-lights flash on his face. I almost have to grin when I think of diamonds in old Bacon Butts's beard. He would pick them out and swap them for bay rum.

We walk.

"Rain all you damn please," I think. "You can't hurt me. I'm as wet as I can get. I'm soaked to the skin. You can't hurt me."

"I'm an old man," whines old Bacon Butts, "an old, old, man, and I gotta go huntin' me a rat-hole at night."

"Yeah, it's hell," I say.

I can't be shedding any tears over old Bacon Butts. I have to find me a rat-hole myself. Besides, he is gassed up.

"I worked hard in my day," he says. "Worked like a horse and broke my health, and now I ain't got a decent place to flop."

His old voice cracks. His puffy eyes fill with tears.

"Yeah," I say, "that's tough. That sure is tough, that is. There ain't no justice in this world. A man just don't get a square deal in this world."

Old Bacon Butts takes another swig from his bottle. He sobs short, cackly sobs in his coat collar.

We turn left down this alley. Half-way down we slip through the doorway of this empty building. We tiptoe upstairs and go into this room. There are other stiffs in this room. We can hear them snore. We strike matches to keep from stepping on them. In one corner is a pile of burlap sacks. They are dry. Good enough for a couple of drowned rats hunting a hole.

I spread my bed upon the floor. I pull off my wet clothes and crawl naked between the sacks. Christ, but it feels good to be lying here. It is cold outside. I can hear the patter of the rain beating down on the tin roof. It is wet outside and cold. But I am not wet or cold. I am warm and dry.

"To hell with you," I say. "Rain all you damn please. I am warm."

It is good to be warm and dry. I had a good beef stew today. My belly is full. What have I got to worry about? Nothing. Nothing to worry about until tomorrow. I pull these sacks up around my chin and I think about those poor bastards out in the rain. They are wet and cold. But I am warm and dry. My eyes get heavy. I fall asleep.

I do not know how long I am asleep. I awake with a jerk. All around me are lights. They flash back and forth. It seems as though there are a thousand lights that flash through the dark. I hear a rat squeal and scurry across the floor. What the hell? I am half asleep, but I know that there is something wrong. My heart pounds. It chokes me. I am afraid. I hear heavy shoes thudding on the floor. I hear stiffs running back and forth and yelling at the top of their voices. A light flashes into my eyes and blinds me.

"Get up out of there," says a voice. "Get up out of there before I kick the living hell out of you."

I know what it is now. It is the bulls. Jesus Christ, can't they ever let a man alone? A man can't even sleep. You can't crawl into an empty rat-hole, for the bulls. This bull grabs me by the throat and yanks me to my feet. I reach over and bundle my clothes up in my arms. He thinks maybe I am reaching for a gat or a club. I feel his fist smash into my mouth. I feel the blood that oozes from my lips. I dress as they shove us outside. There are a bunch of cops out here. There are a bunch of stiffs herded between them. They are red-eyed and sleepy.

"Your paws tough?" this cop says to me.

"They oughta be," I say. "I done enough hard work in my day."

"Well, they better be," he says. "It's the rock pile for you lousy bums."

"Where's the rock pile?" says one of these stiffs.

"They're diggin' a ditch four miles long, and they need some help," this copper says.

"You lousy stiffs will have a place to flop tomorrow night," chirps in this other one.

I want to take this bull by his dirty neck and choke him till his tongue hangs out. The bastard has got himself a place to flop; what does he care about us? I don't say anything, though. They would sap me down proper if I said anything. I am on to their little tricks. I huddle down as far as I can go in my coat collar, but it does no good. The rain beats down in sheets. It drizzles through my clothes. Here I am soggy and miserable. There it was warm and dry.

Down the street shrieks a siren. It is the black Maria come to get us. She pulls up at the curb. They open the door.

"Taxi?" says this stiff with the wooden leg. "I didn't call any taxi."

"All right, haul in, and make it snappy," says this cop.

We get in. I am lucky. I get a seat. They crowd all of us in here like cattle. We are cattle to them. Damn them. Some day they will pay for this. For ten minutes we gasp in here. We are packed like sardines.

"Blow 'em up," yelps old Bacon Butts. He is down on the floor with two stiffs using him for a stool. "Blow the bastards up. Ram a stick of dynamite up their fannies. One stick for every copper. Give me a good dark box car. Give me a good sharp knife, and a copper to use it on. 'So, you bastard, you will throw me into a lousy patrol wagon, will you? Take that and that.' Give me a dark box car and a good sharp knife, and I will pull their yellow guts out with my bare hands."

A stiff crams his hat into old Bacon Butts's mouth. It will not do for the coppers to hear a stiff talking like this. It doesn't matter to a copper if he is gassed up or not.

23

We pull to a stop. We pile out in front of the precinct jail and hurry inside to get out of the rain. More bulls meet us at the door and start frisking us.

"Got a gat?" this cop snaps at the guy with the scarred face.

"What the hell would I be doin' with a gat? I am out of work and cain't find any work," he says.

"You're a goddam liar. You're a lousy bum, and you wouldn't work if you had work."

"Yeah," this stiff says, "that's what you think."

"Open your trap to me again, and I will kick the living hell out of you. Next."

I am next. I walk up in front of this cop. I hold out my arms from my sides. I know how to do it. I have been frisked more times than I got fingers and toes.

"An old-timer, eh?" he says. "How many times you been here before?"

"None," I say.

"Got a gat?"

"No, sir."

The dumb bastard. If I am holding a gat, does he think I will tell him? He goes through my pockets.

"Got a razor?"

"I got a safety razor."

"That's a razor, ain't it. I asked you did you have a razor. I didn't ask you for any of your lip."

"Yes, sir," I say. The bastard.

"Got any money?"

"I got a ten-cent piece."

"You dirty bums never have any money. You never will have any money. You are no damn good, the whole bunch of you. Next."

I go over to the guy at the desk.

"What name did you give the last time?" he says.

"No name," I say. "There wasn't any last time."

"All right, Jesse James, what's the handle this time?"

24

"Thomas Kromer," I say.

Does this smart bastard think I will make up a name? What do I care who knows I am in this lousy can? The tight sons of bitches wouldn't give me a drink of water if my tongue was hanging out.

"My home is in Huntington, West Virginia," I say. I know all of these questions. I want to get it over with. I am sleepy. A guy can't even get a chance to sleep.

"Who in the hell asked you where your home was?" he says. "Your home is wherever you can find some rotten swill to stuff in your bellies."

"Sorry," I say.

"Occupation?" he says. "Anything that pops in your head. Song-writer, sky pilot, anything."

"Mechanic," I say.

"Age?"

"Twenty-six." Will this bastard never be finished with his questions?

"You'll be six months older when you get out. Next."

A cop shoves me into a big room. It is lined on all sides with cells. It will turn your stomach with the stench of unflushed commodes. The turnkey unlocks the door of one of these holes and shoves me in. He locks it and goes back after another stiff. I look around. There are two bunks on the wall. One on top of the other. A drunk is sprawled out in each of them. They have vomited all over the floor. I wonder where in the hell do they expect a guy to sleep. It is two o'clock in the morning. Do they think I am going to stand on my feet all night? If they do, they are crazy. The bastards. What do they care if I have to stand on my feet all night? I hammer on this steel door with my hands. I have to pound a long time before anybody comes to the door.

"What do you want in there?" It is the turnkey.

"Where is a guy going to sleep in here? There's drunks in both bunks, and the floor looks like a privy."

"Sleep on your head, Lily-fingers," he says, "or on your pink teddies."

"I ain't slept in two nights, and I gotta get me some sleep," I say.

"What the hell do I care where you sleep?" he says. "You pound on that door again, and I will come in there and sap you down." He goes away.

A young punk with fuzz on his face sticks his nose through the bars of the cell across the hall.

"What you in for?" he says.

"Vag," I say. "I slept in an empty building to get in out of the rain, and they send me up for vag."

"Vag!" he says. "Hell, you ain't growed up yet. You know what I'm in here for?"

"No, what are you in here for?" I say.

"A hold-up, that's what I'm in here for," he says, "a hold-up."

This is a smart punk. He is not dry behind the ears yet. He is stuck on himself because he got caught pulling a stick-up. I let him gas through the bars. I do not pay any attention to him.

This guy in the next cell sticks his nose out.

"Like your suite, deary?" he yells.

He has a squeaky voice. I can see that his eyebrows are plucked, from where I am. This guy is as queer as they make them.

"Yeah, I like it fine," I say.

"The bitches," he says. "The goddam bitches. They raided my flat and broke up my date. A girl can't even have a decent date without the goddam cops breaking in."

This guy lying on the bunk gets up and shoves this queer away from the bars. He is a wolf. He does not want this pansy to be talking to me. He is jealous.

"For Christ sake, Florence, set down so's I can get me some sleep," he says.

I walk up and down the floor. Up and down. I keep this up for hours. I can't stand it any longer. I sit down in a corner and put my head in my hands. I am all in. Before I know it, I am dead to the world. I do not awake until morning.

"Water," moans the drunk in the top bunk, "for God's sake, won't someone give me some water?"

Nobody pays any attention to him. The drunk in the bottom bunk gets to his feet. I start to crawl in his bunk. I've got to get me some sleep. He clenches up his fists and starts towards me. I could kill him, but I get back in my corner. No use to have any trouble with a drunk.

"You're a bastard," he says. "Ain'tcha a bastard? You're a lousy bum. You're all lousy bums. The bastards won't keep me in here. I got dough. I'll show 'em, the bastards won't keep me in here. Take my money away from me, will they?" He leans over to me. "I'm too smart for these cops. I put most of my money in my shoe."

He takes off his shoe and reaches down in the toe. He pulls out a wad of bills.

"So they think they can outsmart me, do they? I'm drunk, but I ain't nobody's fool."

He waves this dough around in the air. I see one of the bills drop to the floor. I put my foot on it. I figure it is mine by rights of my having my foot on it. He crawls back in his bunk and goes to sleep. I put this fin down in the toe of my shoe and sit back in my corner.

I wait for breakfast. That is a good joke. For two hours I squat in this corner before the turnkey opens the door.

"Where's my breakfast?" I say.

"Breakfast, hell!" he says. "There ain't no breakfast. It's the court for you bums."

They load us in the black Maria and take us to court. We pull in at the back door. They hand us a ham sandwich. We eat it and march to the courtroom and the prisoner's box. There are thirty of us stiffs here. There will have to be two trials.

27

The prisoner's box is not big enough to hold us all. You won't read a better joke than this in a book. Don't they know a stiff has got to sleep?

A guy with a bald head and a black bow tie starts reading a paper. He is telling us what we are charged with. He mumbles something about no visible means of support. He mumbles something about vagrancy. What this guy means is, we slept in an empty building to get in out of the rain. He don't say that, though. He says we have no visible means of support. Does he think I would sleep in that lousy building if I was holding anything? We don't understand all this guy mumbles. We don't listen very close. We are too sleepy. He stops reading. The judge looks up. He has a hard face. Well, hard face or not, what can he do to a guy for sleeping? A guy has got to sleep.

"What have you got to say for yourself?" this judge asks the first guy.

"I am out of work. Last night it was rainin', and I didn't have any place to sleep. I—"

"Next."

"I have been sick. I was afraid of gettin' wet, so I—"

"Next."

"I am out of work and—"

"Next."

These guys don't get a chance to say anything. They no more than get started than he goes to the next guy. He is kangarooing them. They haven't got a chance. I am down near the end of the box. I make up my mind to make a hit. I have a good education. Let me see. I will plead guilty with mitigating circumstances. That sounds all right. This judge will see that I am no ordinary stiff.

"Your honor," I will say very polite, "I am guilty, with mitigating circumstances."

The rest of the stiffs will perk up their ears when they hear this. They will not know what mitigating circumstances are, but the judge will know.

28

"Explain the mitigating circumstances," he will say.

"Your honor, as you know very well, the nation is faced with a world-wide crisis in unemployment. There are three things which are prime requisites of every civilized man, and even savage. These things are food, clothing, and shelter. We are confronted with the necessity of crime or beggary. It is inevitable, your honor, one choice or the other must be made. Rather than degrade ourselves with stealing, we are compelled to beg for the mite we eat. But we must sleep. Somewhere, your honor, we must sleep. In good weather we sleep in the parks. But yesterday it rained. The parks were soaked. This building was empty. We did not break in. It was empty. We had no alternative. We must sleep. We cannot sleep in the rain."

This will give this judge a rough idea. The trouble with these stiffs is they haven't got the guts to speak up. They are scared to death of this judge. Hell, this judge is no better than any other stiff to me. I will stand up for my rights. I will plead guilty with mitigating circumstances. I bet his ears will perk up when he hears a stiff pleading guilty with mitigating circumstances.

He comes on down the line. I go over my spiel in my head. I will be polite, but I will show this guy I am just as good as the next one. He gets to me.

"What have you got to say for yourself?" he says.

"Your honor," I say, "I am guilty with—"

"That's all I want to know. Next."

He don't give me a chance to say anything. I will not stand for this. I don't have to stand for this. Can you imagine a guy like this? They call this a free country, and this guy don't give me a chance to say anything. Maybe they can pull this on some of these stiffs with no education, but they can't pull it on me. I have got a good education. I've had good jobs in my time. I had privileges then, and I got privileges now. I stand up on my feet. Everybody looks at me. This judge gets red in the face. He yells for me to sit down. I do not sit down. All the coppers yell for me to sit down. Everybody is craning their necks to see what is going on. A big, fat woman with a red dress and a pocked face stands up in her seat and thrashes her hands in the air.

"Sock the old judge on the beezer," she yells at me. "Take a poke at the cossacks."

A cop plops her down in her seat. Another cop pulls out a blackjack and starts over to me. What the hell can I do against a cop with a blackjack? He would sap me down proper, and all the rest of these cops would help him. A stiff hasn't got a chance. They know a stiff hasn't got a chance. I sit down.

This judge stands up. He is burned up, and his face is flaming red.

"Sixty days, or a hundred dollars. Take them away."

CHAPTER THREE

I SIT DOWN at the table in this mission. They shove this stew
before us. It is awful. It smells bad. The room is full of the
stench of this rotten stew. What am I going to do? What can I
do? I am a hungry man. Food is food to a hungry man, whether
it is rotten or not. I've got to eat. I take up a spoonful of this
stuff and gag. As hungry as I am, I can't down this swill. This
slop is not fit for hogs. I push it away and pick up the bread.
This bread is hard and stale, but it hits the spot. Who am I to
say it is no good? I've got to eat. This stiff next to me at the
table leans far over his plate and goes after his swill. He is
hungrier than I am.

"Ain'tcha goin' ter eat yer stew?" he says to me.

"No, I can't go this stuff."

"Kin I have it?"

"Take it, and welcome," I say.

He reaches over and takes my stew. He ladles up a spoonful.
He makes a slushing noise when he sucks it in. I don't pay
any attention. If a guy wants to suck in his swill, who am I to
get my stomach turned? I have seen the day when I would
have socked a guy on the kisser who sat next to me and made
a noise like that. But that was before I went on the fritz. I used
to wear spats then. Imagine me wearing spats now. I can stand
on a dime and tell you whether it is heads or tails. That's how
thin the soles of my kicks are.

This guy socks in another spoonful. He gulps and chokes.
He sticks his fingers down his throat and pulls out a yellow
overcoat button. What are these bastards putting yellow over-

31

coat buttons in the stew for? Have they run out of their rotten carrots? Don't they know you can't make a decent stew out of yellow overcoat buttons? This stiff holds this yellow overcoat button up in the air.

"Looky," he yells down the table, "looky what I found. Any you blokes need a button fer yer overcoat?"

"See can you find a gray overcoat button," this stiff at the other end of the table yells. "My overcoat is gray. I can't be puttin' yellow overcoat buttons on a gray coat."

"Today is yellow overcoat button day. You kin not be gittin' yer choice of buttons till comes hash day," this stiff says. "A stiff kin not be gittin' his choice of buttons ever' day."

Another guy digs down in his stew.

"Wait till I see can I find needle and thread. You gotta have needle and thread."

These other stiffs start digging down in their stew to see can they find needle and thread. Not all of them, though. Four or five guys gag and get up from the table. These are hungry men, but the yellow overcoat button turns their stomach. They will soon get over that. I was like that once. That was when I used to wear spats.

This mission stiff who is the overseer of the kitchen walks up the aisle.

"What's eatin' you stiffs?" he yells. "Any more racket out of you, and I will throw you out in the street."

"Cain't a stiff do a little huntin'?" this old guy with all the badges pinned on him says.

"What the hell are you huntin' for?" he says.

"I am huntin' fer me a watch and chain," says one of these stiffs. "How kin I tell what time you feed, if I don't have me a watch and chain?"

"That is good stew," says this mission stiff. "I watched them make that stew myself."

"She ain't sech good stew," says this old man with the

badges. "I cain't find me a overcoat. She is purty frosty out. I sure would like to find me a overcoat." He digs down in his stew.

These other stiffs all start to laugh. This mission stiff is getting his dander up.

"What the hell are you talkin' about?" he says. "Get out of here before I call a cop."

This old guy grins and beats it outside. He does not mind missing his supper. You will find better suppers than this in the sewers.

I sip at this coffee. This dirty-looking stuff in the tin cup is coffee. It is not French drip coffee. You can't taste the coffee in it. You can taste the saltpetre in it, though. It is lousy with this taste of saltpetre. They douse it with this stuff to help you be a good Christian. That is thoughtful of them.

I finish this stuff and go out in the chapel. You get no flop in this mission unless you listen to the sermon. For seven nights a week I have to listen to a sermon. They are long sermons. Sermons that last for three hours. This chapel is a big room. It is filled with stiffs waiting for their flop. Around the walls are religious pictures in fancy colors. It is warm in here. It is damp and chilly in the parks, but it is warm in here.

They have a woman preacher tonight. She stands in the pulpit and waves her arms and jumps up and down. She is going strong. Her voice is like a rasp that grates on your nerves. She is burning up. The sweat pours down her face. She is whooping it up because she is on her favorite subject. She is preaching about getting washed in the blood of the Lamb. They always preach about getting washed in the blood of the Lamb. I am sick of all this. I have heard it so many times.

Now, that girl on the left in the choir is not bad-looking. She looks nice sitting up there with her pink dress, and the violets pinned to her waist. She is too damn good-looking to be wasting her time in this joint. She is daffy like the rest of

33

them, though. She must be daffy, or she would not be in this joint trying to get a bunch of stiffs to get washed in the blood of the Lamb.

This woman preacher has been giving these stiffs plenty of hell, and now she is getting ready to hand out the old soft soap.

"The trouble with you dear men is that you are away from the blessed saving power of Jesus Christ," she says. "You got to get washed in the blood of the Lamb. Only Christ can make you clean. Won't you come up and give your hearts to Christ tonight? Everything will be yours. Peace will be yours. Peace and calm will come into your souls. You will be new men. Christ can give you what you want. Is it a job you want? Christ can give you a job. Ask and you shall receive. How many men will come up to the altar tonight and give their hearts to Christ? Hold up your hands."

We do not hold up our hands. We are old-timers. We have tried this stunt before. Once in Denver I kneeled at the mourners' bench till I had blisters on my knees. I prayed for a job. I thought for sure I'd get me a job. Well, sister, I didn't get any job. I got throwed in their lousy can for sleeping in the park. No, we cannot fall for that stuff. We are old-timers. We are on to your little tricks.

"Will every man in the house bow his head while we ask the blessing of God upon each of you dear, unfortunate men? Let every head be bowed in the presence of the Lord. I see some men in the rear of the room reading newspapers. Put your newspapers away, men. This is no place to be reading of temporal things. You know, men, that is just the trouble with us today. We are too much taken up with worldly things. If we could just get back to God and let the blessed Savior have His way with us, our troubles would vanish like the driven snow. Let every head in the house of God be bowed. Thank you, men."

We bow our heads. We know better than not to bow our

34

heads. We've seen too many stiffs get kicked out in the cold because they didn't bow their heads. We are sick of this drivel this dame is handing out, but it is warm in here. It is cold outside.

"Now, men, while every head is bowed and every heart is lifted, how many of you men would like to have us pray for you? You don't have to come up in front. You don't even have to stand on your feet. Just raise your hand if you would like to have us pray for you. Some of you men have hearts so heavy with burdens you can hardly bear them. Many of you dear souls are standing on the brink of despair, and some even on the brink of eternity. Oh, brother, we know One who will deliver you from the darkness. We know One who will fill that sick heart of yours with new life and new hope. Raise your hands so we will know who to pray for. God hears and answers prayer."

It is the same old stuff. I can see that it is the same old stuff. She is leading them up slow. This is only the first step. Some of these stiffs who are new to this are going to find themselves kneeling up there at the mourners' bench, and wondering how they got up there.

"Raise your hands men," she says. "Just raise your hands. You don't have to come up in front."

Fifteen or twenty raise their hands. They want to be prayed for. I raise my hand. The more hands that are raised, the sooner she will quit harping. She is running true to form tonight. She makes the next step.

"Thank God there are so many men realize the healing power of Jesus Christ. You men who raised your hands, how many of you have the courage to stand up on your feet? I tell you, men, it takes courage to stand up on your feet in the presence of your fellow men, unafraid, and ask God to help you. Some of you men haven't got that courage. How many will stand up and ask God to help you?"

It is the same old stuff. She is soft-soaping them now.

"Come on, men," she says, "who will stand up first for Jesus Christ?"

Some mission stiff in the front row stands up. That's what he's here in the front row for, to lead the lambs to slaughter. Come back here in a year, and you will find this same mission stiff standing up and asking God to help him. As much as these guys ask for help, you'd think they'd get a little help sometimes.

"I am always ready to stand up for the Lord," this mission stiff says.

A couple of young punks stand up. They don't know what it's all about. They feel like I did that time in Denver when I wore blisters on my knees. Pretty soon there are ten standing up. Twenty raise their hands. Ten stand up. That's a pretty good average. This dame is pretty good. She is going strong. She has got them where she wants them. They are standing up.

"Now you men that are standing on your feet, just come up here to the altar. I want to give every one of you a Bible. I want you to study God's word. I want you to know God."

She holds out the Bibles to them. They are standing up. It is easier to go up and get the Bible than to sit back down in their seats while she is holding them out to them. She has got them where she wants them. They march up front and take this paper-backed book. It is not a Bible. It's just one book of the Bible. I know. I've got plenty of them. I was new then. I am an old-timer now. They don't get me to stand up on my feet to be prayed for any more. These stiffs take these books and start back towards their seats. But they don't get away with this stuff. Who do they think they are to get away with this stuff?

"Just a minute, men," she says. "I'd like to ask God's special blessing on each of you dear brothers tonight. Won't you kneel at the altar for just a few seconds?"

These guys stop in their tracks and look funny. They don't

know what to do. Well, what can they do? Kneel at the altar, that's all they can do. She didn't get them up here to give them a paper-backed book. She got them up here to kneel. They kneel.

"Let us pray," she says.

She starts to pray. When she starts to pray, all the choir and the mission stiffs gather around the mourners' bench. They put their arms around these guys that are roped at the altar, and start working on them to give their hearts to God. The young punk on the end of the bench is lucky. He draws the girl in the pink dress with the violets pinned to her waist. I do not blame that guy if he gives his heart to God. For five, ten minutes nobody gives their heart to God. These guys start to squirm on their knees. This mourners' bench hasn't got any soft rug to kneel on. These mission guys are smart. They make you so miserable you will give your heart to God so you can get up off your knees. Pretty soon some guy can't stand it any longer. I see him shake his head. This mission stiff who has his arm around him gets to his feet. He has a grin on his map a yard wide. The punk gets up, too. His knees are all in. He can hardly stand up.

"Praise God," this mission stiff yells, "the lamb was lost, but now he is found."

He shakes hands with the punk.

Everybody shakes hands with the punk.

"Amen," shouts the red-headed woman with the big legs.

"Glory to God!" somebody yells back.

The skinny woman at the organ begins playing a hymn. She is glory-bound. She slams down on the keys with all her might. She wiggles her shoulders and throws her head back. There is a wild look in her eyes. She jumps off the stool and starts dancing a jig. She keeps time with the clapping of her hands. Everyone else starts clapping their hands.

This woman preacher watches this organ-player dance and

37

keeps time by pounding her foot on the floor. Christ, but she's happy. She has got these guys where she wants them. She raises her hand in the air.

"What did all the people say?" she yells at the choir and the mission stiffs.

"All the people said amen," they yell back.

One by one the rest of these stiffs that are roped at the mourners' bench get to their feet. It's hell on your knees to stay there for half an hour.

"Brother, do you give your heart to God?" shouts this woman preacher to the stiff with the purple birthmark on his face.

He shakes his head yes, he gives his heart to God.

"Though your sins be as scarlet, He can make them white as snow," she yells.

She claps her hands together. She has got these stiffs where she wants them.

"Praise God. Washed in the blood," yells one of these mission stiffs. "God will take care of you. Whatever you need, God will give it to you."

"I need a shave," pipes up this stiff in the third row. "Am I next?"

This mission stiff sputters. This woman preacher does not sputter. She walks to the edge of the pulpit and points her finger at this stiff.

"Brother," she says, "the Devil has got you. The Devil is living in your soul. We want nothing to do with the Devil here. Beat it."

This guy grins and goes out. It will be the park bench for him. It don't pay to talk back to a mission stiff.

"Praise God, men," she says, "the Devil is now out of this house. The house of the Lord is no place for Satan. All evening I have felt his presence here. I tell you men, when you get close to Jesus Christ, when you have touched the hem of His garment, you can feel the Devil when he's in the same room with you. You can look into people's eyes and see him. I can see him in some of your eyes now. Oh, sinners, won't you run him out and come up to the mourners' bench?"

Nobody runs the Devil out.

All these guys that went up to the mourners' bench line up and march upstairs. They do not sleep with us sinners. They have been washed in the blood. They sleep in the converts' room. There are clean sheets on the beds of the converts' room. They are not lousy. A stiff who wears blisters on his knees at the mourners' bench deserves a good, clean flop.

This woman preacher wipes the sweat off her face and sits down. She has had a hard night's work. A mission stiff in a purple suit and a pair of red suspenders takes her place in the pulpit.

It is time to testify. After the preaching it is time to testify.

"How many of you men would like to stand up and tell what God has done for you?" yells this mission stiff.

These stiffs are in this joint because they have no place to get in out of the cold, and this bastard asks them to stand up and tell what God has done for them. I can tell him what God has done for them. He hasn't done a damn thing for them. I don't though. It is warm in here. It is cold outside.

Another mission stiff gets up. You can always depend on a mission stiff telling what God has done for him.

"For twenty years I was a dope fiend—"

For Christ's sake, won't someone knock this hophead back in his seat? Every night I have to listen to this guy. Every night he adds a little bit extra. But then maybe you can't blame this crazy slop-swiller. Every guy likes to shine a little bit. Testifying is the only chance he has. Maybe you can't blame this guy for getting up and saying for twenty years he was a dope fiend. When he gets up, he is good for half an hour. He knows he is fixed for half an hour. You can't make a guy sit down when he is telling what Jesus Christ has done for him.

"I just couldn't get along without my shot of snow," he says. "I couldn't sleep, and I couldn't work or eat. Brethren, the

Devil had such a hold on me that I wished I was dead. One rainy night I was crouched all alone in my room. I was just a twitchin' all over. I was out of dope. I just felt as though if I didn't get me some dope, I would go daffy. 'Satan,' I said, 'by the grace of God, I am goin' to lick you.' I pulled out my old dust-covered Bible that had been layin' there in the desk since my angel mother passed over to her reward. I made myself set down at the table and read it. I read for an hour before I closed the good book up. 'Now then, Satan,' I says, 'you and me are goin' to fight it out.' Well, sir, we wrestled there all night, me and Satan. First he would be on top, and then me. Along about mornin' when the sky was gettin' gray in the east, and Satan just about had me licked, I looked out of the window. Brethren, what I am tellin' you is the God's truth. There, lookin' into the window was the face of Jesus Christ, just as plain as that picture of Him on the wall. I see Him look into my eyes pityin' like, and I saw His lips move. 'Satan,' He says, 'this is no child of yours, this is My child. Son, your sins are forgiven. Come into My service.' Well, sir, from that day on, I have never touched a pinch of dope. Praise God, blessed be the name of the Lord!"

He sits down. No one else gets up. Even the mission stiffs are too fagged out to tell what God has done for them. We stand up. This woman preacher says the benediction. We march upstairs to the third floor. Most of the stiffs pull off their clothes and crawl into these dirty blankets. Some of them go in to wash. I go in to wash, myself.

I notice this guy in the gray suit. He is a middle-aged guy. He has not been on the fritz long. I can tell. Up and down, back and forth he walks. He is plenty nervous about something. He does not pay any attention to the rest of these stiffs. He walks from one end of the room to the other. His eyes are glued to the floor. I know what he is thinking. I have walked like that myself. Up and down through the night.

"She is a tough life, buddy," I say.

He does not look up. He does not answer. A nice friendly guy.

"She will all come out in the wash," I say.

"Yeah," he says, "she will all come out in the wash."

He walks into one of these toilets and closes the door. I go on with my washing. I do not think any more about this guy. All at once a roar comes out of that toilet. Smoke curls up over the door. I know what caused that roar. A gun caused that roar. That damn fool has shot himself. That is plain. I run over to the door and try to open it. It is locked from the inside. The stiffs are pouring into this toilet now. They have heard the shot. I get down on my hands and knees and look through the crack in the door.

"What do you see?" some stiff says.

"Plenty," I say.

I am sick in the stomach when I get up. I have seen all I want to see. This guy is sprawled out on the floor with a hole in his head. It is a jagged hole. There is a pool of blood on the floor. His arm is folded up under his head. Some of the blood drips in his hand and runs down the sleeve of his coat. Some of this blood is darker than the rest. That is not blood. That is his brains. This guy is stone dead, all right. His eyes are wide open.

"What's he wanna bump hisself off fer?" says this stiff with the boils on his face. "There ain't nothin' to bump yerself off fer."

"He bumped hisself off because he's got the guts to bump hisself off," says this other stiff. "We are afraid to bump ourselves off, so we live in mission flops and guzzle lousy mission slop."

Somebody has called an ambulance. This stiff does not need an ambulance. He needs a hearse. They run us all out into the hall. We huddle in a bunch and wait to see them carry this stiff out. They bring him out with a sheet spread over him. It is a clean sheet. It came from the converts' room. This is the

41

first time this stiff has had a clean sheet over him for a long time.

I go back to my room and sit on the edge of my bed. It is cold sitting here, but I do not mind the cold. I am thinking about bumping myself off. Why not? It don't hurt. I bet that guy never knew what hit him. Just a jagged hole, and a pool of blood mixed with black, and it is all over. He had the guts, and now everything is all right with him. After a guy bumps himself off, he don't have any more troubles. Everything is all right with him.

I walk over to the window. Down below me is the alley, but I cannot see it. The glass of the window is covered with fly specks, and besides, it is dark and murky down there. It is a long way to the bottom. It is three stories to the bottom. Three stories, with a nice concrete pavement to light on. If a guy was to jump head-first out of this window, it would be all over. Just a few seconds, and it would be all over. I think of that blood splotched with black on the toilet floor. I think of me sprawled on the pavement in the blackness of the alley below.

"Messy," I think, "messy and gooey."

I pull off my clothes and crawl into bed.

CHAPTER FOUR

It is evening. I sit on this park bench and watch the people as they pass. A guy comes down the walk. He twists and wiggles with mincing steps. His eyelashes are mascara'd, and his cheeks are rouged. His lips are flaming red with lipstick. He sits down on this bench beside me. He is perfumed plenty, and he smells pretty good.

"Oho," I think, "this guy is queer, and he doesn't care who knows it."

He pulls out a gold cigarette case and puts a cigarette between his lips. I notice that the lipstick dyes the end of it red. He reaches in his pocket and fumbles for a match. He knows he hasn't got a match. I know he hasn't got a match. We are playing a game.

"Got a match, deary?" he says.

"Sure." I give him a match.

"Care for a smoke?"

I take a cigarette. It is a high-class cigarette. You will not find any like it lying over the curbs. It has a cork tip.

"It's certainly nice in the park this evening," he says.

He purses up his lips and hums like a bird.

"Nicer than last night," I say. "I slept on this bench last night."

This fairy already knows I am on the fritz, but this will make sure he knows it.

"Awful cold?"

"Cold as hell."

"No covers?"

"Newspapers. Newspapers are warm, but the cold comes up through the cracks in the bench."

"That is awful," he says.

"Yeah, it sure is tough," I say.

"How do you eat?"

He knows how I eat, but we are playing a game.

"I eat wherever I can," I say. "Sometimes I get a hand-out from a house. Sometimes a cup of coffee from a restaurant."

"You poor dear," he says. "It must be terrible to live like that."

"What can a guy do?" I say. "A guy has got to live."

"Why, I should think you would be skin and bones," he says.

He lays his hand across my leg. I must not jerk my leg away. He is feeling me out. If I jerk my leg away, he will see that he is not going to make me. This queer will not put out for a meal until he sees that I am a good risk. I leave my knee where it is. These pansies give me the willies, but I have got to get myself a feed. I have not had a decent feed for a week.

"I am not so skinny," I say.

This guy motions around the park.

"Everyone seems to have a girl," he says.

"You have to have dough to get a girl," I say. "Girls are expensive. If you haven't got any dough, you haven't got any girl."

"Did you ever have a girl?" he says.

"Sure, I had a girl," I say, "but I lost my dough, so I lost my girl."

"A good-looking fellow like you ought to get a girl without any money," he says.

He pinches my leg.

I feel the goose-pimples on my leg and the shivers on my back. A pansy like this, with his plucked eyebrows and his rouged lips, is like a snake to me. I am afraid of him. Why I am

44

afraid of this fruit with his spindly legs and his flat chest, I do not know.

"Not so you can notice it," I say. "Girls want the dough."

"Well, sometimes two fellows can have a pretty good time together," he says. "Did you ever go out with any fellows?"

"I never did," I say.

I am lying, but if this queer wants a virgin, that's what he gets.

"I bet you and I could have a wonderful time together," he says. "When two people get to know each other real well, they find they have just a lot in common."

"That's right," I say.

"What are you doing tonight?" he says.

"Not a thing," I say.

"How would you like to go to a good show tonight?"

"I would like that fine, but hell—" I look down at my seedy clothes, and my shoes without soles.

"I can fix you up with clothes," he says. "I have a friend about your size. I will get some from him."

"That will be fine," I say.

"And a bath," he says; "you will feel better after a good warm bath. I have a bath in mauve tile in my apartment. You will feel better after a good warm bath."

His eyes sparkle when he mentions the bath. He licks his lips. I notice that he smears the lipstick when he licks his lips. He takes hold of the end of my belt and fingers it.

"That is a nice belt you have on," he says. "That belt must have cost plenty of money when it was new."

My belt is a cheap belt. It cost two bits when it was new. It is old and frayed at the edges now, but we are playing a game.

"It is a pretty good belt," I say.

He starts to unfasten it. There are people here. They will see him. I pull away. He notices that I pull away. He lets go of my belt.

"Can you meet me here tonight at eight o'clock?" he says.

"Sure, I'll meet you here," I say.

He pulls four bits out of his pocket. He has decided I am a good risk.

"This is for your dinner," he says.

"Thanks," I say. "You are all right."

He pulls out a mirror and straightens the lipstick on his lips.

"Gracious me," he says, "I am a total wreck." He gets up. "Well, deary, don't forget. Toodle-doo until tonight." He wiggles down the walk.

I am a lucky stiff running into this queer. For every queer there is a hundred stiffs to make him. It is seven o'clock. I have an hour to wait. I walk over to this hash-house across the street and order me a beef stew. This joint smells like a slop-jar, but the grub is cheap and hits the spot.

"Did you make her?" this skinny stiff next to me at the counter says.

"Make who?" I say.

"Mrs. Carter," he says. "I see you talkin' to her in the park."

"So her name is Mrs. Carter?" I say. "Sure, I made her for four bits. I got a date for tonight."

"You better fill it. She's in the dough. Lousy with it."

"Any strings on her?"

"Not now. She was livin' with a stiff she picked up off the street, but Geraldine, that big red-headed guy with the scarred face, took him away from her."

"How did Mrs. Carter like that?" I say.

"Mrs. Carter says that Geraldine is a two-timing bitch. She says that if Geraldine didn't look so much like a wolf, she would pull her hair out by the roots."

"Will she treat a guy right?" I say.

"She will treat a guy swell," he says, "if she likes him. You are a lucky stiff making Mrs. Carter. There are plenty of stiffs in this town would give their eye teeth to make Mrs. Carter."

"Where does she hang out?"

"She lives up on the Avenue with the swells. The joint she lives in is lousy with queers, and what is more, they are lousy with jack. Mrs. Carter rooms with a cashier of a bank."

"He queer, too?" I say.

"Sure, she's queer," he says, "but you will not have a chance with her. Mrs. Carter would cut your throat if you tried to pull the wool over her eyes. She is a tough customer. She says she will scratch Geraldine's eyes out does she get the chance. My advice is stick to Mrs. Carter."

I finish my beef stew and go back to the park. There are more people here now. The benches are full. They loll on the grass. It is dark. Every other guy is a queer. The other guy is trying to make her. They twist down the walk. They ogle the guys that pass as they sit on the benches. They wink at the prospects.

An old guy sits on the bench across from me. He is as queer as they make them. He keeps ogling at me. I do not pay him any attention. He purses up his lips. He clucks through his teeth like an old hen.

"Missus," I think, "you are wasting your time. I am waiting for my meal ticket. I am waiting for Mrs. Carter. Mrs. Carter rooms with a cashier of a bank, and what is more, she is lousy with jack herself."

I cannot be bothered with an old queer who clucks through his teeth like a hen.

It is a good thing I am not flirting with this old guy, for I spot Mrs. Carter frisking down the walk. The stiffs are winking as she passes. They whistle low. They cannot whistle loud. The coppers will hear them. The coppers will let you whistle low, but not loud. She does not pay them any attention. She breezes straight up to the bench where I am sitting.

"Right on the dot, deary," she croons. "Your glad rags are waiting at the apartment."

I get up. The rest of these stiffs scowl at me. They are jealous. We walk down the street. We are going to this fairy's room. It is misery for me to walk on the street with this queer. People stop in their tracks and watch her wiggle. They look at her rouged lips and her plucked eyebrows. They laugh.

"Oh ho," they say, "she has got a beau."

I turn my eyes to the ground and try not to pay any attention. What the hell? This guy is my meal ticket. I will go right along to his room. I wish we were there now, though. I do not like to have people winking at me. Maybe they will think I am queer, too. I'd like to see some bastard accuse me of being queer. The first guy that calls me a pansy, it will be just too bad for that guy. That guy will never call anyone else a pansy.

We are getting into the ritzy section. There are big apartments on this street. It will cost plenty of jack to pay rent on one of these joints. I can see that this guy is in the big dough, all right. We turn into the one with the red marquee in front. The floor of the hall is covered with blue tile. There are marble statues, and paintings that are real paintings on the walls. This is some joint, all right. We take the elevator. The elevator boy grins at this queer. I bet this guy is one of his best customers. I bet this guy will make this queer, himself. This is a funny world, and there are a lot of funny people in it. That is one thing I have learned since I have been on the road.

We walk down the hall and stop before room 22. He opens the door. I follow him in. My mouth pops open when I stand inside. Never have I seen such a classy lay-out. The walls are black. The ceiling is black, black satin that hangs in folds to the floor. It is a big room, a big room like a room in a palace. A chandelier of glass stretches from the ceiling. It hangs from bronze chains. The links are as big around as my wrist. My shoes sink far down into this thick, gray rug. My shabby shoes without soles do not belong on such a rug as this.

There is another guy sprawled out on a sky-blue lounge. I can see that this guy is queer, too. He is decked out in a peach negligee. It is edged in gold. He crosses his legs as he reads.

48

There is no hair on them. They are shaved. On one of his ankles is a bracelet, a silver bracelet. On it is a pink cameo as big as an egg.

"Have a good date, deary?" he says without looking up from his book.

"Look for yourself," Mrs. Carter says.

This guy looks up, and squeals when he sees me. He jerks his negligee down over his legs like a woman would do, and jumps up.

"Stay right where you are, deary," Mrs. Carter says, "this is my date. Meet my room-mate, Gloria," she says to me. "She is cashier in a bank."

"How do you do?" I say.

Gloria does not answer. She is sulking at Mrs. Carter. She lies stomach-down on the lounge and pretends she is reading. She is not reading. She is only pretending.

"Wait here until I change my rags," Mrs. Carter says to me.

She goes into the bedroom and closes the door. Gloria winks at me and squenches up her nose at Mrs. Carter in the bedroom. I do not pay her any attention. I remember what the stiff in the hashhouse told me. I cannot take any chances. Those nails of Mrs. Carter's, sharp-pointed and painted a flaming red, were meant for something. I do not wish to have my eyes scratched out.

"Come and sit by me," she whispers.

I shake my head no.

"Afraid of her?" she says. "She couldn't hurt a flea."

She speaks low, but I am afraid Mrs. Carter will hear. I do not answer.

"You are blond," she says, "and Mrs. Carter is blond. You do not go together. I am brunette. My hair is wavy. Mrs. Carter's is straight."

She tosses her head to show me her hair is wavy.

"I come here with Mrs. Carter," I say. "She bought me a meal. What can I do?"

49

"I will buy you plenty of meals, deary," she says, "better meals than she will buy you. How would you like to have a new suit? Your clothes are shabby. How would a new suit be?"

"A new suit would be fine," I say. "I could use a new suit."

"What color do you like?" she says.

"Gray," I say. "I like a double-breasted gray suit with two pants."

"You would look good in a gray suit," she says; "a gray suit would be the thing. I will get you one tomorrow."

"What about Mrs. Carter?" I say.

"Mrs. Carter?" she says. "Who cares about Mrs. Carter. She is an old hag."

"She might hear you in the other room," I say.

She lowers her voice.

"Do you know how old Mrs. Carter is?" she says.

"No," I say, "I don't know."

"Twenty-eight, that's how old. Twenty-eight. If she didn't wear the war paint like a common whore, she'd look fifty."

"You don't use much paint," I say.

"I do not have to use much paint," she says, "I am only twenty-three. When I look as old as Mrs. Carter, I will shoot myself."

"You do not even look twenty-three," I say.

"Do you know what Mrs. Carter will do to you when she is through with you?" she says.

"No," I say. "What will she do?"

"She will kick you out in the cold, that is what she will do. I see her kick plenty of her beaux out in the cold. When she is through, she is through. Now, I like you. I would never kick you out in the cold. You can stay with me as long as you want. I like you a lot. I will take better care of you than Mrs. Carter."

The bedroom door opens. Mrs. Carter comes in. She is wearing a black nightgown that is made of silk.

"You will have to sleep on the lounge tonight, Gloria," she says.

Gloria does not answer. She is burned up.

"Come on in the bedroom," Mrs. Carter says to me.

I follow her in. She makes a face at Gloria as she closes the door.

"She is a cat," she says, "a jealous, two-faced cat."

I sit down on the lounge. She sits down beside me. We are not going to a show. I can see that. That was only a gag.

"Nice place you have here," I say. "I have never seen a classier place." I have to say something.

"Yes, it's nice," she says. "I'm glad you like it. You can stay here for a long time if you want to."

She moves up closer to me and puts her arm over the back of the lounge. Her fingers touch my neck. I feel the cold chills go up my back. I pull away.

She frowns.

"What's the matter?" she says. "Don't you like me?"

"Sure, I like you," I say.

"You don't act like it," she says.

"Well," I say, "a guy likes to get acquainted a little bit first. Sure, I like you fine, but a guy likes to wait a little first."

"Don't you think I'm pretty?" she says.

"Sure, you're pretty," I say. "You're a good-looking guy, all right."

She frowns again.

"I am not a guy," she says.

"Well," I say, "you're a good-looking—you're a good-looking girl."

"As good-looking as Gloria?"

"Better, a lot better than Gloria."

"She is a slut," she says, "a no-good, double-crossing slut. She would take you away from me if she could. Could she?"

"Her?" I say. "Not her. She hasn't got a chance. I just can't see Gloria."

I am ashamed of all this. I am sick in the stomach, I am so ashamed of all this. What can I do? What I am doing is all I can do. A stiff has got to live.

"What did she say about me in there?" she says.

"Nothing," I say. "She didn't say nothing."

"She said something. I heard her mention my name. What did she say?"

"Oh, she said: 'How do you like Mrs. Carter?' That's all she said: 'How do you like Mrs. Carter?' "

"What did you tell her?"

" 'Fine,' I said. 'I like her fine.' "

"Did you just say that or did you mean it?"

"I meant it. Sure, I meant it."

"Were you ever in love with anyone? Did you ever have a girl?"

"Sure, I was in love. Sure, I had a girl. I told you in the park I used to have a girl. But I haven't any girl now. I haven't got any dough. No dough, no girl."

"Are you still in love with her?" she says.

"Well," I say, "what good would it do me? What good would it do a stiff if he was in love with his girl? When a guy loses his job in his home town, he has to go on the fritz. He has to grab himself a drag out of town. A guy can't be dinging back doors for hand-outs and flopping behind signboards when his girl lives in the next block."

"I don't want you to have a girl," she says; "I want you to stay here."

"That is nice of you," I say.

"You won't have to worry about eating here. You won't have to sleep behind signboards, either. I have a nice bed."

Her eyes sparkle when she looks at her bed. It is an oak bed. An oak bed with sky-blue spreads, and pillow slips of silk.

She gets up and crawls into the bed.

"Come on to bed," she says.

"In a little bit," I say.

"It is cold out there. It is nice and warm in here," she says.

I want to put this off as long as possible. But not this guy. He wants to go to bed. He will not talk any more. He yawns.

"I can't sleep with the light on," he says. "Come on to bed."

It is chilly here, and I am sleepy. I will have to go to bed some time. This queer will stay awake until I do go to bed. What the hell? A guy has got to eat, and what is more, he has got to flop.

"Sure," I say, "I am ready for the hay."

You can always depend on a stiff having to pay for what he gets. I pull off my clothes and crawl into bed.

CHAPTER FIVE

IT IS AFTERNOON, and I have not eaten today. I press my hand over this bulge in my coat pocket, and watch this stiff who stands on the corner. I can see that he is going to eat, and he does not need a bulge in his coat pocket to do it, either. He does not need to risk getting a copper's bullet in his guts. He walks over to this skinny guy with the girl on his arm.

"Buddy," he says, "could you spare a little change to help a hungry man get something to eat?"

This skinny guy with the girl on his arm stops and scowls at this stiff. He does not want to part with his change to help a hungry man get something to eat.

"Why don't you get a job and go to work?" he says.

"There ain't no work," this stiff says. "I can't find no work anywhere."

"I ain't got no money for bums," this guy says.

"Go on," this girl says, "give him some dough. Maybe he is hungry. Times is pretty tough."

"They sure are tough, lady," this stiff says.

This skinny guy growls. He does not care if times are tough or not. His belly is full. He is sitting on top of the world. He has a good-looking girl hanging on his arm. What is a hungry stiff to him? He wants to tell this stiff to get the hell out of his sight, but he can't do that. That would not make a hit with this girl. There is only one thing he can do. Shell out, that's all he can do. This stiff is smart. He knows that's all this guy can do. He has got this guy where he wants him. It must feel pretty good to have one of these bastards where you want him.

He reaches down in his pocket and pulls out two bits. He would like to pull out a jitney, but he can't do that. This girl is looking. He does not want to look like a cheap skate in front of his girl. A jitney or a ten-cent piece does not go with a girl. She knows a stiff cannot fill up his belly on a ten-cent piece.

"Thank you," this stiff says. "Thank you, and the lady."

He slouches down the street.

This skinny guy grunts. He does not like parting with his dough.

I admire that stiff. He has got the guts. He does not need to go with a gnawing pain in his belly. I do not need to go with a pain in my belly, either. I have not got the guts to hit me a guy with a girl, but I have got the guts to hit a high-toned restaurant. If I cannot get me a feed in this restaurant, I have got the bulge in my pocket. I am tired of having the pain in my guts. I have made up my mind. This is the last time I will whine for a feed. I am going to show these bastards I will get mine. That is why I have the bulge that I cover up with my hand.

I walk into this joint and stand by the cash register. I look around. I have hit me some high-toned joints, but never one such as this. There are no counters here. Only tables. Women sit at these tables. It is not evening, but they have on evening gowns. On their feet are gold and silver slippers. They glitter with the jewels that are on their fingers and arms. The men are sporting coats with tails. The tables sparkle with the shine of silver dishes. I stand there, and I cannot imagine people living like this. I cannot believe it.

They look up from their tables and stare at me. I do not blame them. I am a crummy-looking customer to be in a joint like this. I know that. But I am here. I am after something to eat. I am going to get something to eat, too, or know the reason why.

"What do you want?" this cashier says.

She has a hard face. She is not going to be friendly. I can see that.

55

"I want to see the manager," I say.

"What do you want with the manager?" she says.

"Private business," I say.

This manager is standing at one of the tables. He sees me talking to the cashier and comes over.

"What do you want?" he says.

"I want something to eat," I say. "I am a hungry man."

All these customers can hear me asking for something to eat. It will not do this manager's business any good to turn down a hungry man for something to eat. He knows that. I know he knows it. That's why I am in this classy joint.

He grins and slaps me on the back.

"Sure, I can give a hungry man something to eat," he says. "Come on back in the kitchen with me."

All these cash customers grin. This manager's all right, they think. We will eat here regular. He deserves our trade. He will feed a hungry man. I can see where this guy is all right, too. I can see where I am going to get a high-class feed. Well, I need a high-class feed. We walk back to the kitchen.

This manager closes the door to the kitchen so these cash customers cannot hear.

"Hey, Fritz," he yells, "give this bum a cup of coffee and send him out the back way."

The lousy bastard. A cup of coffee. Out there he slapped me on the back. He was all smiles out there. He was showing off. I would like to take a sock at this guy, but I cannot. I cannot take any chances on getting pinched while I have the bulge in my pocket.

I walk out the back way without waiting on this coffee.

All right, I think, all right. We will not hit any more restaurants. We will not whine for any more feeds. We will either get it or we won't get it. I walk down the street. I keep my hand in my right coat pocket. There is not so much of a bulge when my hand is there. They will think it is only my hand. But it is not my hand. I have a gat in this pocket. It is heavy and black. It is a good gat. It will shoot straight. It will shoot straight if I can keep my hand from shaking, and I will have to keep my hand from shaking. I will not be caught. I have thought it all out. I have spent the night thinking it all out. I have made up my mind. Before I will be caught, I will shoot. And I will shoot straight. If I cannot get away, if they corner me, just one of these little slugs will be enough for me. My troubles will be over. I will not have any more to worry about. They have starved me to death long enough. I am tired of walking the streets all day long asking for work. They laugh at you for asking for work.

"There is no work," they say. "We cannot keep the men we have. If it's a meal you want, you can go to the mission. You can get a good meal at the mission."

I will stop asking for work. I will quit standing in the soup-lines for hours for a bowl of slop. I have made up my mind to take a chance. You can only die once.

I finger this gat. I have waited a long time to get my fingers on a gat like this. At night, on the cold ground in the jungles, I have dreamed about a gat like this. Blue black. A gat that will shoot straight. A gat that will not miss. Now I have it. The stiff I stole this gat from was drunk. He does not need this gat. He will be soused up for a week. Maybe in a week I will give him back his gat, and a wad of dough besides.

I walk on down the street. It is clogged with people. They do not look at me, and if they do, they do not see me. They do not notice my ragged clothes, and my beard that I have let grow for a week. They have troubles of their own. Some of these guys I pass on the street are wishing to Christ they could get their fingers on a gat. Well, I have my fingers on a gat. They are around the handle now. It is a good handle. It is not smooth and shiny like the rest of the gat, but rough. It is rough so you can get a good grip on it. It will not slip out of your hands.

I have planned it all out. There must be no hitch in my

planning. In my pocket is my razor. After I have pulled this
job and got away, I will shave. You would not know I am the
same guy when I have shaved. I will have plenty of dough in
my kick, too. Stacks of dough like these tellers have in their
wire cages in the banks. That will make me a different guy.

It is time I got down the street. I know the time. I have
picked the best time. I have had my fingers on this gat for two
days now. I have been figuring during those two days. I know
what I am doing. I know just what to do. This cop will be
passing that joint now. There is a box on the corner. He will be
reporting. He will not be back for an hour. Well, an hour will
make lots of difference. There's lots can happen in an hour. In
an hour I will be a rich man. I will be a rich man or I will be
stretched out on a marble slab in the morgue.

I stop across the street. This is not a big bank. It is a branch
bank. I know better than to try to hold up a big bank. I know
what I am doing. I am not crazy. I am not a fool. I look across
through the window. There are men in white shirts working
in there. Their sleeves are rolled up. It is hot in there. I watch
them as they pass out these bills to the line of customers in
front of their windows. In the drawers in front of them are
piles of bills. There are plenty of these piles. One or two of
them will keep me for life. I will not have anything to worry
about. I will be fixed for life. What have I got to lose? Nothing.
What have I got to live for? Soup and stale bread, that is what I
have to live for. That is what I have to lose.

I have thought it all out. There is an alley a little ways from
this bank. It leads to several short streets. There is a barrel in
the rear of one of these stores in the alley. In this barrel I will
throw my gat and my coat and hat. I will walk out on one of
these short streets. Up the street a little ways there is a picture show. I will go in. I will not hand the ticket girl one of
these bills that I get in the bank. That might give me away. I
am taking no chances. I have a two-bit piece in my pants
pocket for that. There must not be any slip. I will stay in this

show while they are hunting for me. I will shave in the toilet. At night I will come out. I will not hang around the streets. I will go to the mission. They will never look for me in the mission. The last place in the world they will look for a guy with plenty of jack will be the mission. I will not spend any money in this town. I will stay in this mission as long as they will let me. Then I will leave town, but it will be on no drag with its hard, cold box cars I will leave on. I will leave on a passenger, and it will not be on the blinds with the roar of the wind, and the sound of the wheels underneath me. It will be on the cushions.

I press my hand over my pocket to cover up this bulge and walk across the street and into the bank. To the left are the writing-tables. Two women are writing checks. To the right are the bank guys' cages. There are five windows here. Through each one I can see a guy dishing out money. I go up to one of these tables and let on like I am writing a check. I am not writing a check. I am seeing if the coast is clear. I have always wondered how a guy felt when he was robbing a bank. Now I know. I am getting ready to stick up this bank myself. I cannot imagine me holding up a bank. I know how these guys felt now. I know the sickish feeling they had in the pit of their bellies. I know the jerky shake of their hands. I am not going to weaken now. I have made up my mind. Shaky hands or not, I will sleep in no more lousy mission flops. I have whined for my last meal. I have the gat and I am going to use it if I have to. No one cares whether I live or die. They would let me starve to death on the streets without lifting a hand to help me. Why should I care about these guys that hand out these piles of bills from their wire cages? What are they to me? If I stemmed one of these guys on the street, he would tell me to get the hell out of his sight before he called a cop. To hell with everybody. I am going to get mine.

I get in this line that waits in front of the first cage. When I go out of here, I will have to do it on the run. I do not want to run in front of any more wire cages than I have to. They have got gats themselves in those wire cages. It is not their dough, but these bastards would take a pot shot at me just to see me drop or maybe get a raise in pay. There are five people standing in front of me. Two women and three men. I stand behind this fat woman with the big wrinkles in the back of her neck. She makes a good screen. They cannot see me holding my hand over this bulge that is in my coat pocket. There are only two people in line at this next cage, but I stay where I am. I want to be near the door.

This line moves up slow. I have never seen a line move so slow. You would think this was a soup-line it moves so slow. It is this fat woman's turn. She steps up to the window. I am right behind her. She shields me so that this guy in the cage in the white shirt-sleeves can hardly see me. At least he cannot see the bulge that is in my pocket. I glance sideways at this guy who is in the next cage. He is through with everyone in his line. He closes and locks this drawer with all the stacks of bills in it. He comes out of his cage and locks the door behind him. He goes into a room in the rear. That is a break for me. I will not have this guy taking pot shots at me from his cage, anyway. I put my hand in my pocket. I press my fingers tight around this gat. I feel the roughness of the handle. The roughness that is rough so that you can shoot it straight. I hope that I will not have to shoot straight. I hope that I will not have to shoot at all. My hand is shaking so. And my legs, too. I can feel them knocking against each other. It will not do to have my legs knocking against each other. My legs are what I am depending on to get me away from here fast.

This fat woman steps away from the window. I step up. I look at this guy. He looks at me.

"Yes, sir?" he says.

I do not say anything. I have nothing to say. I give this gat a yank, but it does not come out of my pocket. Only the handle comes out. Only the handle and a part of the lining of my coat. Something has happened. It is stuck in the torn lining of my pocket. I yank hard again, but it does not come out. This guy back of the wire cage thinks that there is something wrong. He steps closer to the window and peers out. He sees that my hand is in my pocket. He thinks there is something up. His face goes from pale to a sickish green. I know what that guy is feeling. I have the same feeling in the pit of my own belly. It is a sickish feeling, a vomity feeling. He takes a step back away from the window.

"What do you want?" he says. "What are you pulling at your pocket for?"

This guy is scared. He is plenty scared, but he has nothing on me. So am I.

"I have nothing in my pocket," I say. "Can't a guy put his hand in his pocket, if he wants to?"

I cannot take my hand out of my pocket. I am afraid he will see the bulge.

"What do you want?" he says. "What are you standing there pulling at your pocket for?"

"How much," I say, "how much does it take to start a checking account?"

"Twenty dollars," he says. "Twenty dollars."

He is not thinking what he is saying. His eyes are glued to my hand that is in my pocket. I cannot fool this guy with asking questions. He knows that there is something up. He does not take his eyes off my hand that is in my pocket. I cannot pull at this gat while he is looking. He will yell or set off the alarm. I can feel the cold sweat that stands out on my forehead. Christ, but I am scared. I have to get out of here, but how am I going to get out of here?

I turn around and start walking towards the door. I walk fast. I can feel this guy's eyes boring into the back of my head as I walk. I can feel the eyes of everyone that is in this bank on the bulge in my pocket that I cover up with my hand. I strain my ears waiting for the screech of the alarm. I wait to hear

61

this guy yell for me to stop. I turn around and look back. This guy is backing out of his cage. His eyes never leave me. I see him there backing out of his cage, a pale, sickly look on his face. He is going after one of the cops that guard the bank. They must not catch me. They must not catch me with this bulge in my pocket that is the gat. I start to run. I shove this woman out of the way who is coming through the door. I swing round the doorway and hit up the street. The alley is what I want to reach. I must reach the alley before this cop gets to the street with his gat. I cannot have this cop filling me full of holes from behind. I run as fast as my shaking legs will carry me. I hear the slam of my feet on the sidewalk. I do not look back, but I can feel these people stop in their tracks and watch me run. I make it to this alley and the barrel round the corner. I do not stop here. I keep going. I run faster. Halfway up this alley, I glance back. No one has turned the corner yet. I spot this coal-chute that leads to the basement of one of these stores. I dive head-first into this and slide to the bottom. This basement has not been used for a long time. It is thick with cobwebs that stretch from the ceiling to the floor. They cover my face and get into my eyes as I clamber to the rafters from this box on the floor. These rafters are close together. I stretch myself out on them and lie quiet. There is only the sound of my gasping for breath as I lie here.

Outside, on the street, I imagine I can hear the voices of men yelling. I do not know if they are yelling about me or not. I do not even know if they are hunting for me or not. But I cannot forget that look in the teller's eyes as he looked at my hand in my coat pocket. I cannot forget the way he backed to the rear of the cage when he saw the bulge. He did not press the alarm. There was no alarm. I would have heard it if there was. If these guys outside are hunting for me, they are bastards. They would like to try what I tried, but they have not got the guts. They know they have not got the guts. That's why they are hunting for me. They have not got the guts to do what they want to do, so they are taking it out on a guy who has the guts.

I strain my ears for sounds in the alley outside, but there are none. But there are sounds on the street. I imagine I can hear the words "bank-robber." I crouch low on my rafters. I must not make a sound. Even if they crawl into the coal-chute, I must keep my head. I must lie still. I clutch this gat tighter in my hand. I must have it ready. If they come in here, they will have to have a light to see. When they flash that light on me, the guy that does it will not flash any more lights. He will be holding the light in his right hand. I will shoot to the left. But I will make sure. I will shoot once to the left and once to the right. I will show the bastards it does not pay to hunt for me. What do they know what is right and wrong? How can they know? They have not lived for years in lousy mission flops. They have not eaten swill from the restaurant garbage cans. They have good jobs. They do not know what is right or what is wrong.

I crouch here for hours. My body aches from every joint. The cramps shoot up my legs and up my back. The light that comes from the coal-chute grows from dim to pitch-dark. Outside it is night. There is no sound in the alley. Noises still come from the street. That noise would not be for me now. That is just the ordinary noise from the street. I think. Do not be a damn fool, I tell myself. They are not hunting for you. They were never hunting for you. There were plenty of people saw you come down this alley. If they were hunting for you, they would have searched this alley from top to bottom. These cellars would be the first place they would search. If you hide this gat, what can they do to you? Nothing. Nothing is what they can do to me. That teller did not see the gat in my pocket. All he saw was the bulge. He thought it was a gat, but he cannot prove it. You cannot send a guy up because you think he is packing a gat. You have got to see the gat. I did not say for him to fork over the money. I was too busy trying to get the gat out of my pocket to say anything. All I said was how much does it take to start a checking account? You cannot send a stiff up for asking about a checking account. No, even if they catch me, they can do nothing to me. But I will have to get rid of the gat. If they catch me with this gat on me, it will be just too bad.

I climb down off these rafters and stretch my legs. They are so stiff I can hardly move them. I hide this gat underneath a pile of rubbish in the corner. First I rub the finger-prints off. Me and this gat are finished. They can never prove that I owned this gat. I have got nothing to worry about. I climb back up this coal-chute and into the alley. I look around. There is no one here. They are not hunting for me. I brush the cobwebs off me and walk out to the street.

This guy in the tweed suit is standing on the corner. I walk up to him.

"Buddy," I say, "I am down on my luck with no place to flop. Could you spare me a few dimes to get me a flop?"

CHAPTER SIX

I SIT on this curb and watch these kids that stand in line. Their faces pale and pinched, tired and hungry. They wait, and fidget back and forth. Tin buckets, battered and rusty, are in their hands. They have had a lot of wear, these buckets. This is not the first time these kids have come after their suppers. One at a time they go into this mission. One at a time they come out with a bucket of soup and a stale loaf of bread.

This kid walks up to me.

"Mister," he says, "will you watch my bucket of soup and my loaf of bread while I go in and get some more?"

"Buddy," I say, "how much of this belly-wash can you eat, that you want to go after two bucketfuls?"

"One bucket is not enough," he says. "There are six of us. One bucket is not enough. They will only let you have one bucketful in this mission, so I leave one outside while I go in after the other."

"How do you keep them from knowing you?" I say. "Mission stiffs have sharp eyes. I do not see why mission stiffs don't get jobs as detectives, they have such sharp eyes."

"I am too smart for these guys," he says. "One time I wear this cap I have on. The next time I take it off. They do not know me."

"O.K.," I say. "I will watch your bucket."

He sets this bucket of belly-wash down at my feet and gets back in line.

I let my eyes wander over these women that stand in line. In a soup-line like this you will always see plenty of women.

Their kids are too young to come after this slop, so they have to come themselves. I look at them. I look at their eyes. The eyes of these women you will see in a soup-line are something to look at. They are deep eyes. They are sunk in deep hollows. The hollows are rimmed with black. Their brows are wrinkled and lined from worry. They are stoop-shouldered and flat-chested. They have a look on their face. I have seen that look on the faces of dogs when they have been whipped with a stick. They hold babies in their arms, and the babies are crying. They are always crying. There are no pins sticking them. They cry because they are hungry. They clench their tiny fists. They pound them against their mothers' breasts. They are wasting their time. There is no supper here. Their mothers have no breasts. They are flat-chested. There is only a hollow sound as they pound. A woman cannot make milk out of slop. How much milk is there in a stale loaf of bread?

They shift their babies from hip to hip. They do not say anything. They do not talk. They do not even think. They only stand in line and wait. It does not matter how long. At first it matters, but after a while it does not matter. They are not going anywhere. When they have taken this stuff home and eaten it, they will be just as hungry as before. They know that. These babies will keep pounding their fists against their mothers' breasts. Tomorrow they will have the same hollow sound. They are all old, these women in the soup-lines. There are no young ones here. You do not stay young in a soup-line. You get crow's feet under your eyes. The gnawing pain in the pit of your belly dries you up. There are no smart ones in this line. The smart ones are not in any soup-line. A good-looking girl can make herself a feed and a flop if she works the streets and knows how to play the coppers right. She don't mind sleeping with a copper once in a while for nothing if he will leave her alone the rest of the time.

It is getting dark, and still they stand here. Their hollow eyes and their crying babies get on a guy's nerves. When this kid comes out of the mission, I hit down the skid row towards Karl's room. I huddle in these shadows across the street and watch this light in the window. It is the landlady's light I am watching.

This Karl is a friend of mine I met in the park. He has a job carrying out the garbage in a restaurant. He makes two dollars a week. It is dirty work, but two dollars are two dollars. He pays one dollar a week for this room. On the other he eats. He does not have to worry about coppers grabbing him by the scruff of the neck. He can tell all coppers to go to hell. When it is too cold to sleep in the park, I sleep on the floor of his room.

This friend of mine, Karl, is a writer. He is always hungry. You cannot stuff yourself on a dollar a week. It is not his fault he is always hungry. It is that nobody buys the stuff he writes. He writes of starving babies, and men who tramp the streets in search of work. People do not like such things. For in Karl's stories you can hear the starved cries of babies. You can see the hungry look in men's eyes. Karl will always be hungry. He will always describe things so that you can see them as you read.

I see this light in the window go out. Now is my chance. I cross the street and tiptoe up the rickety stairs. I can judge these stairs pretty well in the dark. This is not the first time it has been too cold to sleep in the park and I have used the floor of Karl's room. On cold nights the fifth step will squeak. On other nights it is all right. The one next to the top will always squeak, warm or cold. I am very careful to skip this one. This landlady has sharp eyes, and ears that are even sharper. Karl says she has a heart like a thermometer. Each ten degrees means one day you are behind in your rent. He says he likes to keep three days behind, as she is then nice and cool.

I turn the knob to Karl's room and walk in. It is dangerous to knock. Last night she caught me right in the doorway. I do not want to freeze to death again tonight. This room is only a hole, but it has a roof over it. That is something. It is not so much the cold, as the wet of the dew that you mind in the park. There is no furniture but a narrow cot and a rickety table. Karl is bent over the table writing. His pale, lean face and his deep-set eyes show that he does not sell any of the stuff he writes. You can believe that this one lives on a dollar a week for food. He jumps up when he sees me. He eyes the sack I have in my hand and grins. He has not eaten today. I can tell. When you are on the fritz long, you can tell when a guy has not eaten.

"Toppin's?" he says.

"Toppin's," I say, "and more than toppin's. This is our lucky night."

He takes the sack out of my hand and looks in.

"Great God," he says, "a coconut pie! A real honest-to-God coconut pie!"

He pushes his papers to one side and spreads this stuff out on the table. We are both excited. Our eyes glisten. Our mouths water. Never have I seen a prettier sight than these doughnuts and rolls, and in the center, standing out proudly above all, this coconut pie. It makes a sight for sore eyes. Some of these rolls are filled with jelly. Some are covered with powdered sugar. But this coconut pie is the prize. It is two days old and squashed in the middle, but it is something to look forward to, squashed in the middle or not.

Karl fills the coffee-pot with water. I unscrew the mantle from the gas-jet. It is a small flame. It is a hard job to hold the pot over it. The handle gets red-hot. We take turns holding it. We are both sweating when it is done, but it is good coffee. I do not lose any time screwing the mantle back on. We must have light, and besides, if the landlady found out we were pulling this little trick on her, it would be just too bad for us.

"Werner?" says Karl.

"Why not?" I say. "I saw him on the street this morning. He had a look in his eyes like Jesus Christ. He gets that look when he has not eaten for three days."

Karl goes across the hall to get Werner. Werner is an acquaintance of ours. He is an artist. He paints pictures of people he sees in the park. All the people in his pictures have a hungry look in their eyes. He has no better luck selling his pictures than Karl does with his stories. They are good pictures. People will not buy them, though. I think it is because of the hungry look. Even the picture of the fat millionaire leading the Peke dog had a hungry look in the eyes. Karl says it is more than an empty belly that puts a hungry look in people's eyes. I think that if Werner would take the hungry look out of the eyes of the people in his pictures, he could buy more hamburger steaks and take the hungry look out of his own eyes. Karl and Werner say this would be sacrilege to art. I do not understand such talk as this.

Whenever Karl and me run into some extra money, we buy groceries with it. We keep them in a closet for a rainy day. For a while our groceries disappeared. Not much. Only a little. A can of beans, a loaf of bread, a few stale doughnuts. We locked the door when we would leave the room. It did no good. Any key will fit his door.

"We will have to do something," says Karl. "We can't always be staying in the room."

"Leave that to me," I say. "I know a little trick that will stop a guy from stealing another guy's beans."

I go to the drug store and buy me ten cents' worth of croton oil. We pour this into a bowl of beans and mix it well. We leave this bowl on the table and go down the street. We are gone ten minutes. We come back, and our bowl is there, but our beans are gone.

"Now what?" says Karl.

"The toilet, that's what," I say.

"What about the toilet?" he says.

"We watch the door," I say.

The toilet is across the hall. We can see it from our door. We open the door a tiny bit and watch through the crack. For a half-hour nothing happens. Then comes this commotion down the hall. Werner lives down the hall. We see him shoot out his door. He is headed for the toilet. He is not losing any time. We watch through the crack till he goes back to his room.

"Now for the fun," I say.

"Fun enough already," says Karl. He is doubled up on the floor from laughing. "Did you see the look in his eyes when he turned the knob of the toilet door? 'Oh, God, don't let there be anyone in there,' they said."

"Wait," I say. "You have not seen half. Do you know what I am going to do?"

"No," he says, "what are you going to do?"

"We are going in the toilet and lock the door," I say. "He will be back. There was plenty of croton oil in those beans."

"But," says Karl, "if he can't get into the toilet he will— No," he says, "we can't do that. That is more than he deserves. He has suffered enough."

Karl is too soft-hearted, but we have fun enough through the crack in the door. Three more times Werner dashes through the hall. Each time we roll on the floor and laugh till the tears roll down our face. After that there is no more stealing. We can now put anything in the closet. It is not bothered. But when we run into an extra treat like this coconut pie, we invite Werner.

Karl comes through the door. Close behind him is Werner, with his pale face, and his coal-black eyes in hollow sockets. Tonight he looks even hungrier than ever. His eyes pop when he sees what is on the table. He licks his lips. We should not have put all this stuff on the table at once. A shock like this is not good for him. It might kill him. Werner's masterpiece will never be such a picture as this.

There is but one cup for the coffee, but there is the bowl and the glass. I fill up the cup for Karl. I take the bowl. Werner must take the glass. Karl sits on one edge of the bed. Werner sits on the other. I squat cross-legged on the floor. It would be more comfortable in Werner's place on the bed, but I am making up for giving him the glass. First we pass the doughnuts. One to each. When we finish this one, we pass them again. Each time Werner is finished long before us. He waits until we are finished. He licks his lips and glues his eyes to the table, then shifts them to the only thing on the wall, this sign which says: "Anyone stealing blankets from this room will be prosecuted."

"Who gave you these?" says Karl: "the baker?"

"The baker's daughter," I say.

"Is she beautiful?" he says. "She must be beautiful. None but beautiful women should touch such toppin's as these."

"She is so-so," I say. "Very pretty; but beautiful—I would not say that."

"Marry her," says Karl. "Marry her and bring her and her beautiful toppin's to live here."

"You never can tell," I say.

"How would you like that?" Karl says to Werner. "A beautiful baker's daughter to furnish inspiration to your art, and toppin's to put meat on your skinny shanks?"

Werner does not answer. He keeps his eyes glued to the doughnuts on the table. Before we are too full, we cut the pie. We still want to be hungry when we eat this pie, because it is a treat. Not often do we run into such a treat as a coconut pie.

That was a good guy, that baker. His heart is in the right place. He is not a beautiful girl like I tell Karl and Werner. He has a straggly mustache and wheezes through his nose when he breathes. If he has a beautiful daughter, I do not know about her. I only say she gave me this stuff in order to show off a little bit in front of Karl and Werner.

We finish this stuff and loosen our belts. We are filled to the brim. Already the haunted look is gone from Werner's eyes. He has even smiled a couple of times between mouthfuls.

"Some day there will be an end to all this," says Karl.

"Some day we shall have all we want to eat. There is plenty for all. Some day we shall have it."

"Revolution?" says Werner.

It is the first word he has spoken since he came into the room.

"Revolution," says Karl. "Not now. There is no leader. But some day there will arise a leader for the masses."

"You are right," says Werner. "Some day there will be plenty for all."

He looks at these crumbs still left from the doughnuts on the table, and his eyes light up. If I was a capitalist, I would steer clear of Werner when the day arrives.

I am tired of such talk as this. You can stop a revolution of stiffs with a sack of toppin's. I have seen one bull kick a hundred stiffs off a drag. When a stiff's gut is empty, he hasn't got the guts to start anything. When his gut is full, he just doesn't see any use in raising hell. What does a stiff want to raise hell for when his belly is full?

"It is not right," says Karl. "There is no justice in this world. They do not know, they do not see what I see in the parks and in the soup-lines. Yesterday I sat in the park and watched these clouds that hung low and black in the sky. I like to sit and watch the stiffs that sprawl in the park. I watch them as they look at the clouds that roll through the blackening sky. They sniff the air. They can smell the storm. I watch them scurry to their holes like rats. I am lucky, I think, to have a hole. This woman on the bench beside me has no hole. The baby in her arms has no hole. I can tell. I can tell by the way she glances at the sky above, and the way she frets with the blanket on the baby as she hears the thunder roar. She is a young woman, a young woman who has forgotten what a hamburger steak looks like. I can tell by the look in her eyes. A hungry look. A look like Werner gets, and you and me. A look like Jesus Christ around the eyes.

" 'You had better hit it for cover,' I say to her. 'This is going to be a real storm.'

"She stares at me as though she does not hear me.

" 'Storm?' she says. 'Oh, yes, storm.'

" 'The baby will get wet,' I say. 'The blanket is not much. You had better get in out of the rain.'

" 'No place to go,' she says.

" 'It is hell,' I say.

" 'Yes,' she says, 'for the baby. For me I don't mind. I'm used to the rain and the wet.'

" 'How old?' I say.

" 'Two weeks,' she says. 'Two weeks tomorrow.'

"Straight ahead she looks into the dark. I sit there and wonder what she is thinking. If I knew what she is thinking, I would not be living in a hole in the wall, I think. I would write the book that I will write some day when I find out what they are thinking when they sit in the parks and stare unseeing into the dark.

"This cop comes up the walk and looks at us sharp.

" 'Better get your wife and kid home, Jack,' he says. 'Regular hurricane blowing up. Be here in ten minutes.'

" 'Yes, sir,' I say, 'yes, sir. She sure is blowing up.'

"I get up. The woman sits there staring. In my pocket I am holding twenty cents. I finger it.

" 'Lady,' I say, 'you can't sit here in the storm. The baby will die of the croup.' I hold out one of my ten-cent pieces to her. 'Go over to that coffee joint and wait till she's over. You can get yourself a good meal in there for a ten-cent piece.'

"She holds out her hand and takes the money. I can tell by the way she takes the money that I was right. She is starved.

" 'Thank you,' she says, 'oh, thank you.'

" 'That's all right,' I say.

"I hit up the street. I look back and see her hugging this baby to her and heading across the street to this coffee joint. I

73

stay in this pool hall until the storm is over. When I come out, I go into this joint myself for my coffee. This woman is still there. She sits by the window. I get my coffee and walk over to her table and sit down. She does not notice me. She keeps staring out of the window. Across the street that glistens with the rain, is the park. It is miserable over there now. Miserable and black and wet.

" 'Well, I see you got in out of the wet all right,' I say.

"She turns in her seat quick. She jumps when she sees me.

" 'Oh,' she says, 'I—I thought you'd gone.'

" 'I came back for my coffee,' I say. 'Yo get good coffee in here for a nickel. Up the street they hold you up for a dime. A dime for a cup of coffee, and lousy coffee to boot.'

" 'Yes, yes,' she says. 'Lousy coffee.'

"She keeps staring out of the window. There is a wild look in her eyes.

" 'I got my opinion of a guy who will charge a stiff a dime for a cup of lousy coffee,' I say.

" 'Yes,' she says. 'Yes. Lousy coffee. Lousy coffee.'

"I can see that she is talking batty. There is something wrong. I thought that there was something wrong when I first sat down at this table. I know what it is now. It is the baby. The baby is not here. She has not got the baby.

" 'Where is the baby?' I say.

"She does not answer.

"I follow her stare out the window. Great Christ! Through the blackness of the park I can see a white splotch on one of the benches. I know what that is. It is the baby. She has gone back after the rain and put it there. She waits here to see if anybody picks it up. We do not say anything more for a while. We just sit here and glue our eyes to this white splotch on the bench in the park.

" 'Can he roll off?' I whisper.

" 'He can't roll off,' she says. 'I pinned his blanket to the bench.'

"We watch this stiff come ambling up the walk of the park. He stops by the bench, peers down, and then hot-foots it across the street. He hurries back with this cop who stands on the corner. The cops looks at this white splotch on the bench and then walks back to the corner and makes a call from the box.

"This woman gets up. She has seen all she wants to see. She pulls her hat tight over her eyes. She does not want this cop to recognize her.

" 'Thanks for the money,' she says.

" 'That's all right,' I say.

" 'He was only two weeks old tomorrow. He will not miss me. Do you think he will miss me?'

" 'He is too young to miss you,' I say. 'They will take good care of him. You had better beat it.'

"She goes out the door and hurries down the walk.

"I sit there and sip my coffee. An automobile pulls up at the curb. The cop gets the baby and hands it to a woman in the back seat. When the car pulls out, this cop stands there and looks around the park. He is hunting for someone. He stops several stiffs that pass by. He talks to them awhile, and they go on.

"Christ Almighty! I happen to think. That cop is hunting for me. He thinks that is my kid. They would not believe me if I told them that was not my kid. They would put me in and throw the key away. I get up from the table and beat it outside. I stick close beneath the awnings and beat it home."

Karl stops talking. He thinks this is something new and something awful, this woman leaving her baby in the park because she cannot feed it. Karl is soft-hearted. That is nothing. I have seen worse than that. I know that that is nothing.

I walk to the window and look out. It has started to rain. It splashes and rattles against the panes. Below me the streets glisten and shine in the dark. A stiff slouches under an awning down there. He is soggy and miserable. He presses himself tight against the side of the building, but he cannot get away from the rain. You never can get away from the rain. I know. It is a miserable night, and he is miserable. I imagine him as he walks the streets in the rain. He passes houses and sees into the front windows from the street. He sees the people who live in these houses. They sit by their firesides. They are warm and dry. He is wet and cold. They are reading about him in their papers. They do not know it is about him, but it is.

"I see by the papers," they say, "where they are starting a new soup-line on Tenth Street. Things are tough. Too bad things are so tough."

They turn over to the next page. The stiff in the rain is forgotten. But the stiff in the rain cannot forget. The water trickling down his soggy clothes will not let him forget. The gnawing pain in the pit of his belly will not let him forget. There are many funny things happen in the park, and on the street, too.

I stretch out on the floor by the window and close my eyes.

CHAPTER SEVEN

IT SNOWS. It melts as it hits, and the slush is inches thick on the pavement. The soles of my shoes are loose. The right one flops up and down as I walk. This morning I tied it to the toe of my shoe with a string, but the string wore through in an hour. Tomorrow I will tie it up with a piece of wire. It will stay a week if I tie it up with a piece of wire. My shoes are filled with water. I can feel it oozing through my toes as I walk. I walk and I can see the bubbles slosh from the soles. I am chilled to the bone. I pull my coat collar up around my ears, but it does no good. The chill comes from my soggy feet and the wind that howls round the corners. Besides, my coat is thin. I bummed it from an undertaker. The stiff that owned it croaked in the park with T.B. There's still a smudge of blood on the sleeve from the hemorrhage. I could have had his pants and shoes, too, but they were worse than mine. This coat is my Christmas present. For this is Christmas Eve.

There are lights in all the stores. They are packed with people, buying. A big arch stretches across the street. It is decorated with gold and silver tinsel. Across it, in different colored lights, it says: "Merry Christmas." The streets are choked with people. They crowd and shove. Everybody is laughing. I wonder how it feels to laugh like that? That fellow and his girl in front of me have been laughing for a block. He has bundles piled clear to his chin. When one starts to slip, she gives it a poke back in place, and they both laugh. They do not laugh because she pokes the bundles back in place. They laugh because they are crazy about each other. Besides, it is Christmas

Eve. He is sporting a fur overcoat, and his shoes do not slosh when he walks. It is easier to laugh when you are warm and your shoes do not slosh.

Across the street is a restaurant. The electric sign over the door blinks on and off in the dark: "Eat—Eat—Eat." It looks warm in there. Warm and dry. Out here it is wet and cold. It would be nice to sit in there on Christmas Eve and watch how miserable it is outside. But that is not for me. I am holding a four-bit piece. A four-bit piece to celebrate Christmas Eve with. I stop and listen to this band that plays on the corner. They are playing Christmas music. I know the piece they are playing. It is "Silent Night." My mother used to sing me that song when I was a kid. That was a long time ago. Long before I went on the fritz. Here I am now with the sole of my right shoe flopping up and down. Here I am now huddled down in my ragged undertaker's coat.

I walk towards my flop on the skid road. I am hungry, but I cannot eat. If I eat, I cannot sleep. It is too cold to flop in the park in the snow. It is Christmas Eve and I am hungry.

I pass this dark doorway and see this girl who stands inside. She is on the make. I can tell by her look. She steps out of the shadows.

"You—you want to go with me?" she says.

I look at her in her cheap red dress and her blue tam. I look at the scared look in her eyes. She is not the type. I can tell. I have seen too many. She is nervous. She pulls at her handkerchief.

"Where are you going?" I say. I am only joking.

"I—you—you don't understand," she says.

She looks down at her feet. I notice that her shoes are worse than mine. The runs in her hose start at her shoes and go to the hem of her dress. I can see that she is the same as me.

"You are not used to this," I say. "You are not so good at it. Why don't you go to the mission?"

78

"I am not used to it at all," she says. "You are the first one. I guess I am sort of clumsy, but I'll learn."

"Not if I can help it," I say. "You hungry?"

"That's why I am on the street," she says. "I'm damn near starved."

"I am holding four bits," I say. "Let's eat."

"I should not be bumming meals off another stiff," she says, "but I'd cut your throat for a hamburger steak."

We walk down the street towards the restaurant on the corner.

"I've got an idea," she says. "Two meals in a restaurant will take all that money. Now, I've got a room with a hot plate in it. We will take this money and buy enough groceries for five or six meals."

"That is a good idea," I say. "I will do the buying. I am an old-timer. I know how to do this. I will go in the stores. You wait outside for me."

I go into this cigar store on the corner and change two of my ten-cent pieces for pennies. I am going to penny-up on these store guys. We pass this meat market. There are chickens strung across the window on strings. They look good. We lick our lips as we stand outside and watch them. They would go good doused in mud and baked over a jungle fire. But baked chickens are not for the likes of us. We are only a couple of hungry stiffs, and we are on the make for a beef stew. I walk into this joint. She walks up the street to the corner and waits.

This butcher is red-faced and fat. His belly hangs in folds over his belt. If I was holding what it took to put that belly on him, I would not have anything to worry about. He grins at me when he sees me. He thinks I am a cash customer. It is cash customers who buy the chickens that hang from strings in his window.

"Buddy," I say, "I am on the fritz and only holding three

cents. Could you sell a guy three cents' worth of old baloney butts?"

The grin comes off his face. I knew it would. Nobody has any use for a stiff, not even a pot-bellied butcher. He scowls and reaches down in the box where he keeps his dog meat. He fishes out two baloney butts. They are green at the ends. Not for me, mister. I see a stiff almost die one night from eating green baloney butts. No, sir, there are too many baloney butts in this world for me to eat green ones.

"Jack," I say, "these baloney butts are green. I can't be paying good dough for green baloney butts."

"What do you want for three cents?" he says.

"I want some good baloney butts," I say. "Baloney butts that are not green at the edges."

"You are damn particular for a stiff," he says.

"It is my dough and my stomach," I say.

He cusses under his breath, but he digs up two baloney butts that are not green. I hand him my three cents and he takes it. The tight bastard. Soaking a stiff three cents for a couple of green baloney butts. I walk up to the corner and give this package to the girl. We walk on.

"We have got the meat," I say. "Pretty soon we will have the bread. I know how to do this."

We pass this bakery, and I go in. There is a woman behind the counter.

"Lady," I say, "I've only got two cents. Could you maybe sell me a stale loaf of bread for two cents?"

She hands me a stale loaf of bread. She does not reach out her hand for the two cents.

"Keep the two cents for the onion," she says. "You can't make a decent stew without an onion."

I can see that this woman is all right. I can see that she knows what it is to be hard up. She is not like that pot-bellied butcher. He is a bastard. I go outside and give this bread to the girl to carry. I do not want to be carrying anything when I go in the stores. It does not pay to look too prosperous when you are pennying-up on the store guys. When we pass a place that looks good, I go in. Pretty soon we have all the stuff we can carry. My twenty cents are gone, but we still have thirty cents to use when this stuff is gone. You cannot beat pennying-up. Once in St. Louis I ate for a week on three cents. I made the restaurants.

"Could you maybe give a hungry stiff a half a cup of coffee for three cents?" I would ask them.

I am not begging anything. If a whole cup of coffee costs five cents, a half a cup will only cost two and a half cents. I am giving them a chance to make a half a cent on me. But they do not give me a half a cup. They give me a whole cup, and something to eat with it besides. I would be eating yet on that three cents only some bastard like that pot-bellied butcher took my capital away from me. Some guy like that is always taking a stiff's capital away from him.

We walk towards her room.

"How long have you been doing this?" she says.

"So long I have forgotten how long," I say.

"Do you mind it very much?" she says. "Do you mind asking for two old baloney butts when there are people to hear you ask?"

"I used to mind," I say. "I used to live on doughnuts and coffee because I was ashamed for people to hear me ask. But you can't live forever on coffee and sinkers. You get all greasy inside. Some time you have to get a square meal to hold your stomach in shape. It will shrivel up on you on coffee and sinkers."

"Does it take long to get used to it?" she says. "Don't you always mind a little?"

"It is the bastardly butchers who take your pennies away from you and cuss you under their breath that you mind," I say. "You don't mind the ones like the woman in the bakery. She knows that times are tough. She has been hard up herself. She will help a hungry stiff with a stale loaf of bread."

"Why don't you hit the houses for something to eat?" she says. "Won't they feed you at the houses?"

"I will always hit me a house if I can find me a yellow house," I say. "I have good luck at a yellow house, but not too yellow. Some stiffs will not hit any but a green house, but give me a yellow every time, but not too yellow. It must be just the right shade of yellow."

"Do you ever hunt for a job?" she says. "Don't you ever try to get off the bum and live decent again?"

"Sure, sometimes I try," I say. "But what can a stiff do? You ask for work and they laugh at you for asking for work. There is no work. I hardly ever ask for work any more. Sometimes as I sleep in the park at nights, I wake up. I light my pipe and look at the stars in the sky above. 'I am a man,' I think; 'this is no way for a man to live. Tomorrow I will get me a job. I will keep on asking until they give me a job. I will make them give me a job.' I puff at my pipe through the night, and I can hardly wait for morning so that I can get me a job. When the morning comes, it is cold. I shiver on the street in my thin undertaker's coat. I go to the factories on my empty stomach, I go to the stores and the restaurants. 'Give me a job,' I say, 'any kind of a job. I will work for whatever you will give me. I will work for almost nothing.' They shake their heads; there are no jobs. Finally I can't ask at any more places. I am too hungry. A man hasn't even the guts to ask for a job when he is hungry. Besides, it is day. Things look different in the day than they do in the night. At night as you lie in the park and look at the stars, it is easy to find a job. In the day, in the heat and the glaring light of the sun, it is not easy. It is hard."

We are hitting the red-light district. Her room is here. The red-light district is the only place where you can get a room for a dollar a week. I look at her. She looks at me. We are two people in the world. We are the same. We know that we are the same. Our gnawing bellies and our sleepy eyes have brought us together. We do not say any more. We do not need to. I have these bundles piled up to my chin. She takes my arm, and we walk.

We turn into the doorway of this ramshackle red brick building and climb the stairs to the fourth floor. The rug in the hall is ragged and dirty. The people who live here do not live here for the scenery. They live here because they have no other place to live. The cops will not bother you for working the streets here. That is what these streets are for. We go into her room. It is only a two-by-four hole, but is clean. She keeps it that way herself. It has a bed and a chair. A hot plate sits on a box. You eat on the bed or the hot plate. It does not matter which so long as you have something to eat. I notice that the bed is a double bed. That is thoughtful of the landlady, because if the beds in the rooms were not double beds, there would be no use for the hot plate. There would be nothing to eat.

"This," she says, "is my boudoir and kitchenette. How do you like it?"

"It looks like a mansion to me," I say. "I have lived in the missions for two years."

I put the bundles down on the edge of the hot plate and sit down on the edge of the bed. I have walked the streets all day hitting the stem. I am tired. A four-bit piece is hard to ding.

She takes off her tam and starts to cook. I watch her as she cooks. She is pretty. Her hair, that is brown, and her eyes, that are blue, make her pretty. What she needs is a couple of square meals to fill up the drawnness of her cheeks and take the paleness from her skin. We talk as she cooks. I tell her about that bastardly butcher who took my capital away from me. She laughs. I laugh. We understand each other. We like each other. I am not like this because I want to be. She is not like this because she wants to be.

She peels the spuds. I clean the coffee-pot.

"James, the salt," she says.

"Yes, m'lord, and the pepper besides," I say.

We are having a good time. It does not take much for a couple of hungry stiffs to have a good time. The spuds that begin to sizzle on the hot plate are enough. The pot of coffee that fills the room with its smell is enough.

"People meet in funny ways, don't they?" she says. "It was funny the way I met you, stopping you on the street."

"A stiff is always doing funny things," I say. "We can't act as other people act. We have got to do what we can. A woman turned me down for something to eat one time. I went out in front of her house and sat there on the curb all day with my head in my hands. In the evening she came out and gave me my supper. I worked in her garden for two weeks straight. I write to her yet sometimes. We have to act the best way we can."

"What did you think of me when I stopped you?" she says. "What do you think of a girl who will go as bad as that?"

"I think she was awful hungry for a hamburger steak," I say. "I think she has not had a hamburger steak for a week."

She laughs.

"And you are right," she says. "Not for more than a week. Two weeks. I had some turnips here and some beets. For three days I ate them. For two days there has been nothing."

"You look at things different when you have not eaten for two days," I say. "I know. I have gone that long myself. I have stolen. I have done worse than steal when I have gone that long."

"Yes, you look at things different," she says. "What is supposed to be wrong does not look wrong when the only right thing looks like something to eat. When I stepped out of the doorway to you, I wanted something to eat. Nothing was wrong that would give me something to eat."

"That is the way I felt when I started to knock a guy in the

84

head once," I say. "That is the way I felt when I started to hold up a bank once."

"But you didn't knock a man in the head or hold up a bank?" she says. "You only started to. You didn't really do it?"

"No, I didn't do it," I say. "I only started to. I lost my nerve on the man. My gun got caught in the lining of my pocket, or I would have held up the bank. Maybe it is a good thing it did get caught. Maybe if it hadn't of got caught, I wouldn't be here. I am glad that I am here."

"I am glad that you are here," she says. "I am glad that I am here. I am glad that I stopped you on the street."

"I am glad you stopped me instead of someone else," I say. "Maybe this other guy would not know how to penny-up on the store guys."

"We will penny-up some more," she says, "but there must not be any baloney butts that are green at the edges. We can't be paying good dough for green baloney butts. There are too many baloney butts in this world for us to be eating green ones."

She is mocking me. We laugh.

"And the bread from the bakery," I say. "That bread was a little too stale. I am afraid that after this we will have to do our trading farther round the corner. For two cents we should get a fine loaf of rye bread that will be fresh, and not stale."

"We will trade at no place where they do not throw in some good cow's butter when you buy an onion for the stew," she says. "Cow's butter and cow's milk."

I walk to the window and look out. Through the murk a million lights flash on and off through the haze of the snow. She comes to the window and stands beside me.

"On Christmas Eve a roof is something," she says. "There are worse than us out there."

"Tomorrow where is the roof?" I say.

"Tomorrow is tomorrow," she says. "Tonight there is the roof."

I point to the rows of lights that span the bridge to the right of the town.

"There are a hundred stiffs live under that bridge," I say. "I have slept under there myself. I know. Men with wives. Men with children live under that bridge. That is their roof on Christmas Eve."

She takes my hand in hers.

"If you like, if you love the person you are under the bridge with," she says, "the bridge would not be bad. Even on Christmas Eve it would not be bad."

We stand hand in hand by the window.

"I like you," she says. "My name is Yvonne."

We laugh.

"My name is Tom," I say.

"Where are you staying at nights?" she says.

"In the park," I say.

"You can stay here," she says, "until the landlady kicks us out."

CHAPTER EIGHT

I WAIT, and, Christ, but the hour goes slow. I stand in this soup-line. Back of me and before me stretch men. Hundreds of men. I huddle in the middle of the line. For two hours I have stood here. It is night, and ten minutes before they start to feed. The wind whistles round the corners and cuts me like a knife. I have only been here for two hours. Some of these stiffs have been here for four. Across the street people line the curb. They are watching us. We are a good show to them. A soup-line two blocks long is something to watch. These guys on the curb are not in any soup-line. They have good jobs. They have nothing to worry about. It must be pretty soft not to have anything to worry about.

Sixty seconds in a minute, I think, and ten minutes. That makes six hundred seconds. If I count up to six hundred, slow, they will be started when I finish. I begin to count. I count to a hundred, but I can get no further. I have to stop. I am too cold to count. I stomp my feet on the concrete walk. I swing my arms high over my head. It is a damn shame to stand in this line as cold as I am, but I have to stay. I am hungry. I have to get a little something in my belly. I wait. We stiffs in the soup-lines are always waiting. Waiting for the line to start moving. The bastards. They keep us standing out in the cold for adver-tisement. If they let us in and fed us, where would the adver-tisement be? There wouldn't be any. They know that. So they keep us out in the cold so these people on the curb can have their show.

There is a commotion up in front of me. Stiffs bunch around in a knot. A cop pushes them back in line. There is a stiff stretched out on the ground. He is an old stiff with gray hair. His eyes are wide open, but he does not move a lick. He is tired of waiting for this line to start moving. He is stretched out on the concrete, and dead as four o'clock. I can see that this stiff is lucky. There will be no more waiting for him. They cover him up with a sheet and load him in the mission truck. He is off to the morgue. There is no fuss when a stiff kicks off in a soup-line. There is no bother. They throw a sheet over him and haul him away. All he needs now is a hearse and six feet of ground, and they will have to give him that. That is one thing they will have to give him. And it will not make any difference to him how long he has to wait for it. It must burn them up plenty to have to give a stiff six feet of ground for nothing.

This old stiff croaking like this out in the cold puts this bunch in a bad humor. They shove and cuss at these guys in the mission who make us stand in the cold. They can see that we mean business. They open the doors and let us in. A mission stiff hands us a pie pan, a tin cup, and a spoon. We carry them up to where these guys are standing over these tubs of stew. It is scorching hot in here. These mission stiffs that are ladling out the stew are sweating. The sweat drips from their faces and falls in the stew. But that is nothing. What is a little sweat to a stiff? What can a stiff do about it if it maybe turns his stomach?

We get our pan of stew and our cup of water and sit down at the table. The room is filled with these tables. A mission stiff walks along the aisles with a basketful of stale bread. He throws it to us like a guy throwing slop to hogs, and we catch it. This stew is made of carrots that were rotten when they were cooked, but we eat it. We have to. A stiff can't stand the cold outside unless he has a little something in his belly. I bolt down this stew and get out. The smell of this place will turn a guy's stomach. It smells like a slop-jar.

Now for a smoke. I am dying for a smoke, but I am not

holding any smoking. I keep my eye peeled over the curb. A guy will throw a snipe on the walk, and a wind will come along and blow it over the curb. You will find your biggest snipes over the curb. I spot one in front of this drug store. It is a big one. It is not half smoked. I can see that the guy who threw this butt away was in the big dough. I slouch up to this snipe and stop. I put my feet between it and the store. I lean down to tie my shoe. I am not tying my shoe. I am picking up this snipe. What these guys in the drug store don't know won't hurt them.

I walk back to this mission and stop by this stiff who leans up against the telephone pole. He is sporting a pretty good front. He carries a roll of chicken wire under his arm. You can hardly tell this guy is a stiff.

"That was awful stew," I say.

"What was?" he says.

"That slop they feed you in the mission."

"You eat that slop?"

"What else is a guy going to eat?" I say. "A guy can't starve."

"A stiff with brains don't need to eat slop, and he don't need to starve," this guy says.

"Sez you," I say.

"Sez me," he says. "I have got a ten-cent piece." He pulls this ten-cent piece out of his pocket. "What would you buy if you had a ten-cent piece?"

I think. What can a stiff buy with a ten-cent piece when he is half starved? Well, a good cup of coffee will hit the spot right now. A good cup of warm coffee will go a long way when you are hungry.

"Coffee and sinkers is what I would buy if I had a ten-cent piece," I say.

"And that is just why you have to eat slop," he says.

"What has that got to do with me eating slop?" I say.

"You do not use your brains," he says. "Why do you think I lug a roll of chicken wire under my arm?"

"I have been wondering about that ever since I see you on the corner," I say. "Why do you lug it?"

"The coppers," he says, "that's why."

"What do coppers have to do with chicken wire?" I say.

"When you walk up the main stem," he says, "how do you go, fast or slow?"

"Any stiff knows that," I say. "I go as fast as hell. If you do not go fast, the goddam coppers will stop you and frisk you on the street."

"You are right," he says. "But I don't walk fast on the main stem or anywhere else, and the coppers don't bother me."

"They don't bother you?" I say.

"They do not," he says. "They don't think I am a stiff. What would a stiff be doin' with a roll of chicken wire under his arm?"

"You are a smart stiff," I say. "I have never tried that."

"It's just as easy to be a smart stiff as a dumb stiff," he says. "All coppers are dumb. A smart stiff will fool a copper every time."

"You didn't say what you were going to do with your ten-cent piece," I say.

"I will show you some brains that are real brains and not imitations," he says. "We blow this dough for two doughnuts, see? Then we hot-foot it to a corner where a bunch of dames is waitin' for a street-car. We plant one of these doughnuts on the curb and go across the street. When enough dames is waitin' there, I duck across the street, dive at this sinker, and down it like I ain't et for a week. Dames is soft, see. This racket is good for a buck and sometimes two bucks."

I can see that this stiff has got brains, and what is more, he has got imagination.

"How long have you been working this little trick?" I say.

"Since I have been on the fritz," he says.

"And the bulls, don't the bulls ever break up your racket?" I say.

"Bulls!" he says. "I am too smart for the bulls. Come on, and I will show you why I don't eat the slop they throw out in the mission."

We go into this bakery and buy two doughnuts. They are no ordinary doughnuts. They are big and honey-dipped. I have never seen a prettier picture than these two doughnuts. That is because I am damn near starved. I want to sink my teeth into one of them, but I know that that is foolishness. After I was through eating it, I would be hungrier than ever. When you are starved and get a little something to eat, you are hungrier than ever. We can't waste any time eating one of these doughnuts. We are on our way to try out a little scheme that took lots of brains to think up.

We slouch down the street until we spot a good corner. There are a bunch of women waiting there for a street-car. When it comes along and they get on, we take this chance to lay one of our doughnuts on the curb. We put it in plain sight. Anyone waiting for a car can see it. I carry the other one, and we walk across the street and wait. In a little while there is another bunch of women on this corner. There are some men too, but we are not interested in the men. Men are hard, but women are soft. A woman does not like to see a hungry stiff starve to death. A man does not care if a stiff starves to death or not.

"Now is my chance," this stiff says.

He slouches across the street. I stand here and watch him. He has got the guts, all right. There is no doubt that this guy has got the guts. I can see now why this guy does not need to eat mission slop. A stiff with this much guts can live like a king. He stops across the street and lets his eyes fall on this doughnut on the curb. It is a picture sitting there. I expect to see him make a dive for it, but he does not. This stiff is deeper than that. He knows how to do it. He just stands there and watches it. These women see him looking. I can see they are thinking why will a guy stand on the street and watch a doughnut? He walks on by and stops a little ways up the street. Pretty soon he comes back. He walks far over to the curb and snatches it up on the fly. He hits it over behind a telephone pole. By the way he acts, you would think this was the first doughnut this stiff ever snatched off the curb. You would not think this guy has been pulling this gag for years. He downs this doughnut almost whole. It looks as though this stiff is plenty starved. You would think he has not eaten in a month of Sundays. That is what these women think. That is what he wants them to think.

This big fat woman in the brown coat reaches down in her pocketbook and fishes out some change. She walks over behind the post and hands it to this stiff. He shakes his head no, but he holds out his hand yes. This guy wants it to look as though it hurts his pride to take dough from this woman. I can see that this guy will never need to swill slop in a mission. If one person is going to be big-hearted, everybody wants to be big-hearted. Four or five of these women fish around in their pocketbooks and walk over to this stiff who hides behind the post. This is real money. This is not chicken-feed that this guy is taking in. One of these women shells out a buck. I can see the green of it from across the street. If I had the guts, I can see that there would be one more dummy-chucker in this town tomorrow than there is today. You just dive down on a doughnut, and these women do the rest.

He thanks these women and walks up the street. In a little while I walk after him. I do not want these women to think I am with him.

"You are the stuff," I say. "That is the prettiest little trick I have seen in a long time."

"You will go a long way before you find a prettier little racket than dummy-chucking," he says. "How much do you think I cleaned up on that doughnut?"

"I don't know," I say, "but I saw you get a buck."

"Two bucks and sixty-five cents," he says. "That is how

much I made on one doughnut, and you wanted to spend that ten-cent piece on a cup of lousy coffee. You have got to have brains and imagination to get along on the fritz."

Me and this stiff hot-foot it to a restaurant and order up a good meal. This guy is all right. When he leaves he slips me a four-bit piece.

"Any stiff that eats mission slop ought to have his fanny kicked," he says. "There is too many doughnuts in this world for a stiff to eat mission slop."

I sit here in this restaurant and think. Why can't I do what this stiff does? I have as much brains as he has. I have the imagination, too. But I cannot do it. It is the guts. I do not have the guts to dive down on a doughnut in front of a bunch of women. There is no use talking. I will never have the guts to do that.

CHAPTER NINE

I CROUCH here in this doorway of the blind baggage. For five hours I have huddled here in the freezing cold. My feet dangle down beneath the car. The wind whistles underneath and swings them back and forth. The wheels sing over the rails. Up in front of me the engine roars through the blackness, that is blacker than the night. The smoke and the fire belch into the sky and scatter into scorching sparks that burn my back and neck. I do not feel the wind that swings my legs. They are frozen. I have no feeling in them. I slink far back in this door and put my hands over my face. Great God, but I am miserable. I cannot stand this much longer. I was a fool for nailing the blind baggage of this passenger. I was a fool, and now I am freezing to death.

I think. How am I ever going to get off this drag if it ever does stop? I can't walk. My feet, that are frozen, will not hold me up. I sit here and think, and I doze. I awake with a jerk.

"You damn fool," I say, "you can't go to sleep here. You will fall under those wheels that sing beneath you. Those wheels would make quick work of you, all right. Those wheels would make mincemeat of you. You would not be cold any more."

I begin to sing. I sing loud. I yell at the top of my voice, because of the roar of the wheels and the sound of the wind underneath me. I don't want to fall under those wheels. I am only a stiff, and I know that a stiff is better off dead, but I don't want to fall under those wheels. I can feel myself getting dopey. I try to sing louder. I try to hear my voice over the sound of the wind and the cars, but I cannot. I cannot keep

94

awake. I can see that I cannot keep awake. I am falling asleep. I wonder if this is the way a guy freezes to death. I am not so cold now. I am almost warm. The wind roars just as loud as before. It must be just as cold as it was before. But I am not cold. I am warm. Great Christ, I must not let myself freeze to death. I swing my arms. I reach my head far out over the side of the car. The wind tears at my face, but I keep it there until the tears run down my cheeks. Oh, Christ, won't this drag never stop?

I feel the buckle of this drag beneath me. I feel it jerk and throw me forward. I hear the whine of air for brakes. I grab the sides of this car with all my might. My frozen fingers slip, then hold. I am not scared. I am not afraid. I just grab the sides of the car and hold. I feel this train slacken speed. I see the scattered lights of a town. Only a few lights, but I see that this drag is going to stop. I begin to laugh. I laugh like a crazy man when I see that this drag is going to stop.

I hang on with all my might. There will be a jerk when this drag stops. I do not want to go under those wheels. We pull to a stop in front of this jerkwater station. There will be no bulls in this place. The thing to do is to get off this drag before it starts again. It will not stay here long. How am I going to reach the ground? My legs are numb. They are frozen. They will not hold me up. I rub them fast and hard. I feel them sting and burn as the blood begins to run. I try to move them. I can move them. I can see them move. But I feel nothing when they move. I pull myself to my feet. I am standing. I can see that I am standing, but I cannot feel the car beneath my feet. I reach out over the side of this car and grab the ladder. I climb down. I hold with one hand and guide my legs with the other, but I climb down. I stop at this last step. It is a long way to the ground for my frozen feet. I jump. I fall face-down in the cinders at the side of the track. This drag whistles the high ball. She pulls out. I lie here in the cinders with my bleeding face and watch the coaches go by. I lie here in the cinders with my frozen legs that have no feeling in them. I shiver as I think of that blind baggage with the roar of the wheels and the sound of the wind underneath. I push my fists into the ground and get to my feet. I grimace at the pain that shoots through my legs, but I grit my teeth and walk.

What I want right now is a cup of coffee. A cup of good hot coffee will always warm a guy up. I am too cold to want to eat. I make it to the main stem of this town. There are lights in the few stores that are still open. I pass a restaurant. There is a sign in the window. It says: "Try our ten-cent hamburgers." I wonder if they would let a frozen stiff try their ten-cent hamburgers. I walk in. There are two customers eating. I walk up to this bird behind the counter. He backs away. He glances at his cash register. He has a scared look on his face. I look in the mirror that lines the wall. I do not blame this guy for being scared. What I see scares me, too. My face is as black as the ace of spades. It is smeared with blood from the cuts of the cinders as they scraped my face. I hit those cinders hard.

"Buddy," I say, "I am broke. Could you spare me a cup of coffee?"

"I can't spare you nothin'," he says. "Beat it before I throw you out."

Imagine this bastard. I am half starved and half froze, and he turns me down for a lousy cup of coffee. I am too cold to even cuss him out. I want to cuss him out, but I am too cold. I walk down the street and hit these other two restaurants. They turn me down flat. I can't get me anything to warm me up. But there is one thing I will have to get, and that is a flop. In weather like this a stiff has got to have a flop.

"Where is the town bull?" I say to this guy on the corner.

"You will find him in the garage," he says. "He will be shootin' the bull by the stove in the garage."

I walk over to this garage and find this hick cop by the stove in the office.

"Chief," I say, "I want to get locked up in the can. I am on the fritz with no place to flop."

"The jail ain't no hotel," he says. "I can't lock you up. I can't louse the jail up by locking you up."

Well, if this is not a hell of a note! A stiff can't even break into a lousy can. They call this a free country, and a stiff can't even break into jail to get away from the cold and the wind.

"Can I warm up a little by your fire?" I say. "I am froze."

"Get this straight," this bull says; "we have no use for lousy stiffs in this town. The best thing you can do is to hit the highway away from here."

"What is a stiff supposed to do, shoot himself?" I say.

"If I catch you in this town tomorrow, it will be a good thing if you do shoot yourself," he says.

I go out to the street and walk. I walk fast. I do not feel like walking fast, but I have to to keep from freezing to death. That's how cold I am. I pass a pecan grove. Over away from the road I can see a shack with a light in it. I knock on the door. An old man comes to the door with a lantern in his hand.

"Hello," I say. "Have you got somewhere a guy could flop for the night around here? I am freezing to death, with no place to flop."

He puts his hand on the top of my head.

"Son, do you believe in Christ?" he says.

"Sure," I say, "I believe in Christ. Have you got some place I could flop around here?"

"The last days are upon us," he says. "The sound of the trumpet is soon upon us. Repent or you burn in everlasting flame."

This guy is as batty as a loon. I can see that.

"Have you got some place I could flop outside?" I say. "An old shed or something?"

Outside will not be too far away from this guy. He is ready for the booby-hatch.

"The lamb that is lost is the care of the Lord," he says.

He leads the way to this building where they store the pecans. It is a big place. The floor is covered with piles of these pecans. He takes a shovel and digs a hole down in one of these piles. He puts two burlap sacks in the bottom of it.

"Son," he says, "lay down in this hole and rest."

I get in.

He covers me up with pecans, and piles sacks on top of me. My face is all that is sticking out of the hole. He puts a sack over my face.

"Rest that you may better fight the battles of the Lord," he says.

He takes his lantern and goes back to his shack.

It is pitch-dark in here now. I lie under these pecans and think. Here I am lying down in a hole. Here I am covered up with pecans. Before I went on the fritz, I was lying nights in a feather bed. I thought I was hard up then. I had a decent front. I had my three hots and a flop. Can you imagine a guy thinking he is hard up when he has his three hots and a flop? That was two years ago, but two years are ten years when you are on the fritz. I look ten years older now. I looked like a young punk then. I was a young punk. I had some color in my cheeks. I have hit the skids since then. This is as low down as a guy can get, being down in a hole with pecans on top of him for covers. If a guy had any guts, he wouldn't put up with this. I think. Why should one guy have a million dollars, and I am down in a hole with pecans on top of me for covers? Maybe that guy has brains. Maybe he works hard. I don't know. What is that to me if he is there and I am here? Religion, they say in the missions. Religion and morals. What are religion and morals to me, if I am down in a hole with pecans on top of me? Who is there to say that this world belongs to certain guys? What right has one guy to say: This much of the world is mine; you can't sleep here?

I lie here in the darkness and think. It is too cold to sleep. On the blind baggage of the drag I could not keep my eyes open. Now I cannot close them. I listen to these rats that rustle across the floor. I pull this sack off my face and strain my eyes through the blackness. I am afraid of rats. Once in a jungle I awoke with two on my face. Since then I dream of rats that are as big as cats, who sit on my face and gnaw at my nose and eyes. I cannot see them. It is too dark. I cannot lie here and wait with my heart thumping against my ribs like this. I cannot lie here and listen to them patter across the floor, and me not able to see them. I pull myself out of these pecans and get to my feet. I tiptoe out to the road. I do not want to wake this crazy old codger who dug the hole for me. I do not want to hurt his feelings, and besides, he might go off his nut.

I walk. I lower my head far down to keep the whistling wind from cutting my face like a knife. I listen to the creak of the trees as the wind tears through them. I keep to the left of the road. I cannot hear the sounds of the cars as they come up behind me. You can hear nothing for the roar of the wind. From time to time I turn my head to stare through the night for signs of a headlight. When I see one, I stop in my tracks and hold out my hand for a ride. They do not stop when they see me raise my hand. They step on the gas and go faster. They do not care to pick up a worn-out stiff with blisters on his feet. It is night. They are afraid. They are afraid of being knocked in the head. I do not blame them for being afraid. You cannot tell what a stiff might do when he is as cold and fagged as I am. A stiff is not himself when he is as cold as I am.

I reach the town and skirt it. I am afraid of rats, and this town bull has a face like a rat. I reach the yards and crawl into one of these cars that line the tracks. I shove the door almost shut. I do not shut it tight. If they start moving these cars during the night, I want to be ready for a quick get-away. I take this newspaper out of my pocket and spread it on the floor. I take off my shoes and use them for a pillow. I lie down. I am all in. I am asleep in a minute.

I do not know how long I am asleep. I awake with a jerk. Something has awakened me. All at once I am wide-eyed and staring. There is a feeling of queerness in the top of my head. I know that feeling. I get that feeling when there is something wrong. I had that feeling once when a drag I was on went over the ditch. That feeling was in the top of my head just before a guy I was talking to on the street dropped dead. My breath comes in short gasps. There is a crawling feeling all over me. A tingle starts at my feet and runs to my hair. I feel a chill in the roots of my hair. I know what that is. My hair is standing up. I raise up on my elbow. The rustle I make as I move on the paper sounds like thunder in the quietness of the car. A ray of light comes through the opening in the door. It is not strong enough to reach to the other end of the car, but I know that there is nothing there. It is in back of me. Whatever it is that is in this car is in back of me.

I tell myself that there is nothing to be afraid of. There is nothing in this car but me, I tell myself. It is only a nightmare. You have ridden the blinds too long at a stretch. You are as nervous as a cat. You will have to take time out from the drags for a while and rest up in the jungles. You have been going at too steady a clip. But I only tell myself this to stop the tingle in the top of my head and the shivers that crawl up my back. Riding the drags does not do this to me. I have been doing it too long. I would not know what to do if I was not riding the drags. I know that there is something in this car. There is something near me. There is something in back of me. I can feel the eyes boring into the back of my head. When I feel like this I know that there is something wrong, something terribly wrong. Great Christ, but I am afraid. My flesh is goose-pimply. I want to scream at the top of my lungs. I want to make a wild dash for the door. I want to dash out into the night and run. I reach out and find my shoes in the dark. I put them on. I cannot tie them. My fingers tremble too much to tie them. I sit there and tremble and shake and try to get hold of myself.

"You are a fool," I tell myself, "a damn fool. The door is almost closed. You can't dash for that door. The thing that is in back of you would grab you before you could begin to get it open. Besides, who would want to hurt you? You are only a stiff. You are not holding any dough. What would anybody want to hurt you for? You must stay here. You must stay here and wait."

For five, ten minutes I wait here, tensed on my elbow. Nothing happens. I feel the sweat pouring down my face. I feel it drip from my chin. It is cold in here, but the sweat drips down my face. I cannot stand this waiting in the dark. I will go crazy if I wait here any longer. I get to my hands and knees and start crawling towards the door. I crawl slow. Slower than I have ever crawled before. If you could see me, you would not think I was moving at all. Then I hear this sound. I stop in my tracks. It is only a little sound. A sound as though something were slipping up nearer and nearer. A sound as though someone was raising one foot and then putting it down. Then sliding the other foot up. Nearer and nearer.

Then, through the dark, comes this squeal. It is a wild squeal. A squeal like something is mad and crazy. It is like something that has lost its mind. I feel it bound through the air and land on my back. It knocks me down to the floor. These sharp claws bite into the nape of my neck. The long fingers grip my throat so that my breath comes in sobs. I am strangling. I grab at these claws. I feel a man's wrist. A strong wrist. A wrist that is all covered with hair like an animal's. I am down on my belly on the floor of the car. These fingers like hot iron press tighter and tighter. I feel these knees that bore into the small of my back. My neck wrenches backward. So far back I wait to hear it snap. Dizzier I get, and dizzier.

Like in a dream I know that these claws that bite into my neck are trying to kill me, to choke me to death. I struggle blindly in the darkness.

I throw myself to my back. I feel the claws loosen their grip. I feel them slide off my neck and tear the flesh off in strips. I feel the burn on my throat and the moistness that I know is blood. I stumble to my feet as he sprawls on the floor. I am facing him now in the dark. He scrambles to his feet. He is only a shapeless mass in front of me. It is a shapeless mass that wants to kill me, to choke me till there is no life in me. I see it hurl itself through the air. I brace myself against the side of the car and kick out with my foot with all my might. I feel it hit, hard. I hear a grunt, a squeally grunt that a pig might give. My foot is buried in his belly. He thuds to the floor. He rolls over and over, but he is up again in a second. There is a flash in his hand. Through the ray of light that comes through the door I see this flash. My spine creeps. I know what that flash is. It is a knife. I cannot let him get at me with the knife. I cannot let him rip me open with the knife. He is going to murder me with the knife. I have to get out of here. Great Christ, I have to get out of here. I leap towards the door and reach it. I claw at it and try to pry it open. It is caught. The splinters bury themselves in my finger-nails. I do not notice the pain. I am too afraid to notice the pain of a splinter in my nails. Again behind me I hear that scream.

I swing around. The knife flashes through the air above my head. I grab at the hairy wrist that holds the knife. The razor-sharp edge slashes my arms. I know it slashes my arms because of the scorched feeling and the wet that spurts against my face. I struggle with the wrist that holds the knife and the arm that clubs at my head. I am getting weak. The loss of blood has made me weak. I cannot hold the arm that clutches the knife. I glue my eyes to this flash that quivers and shakes over my head as we strain in the ray that comes through the door from the moonlight. Nearer it comes and nearer. I twist the wrist with all my strength. I twist till I hear the snap of it through our panting and scuffling. I hear this scream again as the arm goes limp and the knife clatters to the box-car floor. I start to dive for the knife on the floor and feel this fist that smashes to my face. I sprawl to the other end of the car. I grope in the dark and try to get up. I cannot. I am too weak to get to my feet. I lie here and tremble on the floor.

Through the ray of light that comes from the door I see this guy stand and stare at the floor. The gleam of the knife is there. He does not pick it up. He is not looking at the knife. It is this pool of blood from my slashed-up arm he is staring at. He stares like a guy in a trance at this blood. He flops to his knees and splashes his hands in the blood and screams. He splashes his hands in the pool of blood and smears it all over his face. I can see him quiver and shake and hear his jabber as he smears the blood. I lie here and wait for the flash of the knife, but it does not come. He leaps to his feet and jumps towards the door of the car. He jabbers and babbles as he shoves against it. He slides it open and leaps to the tracks. I can hear his screams as he crashes through the thickets.

I lie in the darkness with my bloody arm and shiver and sob in my breath.

CHAPTER TEN

WE CRAWL on our hands and knees and ease up towards the yards. It is so dark you can hardly see your hand in front of you. We can hear them banging these cars around inside this high board fence that separates us from the yards. We can hear the switch engines chugging as they make up our drag. We do not have long to wait. We hear this drag give the high ball. We ease up as close as we can get without being seen by the bulls. We scrape our knees and our hands on the sharp pebbles in the tracks and stumble over the ties that are higher than the rest. We cuss under our breath. We crawl to the side of the tracks and press up tight against these piles of ties. We are nervous. A stiff is always nervous when he knows he has to nail a drag in the dark. This drag is pulling out. We see this shack on the tops wave his lantern to the engineer. We can hear her puffing as she comes. I cock my ear and listen to the puff. You can judge how fast a drag is coming by listening to the puff. This one is picking up fast. She will be balling the jack when she gets to where we are. I keep one eye peeled for the bulls. If they are riding this drag out, they will be laying for us. I have too many scars already from being sapped up by the bulls.

I can see her coming now. I can see the sparks that fly from her stacks, and the flames that leap above her. She is puffing plenty. She is a long drag, and a double-header. I can make out the sparks from the two engines. That is why she is balling the jack so much. This is a manifest. She won't lose any time going where she is going. Passenger trains will take a siding and let these red balls through.

This old stiff picks up his bindle, and starts back towards the jungle.

"This one is too hot," he says. "There will be another drag tomorrow. I do not like to sell pencils."

Four or five stiffs follow him. They know when a drag is too hot, too. They do not want to sell pencils, either.

I crouch here in the dark and wait. Farther up the track I can see these other stiffs crouching beside the tracks. They are only a shadow through the dark. I hope I can make it, but I am plenty nervous. It is too dark to see the steps on the cars. I will have to feel for them. I pick me out an even place to run in. I look close to see that there are no switches to trip me up. If a guy was to trip over something when he was running after this drag, it would be just too bad. That guy would not have to worry about any more drags.

These engines bellow past us. I can see now that I have waited in the cold for nothing. I can see that a guy can't make this one. It is just too fast. The roar she makes as she crashes over the rails, and the sparks that shoot from her stacks, tell me she is just too fast. A stiff is foolish to even think about nailing this one. Christ, but I hate to wait all night for a drag and then miss it because it is too fast.

This stiff in front of me does not think this drag is too fast.

"Brother," I think, "I hope you are right, because if you are wrong you will not do any more thinking."

I see him run along by this drag. I see him make a dive at this step. He makes it. It swings him hard against the side of the car. I can hear the slam of his hitting from where I am. He does not let go. He hangs on. I see him begin to climb the steps to the tops. Damn, but that was pretty. No waiting all night for a drag and then missing it for this guy. He is an old-timer. I can tell by the way he nailed this drag that he is an old-timer.

Another stiff runs along by this drag. I can tell that he is scared. He reaches out his hand after this step as this drag flies by, and then he jerks it away. This stiff will never make it. I can tell. He has not got the guts. A stiff has got to make up his mind to dive for those steps and then dive. This stiff makes up his mind to take a chance. He reaches out and nails this step. The jerk swings him around and slams him against the car. He hits hard. If he can hold on, he is all right, but he cannot hold on. He lets loose and flies head-first into the ditch at the side of the track. The bottom of that ditch is cinders. Christ, but there's a stiff that's dead or skinned alive. I cannot tell if he is moving in the ditch or not. It is too dark to see. I cannot go over there and see. I have waited all night in the cold to make this drag, and I am going to make it. That first stiff made it. If he can make it, I can make it. I have nailed as many drags as the next stiff.

"Be sure and nail the front end of the car," I tell myself. "Be sure and nail the step on the front end of the car. If you lose your hold, you will land in the ditch like that other stiff. That will be bad enough, but if you nail the rear end and lose your grip, you will land between the cars."

It is just too bad for a guy when he goes between the cars. I saw a stiff once after they pulled him out from under a box car. That stiff did not need to worry about nailing any more red balls at night.

I judge my distance. I start running along this track. I hold my hands up to the sides of these cars. They brush my fingers as they fly by. I feel this step hit my fingers, and dive. Christ, but I am lucky. My fingers get hold of it. I grab it as tight as I can. I know what is coming. I slam against the side of the car. I think my arms will be jerked out of their sockets. My ribs feel like they are smashed, they ache so much. I hang on. I made it. I am bruised and sore, but I made it. I climb to the tops. The wind rushes by and cools the sweat on my face. I cannot believe I made this drag, she is high-balling it down the tracks so fast. I am shaking all over. My hands tremble like a leaf. My heart pounds against my ribs. I always get nervous like this when I have nailed a drag at night going as fast as this one is.

I lie up here on the tops in the rush of the wind and wonder about that poor bastard over in the ditch. I wonder if he was killed. I know that these other stiffs who missed the drag will see to him, but I cannot get my mind from him. A stiff like that has no business on the road. That guy should be a mission stiff. He has not got the guts to nail a drag at night. He should stick to the day drags. A stiff can't expect to reach up there and grab hold of those steps. You have to feel them brush your fingers, and then dive for them. If you make it, you are lucky. If you don't make it, well, what the hell? What difference does it make if a stiff is dead? A stiff might just as well be dead as on the fritz. But just the same I am glad I am here on the tops and not smashed all to hell underneath those wheels that sing beneath me.

For two hours I lie up here before this drag pulls to a stop at a red block. I am as stiff as a board from the rush of cold wind and the frost that covers the tops. I will have to find me an empty. It is just as cold in an empty as it is up here, but there is not the rush of the wind that cuts through you like a knife. I climb down to the ground and run along by the tracks until I hear the voices of stiffs in one of these cars. I shove the door open and climb in. There are about ten stiffs already in this car. They are walking back and forth and stomping their feet from the cold. It is miserable in this car, and they are miserable. I am miserable myself. But then, what the hell? A stiff is always miserable. If he was not miserable, he would not be a stiff.

Some of these stiffs lie on the floor with last Sunday's newspapers around them for covers. They are not so cold. You will find a worse blanket than last Sunday's newspaper. I have no newspaper. I sit down in this corner and shiver. My teeth click together. On all sides of me I can hear other stiffs' teeth clicking together. The click keeps time with the song of the wheels on the rails. I close my eyes and try to sleep. But all I can do is lie here and think. I think: Here I am. I am in a box car. I am heading west. Why am I heading west? Well, it is warmer out west. There will not be the snow and the rain. You will not have to be listening to your teeth clicking together every time you try to get a little sleep. It is too cold to lie here. I get up and go over where these other stiffs are.

We huddle in a bunch. There is a pile of tar paper on the floor. We tear this up into small pieces and light it. The flames flicker up and light up our faces, grimy and sunken. The black smoke roars up and fills the car. We crouch around this fire and choke for breath. We do not mind the smoke if we can get a little heat. We stomp on the floor with our numbed feet. We swing our hands back and forth. We are just a box-carful of frozen stiffs. We do not make a pretty picture with our red-rimmed eyes and our sunken cheeks. We do not care whether we make a pretty picture or not. What we want is to get warm. I take off my shoes. I hold one of my numbed feet over the flames. I cannot feel the flame that burns my foot, but I hold it there until my sock is scorched and burning. Then I change to the other foot. Back and forth, back and forth.

We huddle here and hack and cough in the smoke. We do not dare to open the door. It will not do for the shacks to see the smoke pouring out of this car. They would sick the bulls on us at the next stop. These bulls would put you in and throw the key away if they ever caught you building a fire on a box-car floor. Pretty soon we are out of tar paper. We get out our knives and start cutting splinters from the beams of the car. The beams are hard. It is a tough job to cut fast enough to keep the fire going. It goes out.

I crawl back in my corner and wait for morning. The desert! That is a good joke. The books say the desert is scorching hot. I wonder did any of these guys that write the books ever ride across it at night in a corner of a box car? I lie here in my corner and listen to these stiffs' teeth clicking together. Even above the roar of the wheels I can hear them.

"Goddam it," says this stiff in the corner across from me, "I am not goin' to stand for this much longer. I will get my hands on a gat, that's what I will do. I will show the bastards I am not goin' to freeze to death in a box car."

He stomps his feet on the floor to get the blood to running.

"Up your fanny," says this stiff he is with. "I have heard that old bull for years. If you are a stiff, you will freeze in box cars and like it. That's where a stiff belongs, in the corner of a box car."

"If I ever get my fingers on a gat I will show the bastards where I belong," this stiff says. "It will be just too bad when I get my fingers on a gat."

"Yeah, I said that, too," this other stiff says. "But I have got my fingers on a gat, and what did I do with it? Nothin', that's what I did with it. Nothin'. A stiff hasn't got the guts to do anything but eat slop and freeze to death. That's all he's good for. That's why he is a stiff."

I lie here in my corner, and I know that that stiff is right. That is all that a stiff is good for. I had my fingers on a gat, too. What did I do with it? Just what he did. Nothing. I maybe could have been on easy street now if I had gone through with that bank job. I would have either been on easy street or been under six feet of ground. And what difference would it make if I was under six feet of ground? Is six feet of ground any worse than lying here with my teeth clicking together to the tune of the wheels that sing over the rails beneath me? There is nothing worse than this unless maybe it is being down in a hole with pecans on top of you for covers.

This drag pulls to a stop at this water tank. A draft of wind hits me. I can hear the door slide open. It would just be our luck to have some shack kick us off in this God-forsaken place. But it is not that. Two new stiffs are climbing into the car. They carry big flashlights in their hands. I can see from the flash of the lights as they flash them around in the car that they are a couple of mean-looking eggs. Their faces are covered with dirty whiskers. They have not had a shave in a long

109

time. They are filthy. There is no sense in a stiff letting himself get this filthy. There is too much water in the world. One of these stiffs has a black patch over one eye. He is wearing an old raincoat. The other one is wearing a ragged brown overcoat and a blue toboggan.

This drag gives the high ball and pulls out. I lie here and listen to her puff, and wonder how many more miles.

"All you bastards get over in the other end of the car, and make it snappy."

I raise up quick. These two stiffs that just got on are standing there in the doorway facing us. They are holding their gats in one hand, and their flashlights in the other. They look plenty tough standing there. These big, black gats look plenty tough, too. One of these guys has got his gat pointed straight at me. This drag is jerking and swinging over the rails. That gat is liable to go off any minute. I do not lose any time getting to the other end of the car. I can see that these two mugs mean business. If they do not mean business, why have they got these gats? And why does this guy have to pick on me to point his gat at? Why don't he point it at one of these other stiffs? There are plenty of other stiffs in this car besides me. These other stiffs do not like the looks of these gats, either. They get to the end of the car as fast as I do.

We know what this is. We know what we are in for. These stiffs are a couple of hi-jackers. This is a hold-up. I have got my opinion of any stiff who will hold up another stiff and take his chicken-feed away from him. Any guy who will do that is a low-livered bastard. I do not say that out loud, though—not with those gats pointed at us like that.

"Hold up your hands," this guy in the blue toboggan says.

We do not lose any time holding up our hands.

"You with the red hair, come out here," says this other stiff. "Any of you other mugs try anything funny and we will drill you full of holes."

This red-headed guy walks out to the middle of the car. He

is holding his hands high in the air. They are shaking plenty. He is scared, and I can't say that I blame him. I am plenty nervous myself. These two are the toughest-looking mugs I have seen in a long time. One of them frisks this red-headed guy while the other one keeps us covered with the gat and flashes his light upon us.

"Where do you keep your dough?" this guy that's doing the frisking snaps.

"In my pants pocket," this red-headed stiff says. "In my left pants pocket. I've only got some chicken-feed."

"I will soon see how much you got," this hi-jacker says. "If I catch you holding out on me, I'll beat the living hell out of you and throw you out on the desert for the buzzards."

I can see that this stiff who is doing the frisking knows his business. I can see that he is an old-timer at this little trick of robbing stiffs of their chicken-feed. He not only looks in your pockets. He looks in the sweat-band of your hat and feels in the lining of your clothes. He does not find anything but chicken-feed on this red-headed guy.

"Get back in the corner," he says, "and keep your hands in the air."

He starts on the next guy. In the lining of this stiff's coat, fastened with a safety pin, he finds five bucks. Can you imagine that? This stiff has got five bucks pinned to the lining of his coat, and he has been bumming smoking off the rest of these stiffs. A tight stiff like that deserves to lose his dough.

"You will lie to me, will you?" says this hi-jacker.

He slaps this stiff across the face with the butt of his gat and knocks him clear across the car. This stiff sprawls on the floor and does not get up.

"Any of you stiffs make a move, and I'll drill you," says this stiff who is covering us.

We do not make a move.

One at a time he goes through the rest of us. I am the last guy. It is my turn.

"All right, you," he says.

I walk out to the middle of the car and hold out my hands. He goes through me. Four bits is all I got in my pockets. He does not find anything in my clothes.

"Where are you hidin' your dough?" he says. "Come clean or you will get what that other stiff got."

"Four bits is all I am holding," I say. "You've already got all the dough I'm holding."

"All right, get back to your end of the car," he says.

I get back. I feel pretty good. This bastard doing the frisking is not so smart. I bet I am the only stiff in this whole car who is holding a cent now. I am too smart for this bastard. I got two bucks hid under that bandage on my arm. I got iodine smeared over the tape. It looks like I got a plenty sore arm. But there is nothing the matter with my arm. That is only a way I thought up out of my head to keep these hi-jackers from stealing my dough. This is not the first time I have run into hi-jackers since I have been on the fritz.

This drag pulls over to a siding and slows down. She is going to let a passenger through. These hi-jackers pull the door open. They know she is going to stop here. I bet they pull this little trick every night.

"Lay down on the floor with your heads to the wall," one of them snaps.

We lie down. This drag stops. We hear these guys pile out the door. We hear the door close and the lock snap. They have locked us in. All these stiffs in the car get up to their feet and start cussing these hi-jackers. All but me. I do not say anything. I have got me two bucks under that bandage, with iodine smeared on top of it.

CHAPTER ELEVEN

IT IS NIGHT, and we are in this jungle. This is our home tonight. Our home is a garbage heap. Around us are piles of tin cans and broken bottles. Between the piles are fires. A man and a woman huddle by the fire to our right. A baby gasps in the woman's arms. It has the croup. It coughs until it is black in the face. The woman is scared. She pounds it on the back. It catches its breath for a little while, but that is all. You cannot cure a baby of the croup by pounding it on the back with your hand.

The man walks back and forth between the piles of garbage. His shoulders are hunched. He clasps his hands behind him. Up and down he walks. Up and down. He has a look on his face. I know that look. I have had that look on my own face. You can tell what a stiff is thinking when you see that look on his face. He is thinking he wishes to Jesus Christ he could get his hands on a gat. But he will not get his hands on a gat. A gat costs money. He has no money. He is a lousy stiff. He will never have any money.

Where are they going? I do not know. They do not know. He hunts for work, and he is a damn fool. There is no work. He cannot leave his wife and kids to starve to death alone, so he brings them with him. Now he can watch them starve to death. What can he do? Nothing but what he is doing. If he hides out on a dark street and gives it to some bastard on the head, they will put him in and throw the keys away if they catch him. He knows that. So he stays away from dark streets and cooks up jungle slop for his wife and kid between the piles of garbage.

I look around this jungle filled with fires. They are a pitiful sight, these stiffs with their ragged clothes and their sunken cheeks. They crouch around their fires. They are cooking up. They take their baloney butts out of their packs and put them in their skillets to cook. They huddle around their fires in the night. Tomorrow they will huddle around their fires, and the next night, and the next. It will not be here. The bulls will not let a stiff stay in one place long. But it will be the same. A garbage heap looks the same no matter where it is.

We are five men at this fire I am at. We take turns stumbling into the dark in search of wood. Wood is scarce. The stiffs keep a jungle cleaned of wood. I am groping my way through the dark in search of wood when I stumble into this barbed wire fence. My hands are scratched and torn from the barbs, but I do not mind. I do not mind because I can see that we are fixed for wood for the night. We will not have to leave our warm fire again to go chasing through the night after wood. A good barbed wire fence has poles to hold it up. A couple of good stout poles will burn a long time. What do I care if this is someone's fence? To hell with everybody! We are five men. We are cold. We must have a fire. It takes wood to make a fire. I take this piece of iron pipe and pry the staples loose.

This is good wood. It makes a good blaze. We do not have to huddle so close now. It is warm, too, except when the wind whistles hard against our backs. Then we shiver and turn our backs to the fire and watch these rats that scamper back and forth in the shadows. These are no ordinary rats. They are big rats. But I am too smart for these rats. I have me a big piece of canvas. This is not to keep me warm. It is to keep these rats from biting a chunk out of my nose when I sleep. But it does not keep out the sound and the feel of them as they sprawl all over you. A good-sized rat tramps hard. You can feel their weight as they press on top of you. You can hear them sniffing as they try to get in. But when I pull my canvas up around my head, they cannot get into me.

"Sniff and crawl all you damn please," I say. "You can't get into me."

When I look at these stiffs by the fire, I am looking at a graveyard. There is hardly room to move between the tombstones. There are no epitaphs carved in marble here. The tombstones are men. The epitaphs are chiseled in sunken shadows on their cheeks. These are dead men. They are ghosts that walk the streets by day. They are ghosts sleeping with yesterday's newspapers thrown around them for covers at night. I can see that these are ghosts that groan and toss through the night. I watch. From time to time a white splotch gets up off the ground. He cannot rest for the rats and the cold. This is a restless ghost. Or maybe it is the gnawing pain in his belly that makes him restless and sleepless. The ground is hard. Damp and hard. There are many things will make a restless ghost at night in a jungle. I am a restless ghost myself.

I look from face to face about our fire. We are not strangers. The fire has brought us together. We do not ask questions about each other. There is nothing to ask. We are here. We are here because we have no other place to go. From hollow, dark-rimmed eyes they watch the fire. Their shoulders sag and stoop. Men come to look like this when night after night they hunt for twigs through the dark to throw on a jungle fire. This hunchbacked guy across from me squats on his legs and talks. His voice is flat and singsong.

"I hit this state in 1915 with a hundred bucks I made in the harvest in Kansas. I pulled off this drag and made for a saloon in town. It was cold riding those rails, and I needed a drink to warm me up. Before I knew it, I was drunk and nasty. This spick lunged up against me at the bar, and I pushed him away. I never liked a greaser, anyway. Before I knew it, we were going after each other with our knives. I jabbed him one in the ribs. He dropped his knife to the floor and yelled. He wasn't hurt bad. Just a jab, but it scared him. Someone grabbed me and pinned my arms from behind. I thought they were ganging me. I was big and strong then. My back was hunched, but strong. I pulled away and let this guy have it. I got him right through the heart. He sagged to the floor. His hands rubbed against my face as he fell. Not hard. Just light. Light and soft like a woman's or a ghost's. I dream about those hands rubbing against my face light and soft when I sleep. I didn't know this guy was a deputy until they locked me up in the jug.

"Well, I got twenty years. That is a long time. It is a lifetime. I wrote my mother I was going down on a construction job in Mexico. That's the last time they ever heard from me. I wanted them to think that I had died down there. Fifteen years in the big house is the stretch I did. It ruined me. It would have ruined anybody. I was like I am now when I got out. My blood is all turned to water. I can't stand the cold any more. My blood is all turned to water.

"I bummed around on the rattlers after I got out. A bindle stiff was all I was. That's all there was to do. I was an old man. Then I got this crazy notion to go home and see how things looked. I hopped myself a drag and headed east. Well, it was the same old town. You know the type. Hardly a new building put up in years. I didn't hang around town much. The first thing I did was to go out to the cemetery. I was hunting a grave. My mother's grave. I didn't hunt long until I found what I was looking for. I knew it would be there. Fifteen years is a long time. I had a sister in that town, and a brother, but I had seen all I came to see. I turned around and walked back to the tracks. There was a west-bound due out of there at night. I nailed it."

He finishes. We do not say anything. We just sit here and stare into the fire. There are a lot of things will put a guy on the fritz. One minute you are sitting on top of the world, and the next you are sitting around a jungle fire telling about it. The rest of these guys could tell their stories too, if they wanted to. They have stories to tell. But they do not say anything. Some stiffs do not tell their stories. They walk up and down the garbage heaps at night with the look on their face.

We hear the sound of voices over at the other side of the
tracks. They are coming our way. We raise our heads. More
frozen stiffs hunting a warm fire, we think. But there is no
such luck for us. Four men are hot-footing it over the tracks.
They swing blackjacks in their hands. From their hips swing
gats in holsters. It is the bulls. By God, a man can't even crawl
into a filthy garbage heap for the bulls.

"Line up, you lousy bums," the leader says.

He swings his blackjack high. He is aching for a chance to
bring it down on some stiff's head.

We line up. There are twenty of us. We are twenty, and they
are four, but what can we do? We kill one of these bastards,
and we stretch. They kill one of us, and they get a raise in pay.
A stiff hasn't got a chance. They know a stiff hasn't got a
chance.

"Hold up your hands," this leader snaps.

We hold up our hands, and they go through our pockets.
They do not find anything. It makes them sore.

"I have a good notion to knock every one of you sons of
bitches in the head and leave you for the rats," this guy says.
"You are nothin' but a bunch of sewer rats, anyway."

He glances around the jungle. He sees our suppers that cook
on the fires. He walks from one fire to the other and kicks
everything over on the ground. I want to pull this bastard's
guts out with my bare hands. We are twenty hungry stiffs in a
jungle. We had to work hard to get that grub. A stiff always has
to work hard to rustle up his grub. It is almost ready to eat,
and he kicks it over on the ground.

"Get out on the highway before we sap you up," this guy
says.

"You are a bastard," says this guy with the wife and kid, "a
no-good bastard."

This bull walks up to this stiff and brings his blackjack
down on the top of his head. It makes a thudding sound when
it lands. He topples to the ground. The blood spurts from the
cut in his head. He gets to his feet and staggers around the

fire. This woman with the kid starts to cry. We close in towards these bulls. We fumble on the ground for sticks and
rocks.

"Let's hang the sons of bitches," says this old stiff, "let's
skin the bastards alive."

These bulls see that we mean business. They go for their
gats in their holsters. They cover us.

"I will bore the first bastard that lays a hand on me," this
leader says.

We stop crowding in. What can we do when they have us
covered with these gats? There is nothing we can do.

"Hit it down the pike as fast as you can go, and don't come
back," says this bull.

We head down the road. It is the cold night for us with our
blistered feet and our empty bellies.

Five miles down this road there is a water tank. Sometimes
the drags stop there for water. If we are lucky, we can nail a
drag out of there tonight. We walk. We have covered a mile
when the man and the woman with the kid drop out. It is a
rough walk over the ties in the night, and they are tired and
hungry. They flop down on the side of the road to sleep. We go
on. We can hear the baby strangling for breath behind us. We
can hear the woman slap it on the back.

We stumble over the ties. It is too dark to see them. We get
over to the side of the tracks and walk. The burrs come up
through the soles of my shoes, but I go on. I cannot stop. If I
stop, I will not be able to get started again. My feet will swell.
I trudge on, and when I take a step it drives the sharp points of
the burrs far into my feet. I straighten my pack over my back
and limp. I look at the stars in the sky above, and I see no
comfort there. I think of that poor bastard lying back there in
the weeds with his wife and kid.

"Oh, God," I say, "if there is a God, why should these things
be?"

We hobble for hours with our heavy packs before we reach

the tank. We flop to the ground beneath it. We pull off our soleless shoes and rest our blistered feet. We lie here like men that are dead, and look at the sky overhead. We talk back and forth through the night. We talk and we do not care whether anyone is listening or not. We do not care. We have to talk. That is the only way we can get our thoughts out of our minds. This hunchback tells his troubles to the stiff in the ragged red sweater. This guy in the red sweater does not care about the troubles of this hunchback, but he sees in his troubles some of his own. So he listens. This hunchback is not talking for himself. He talks for all of us. Our troubles are the same.

"For three years," says this old stiff, "I have laid in the cold and the dark like this. Is this goin' to last forever? Ain't things never goin' to be different? How long is a guy supposed to put up with this?"

"You'll croak in a jungle, and I'll croak in a jungle," this hunchback says. "Times'll never get any better. They will get worse. I got a paper in my pocket." He taps the newspaper in his pocket. "There is an editorial in this paper. It says this depression is good for people's health. It says people eat too much, anyway. It says this depression is gettin' people back to God. Says it will teach them the true values of life."

"The bastards," says this stiff gnawing on the green baloney butt, "the lousy bastards. I can just see the guy that wrote that editorial. I can see his wife and kids, too. They set at their tables. A flunky in a uniform stands back of their chairs to hand them what they want at the table. They ride around all day in their Rolls-Royces. Will you ever see that guy in a soup-line? You will not. But the bastard will write this tripe for people to read. True values of life, by God! If this guy wants to get back to God so much, why don't he swap his Rolls-Royce for a rusty tin bucket and get in line? The bastard."

"He says you can live on nothin' but wheat," this hunch-back says. "He says this depression is nothin' to get excited

119

about. People will not starve. There is plenty of wheat. If a guy says he is hungry, give him a bushel of wheat."

"Where is the wheat?" this old stiff says. "When I come through Kansas, they was burnin' the goddam stuff in the stoves because it was cheaper than coal. Out here they stand in line for hours for a stale loaf of bread. Where is the wheat, is what I want to know."

"Try and get it," this stiff says, "just try and get it. They will throw you in so fast your head will swim."

Far away we hear this drag whistle in the night. It is a lonesome and dreary moan. We put on our shoes and go out to the tracks and wait. We lie down on the tracks and place our ears to the rails. We can hear the purr that rumbles through them. We look at each other and shake our heads. Too fast. If she does not stop for water at this tank, she is too hot to catch on the fly. A stiff just can't nail this one on the fly. We are old-timers. We know by the sing in the rails when a drag is too hot. We go back to our bindles and sit down. If she does not stop, there will be another drag tomorrow. What is a day to us, or a month or a year? We are not going any place.

We see her belch round the bend. She is not going to stop here, that is sure.

"She is coming round the bend," this kid yells. "Ain't you stiffs goin' to nail her?"

We shake our heads. Too fast. We know. We can tell by the puff, and the sparks that fly from her stacks.

He hits it over to the tracks and waits. Is this damn punk going to try to nail this one? If he does, he is crazy. But what the hell? All punks are crazy. They make it harder for us old ones. This drag whistles. She is batting plenty. The engine and a dozen cars pass us before we know it. She can't waste any time slowing up for a bunch of stiffs. This kid stands there by the tracks and watches her whiz by. He is making up his mind whether to nail it or not. He is a damn fool to even think about nailing this one. I have seen too many guys with stumps for legs to even think about nailing this one. I can still walk. That is something.

I sit here on my bindle and watch him. He is only a shadow by the tracks. The cars whiz by. He runs along beside her. He makes a dive for this step, the rear step. What is this damn fool diving for the rear step for? Don't he know enough to nail the front end of a car? She swings him high, and in between the cars. He loses his grip. He smashes against the couplings. He screams. He is under. Oh, Jesus Christ, he is under! He is under those wheels. We run over. He lies there beside the tracks. He is cut to ribbons. Where his right arm and leg were, there are only two red gashes. The blood spurts out of the stumps. It oozes to the ground and makes a pool in the cinders.

We drag him over to the side. He is through. I can see that he is through. His eyes are half shut. They are dopey-looking. There is a grin on his face. It is a foolish, sheepish grin. No stiff likes to have a drag throw him. It hurts a stiff's pride to have a drag throw him. It hurts this kid's pride, too, so he has a sheepish grin on his face, and him with his two stumps oozing blood to the cinders.

I lean over him.

"Want a cigarette, buddy?" I say.

"Hello, there," he says. "Sure, I want a cigarette."

I put it between his teeth and light it.

"My arm feels funny," he says. "Kind of numb and tingly. That old drag was balling the jack. I must have bumped it pretty hard."

"You got a rough bump," I say, "but you will be all right in a minute. She was a hot one, all right."

"She was plenty hot, all right," he says. "I thought I was a goner when I slipped."

He does not know he is hurt. He cannot see his two stumps that are oozing blood on the cinders. I lean over so he cannot see. What is the use to let him know? He will be gone in a minute. There is nothing we can do. His troubles will soon be over.

I watch him. I am sick all over. I am watching a kid die. It is hard enough to watch anybody die. I even hate to watch an old stiff die, even when I know he is better off dead. But a kid is different. You kind of expect a kid to live instead of die.

There is no color in his face now. All the color is on the ground mixed with the cinders. He closes his eyes. The cigarette drops out of his mouth. He quivers. Just a quiver like he is cold. That is all. He is gone. I unfold a newspaper and cover up his face.

We sit there in the dark and look at each other.

CHAPTER TWELVE

I AM in this mission. I lie up on top of this bunk. It is a high bunk. It is a three-decker. If I should turn over on my stomach in my sleep, I would fall out and break my neck. This is a big room. There are a thousand here besides myself. I lie up here and listen to the snores of a thousand men. It is not funny. I lie here and listen to them snore, and I cannot sleep for thinking. I look at the rafters overhead and the shadows that play across them. I think of vultures hovering in the sky, waiting. They dart across the rafters and onto the walls. I see them swooping down on their prey that lie sweating in the lice-filled bunks. Their prey is a thousand men that lie and groan and toss. I lie here and listen to them groan and toss, and I try to figure it out.

"There is no God," I say. "If there is a God, why is such as this? What have these men done that they live like rats in a garbage heap? Why does He make them live like rats in a garbage heap?"

It is all dark in here. Dark save for the light and the shadows that come from the electric sign outside. It is a big sign. It hangs from wires in front of this mission. "Jesus Saves," it says. I can hear the shuffle of stiffs as they slouch in front of the door outside. They lean up against the sides and sprawl on the curb. They are waiting for nothing. There will be no flop in this joint for them tonight. They are too late. There are plenty of beds left in here, but they are too late. You have to come early and listen to the sermon if you want a flop in this joint. They are too late. I lie here and wonder since when did Jesus Christ start keeping office hours?

There are gas hounds out there, too. I can hear them. They snore and groan in the doorway. They do not care where they flop. They do not care if they flop at all. They do not have a care in the world. I do not blame these guys for being gas hounds. They do not know what it is to be hungry. They never have to eat. What's the use of blowing a good ten-cent piece on a feed? You can blow it on a can of heat and forget you are hungry. You can forget a lot of other things besides.

I turn my eyes to the stiff in the bunk next to mine. Through the shadows I can see him lying there. His face is pasty white. The bones almost stick out of his skin. All you can see is the whites of his eyes as he rolls them back and forth. They are big eyes. Big eyes set in a skull with only a little meat still left. And they are all white. That's what gives me the willies when he rolls them about like that. There is no color in them. They are all white. I turn my head away from him, but still I can hear him groan. It is a hollow groan. It comes from a hollow chest. I cannot keep my eyes away from him. I cannot help looking at him. His hands are like claws lying there on the dirty blankets. He does not breathe. He only rattles. Why don't someone do something for this poor bastard? Do something! That is a good joke. When he rattles to death on top of this lousy bunk, it will only be one less to swill down their lousy carrot slop. God damn them. Some day they will pay for this.

"For Christ sake, what is the matter with that stiff?" says this stiff in the next bunk.

"He is croaking up here in his lousy bunk, that's what's the matter with him," I say.

"Does he have to make that much racket to croak?" he says. "I see plenty of stiffs croak, but I never see one make that much racket at it."

"I guess a stiff has got a right to make as much noise as he wants to when he is croaking," I say. "Why should he care if a bunch of stiffs get their sleep or not? Nobody is worrying their heads off about him."

"Give him a swig of heat or knock him in the head," this stiff says. "They are kickin' me out of this joint tomorrow. I got to get me some sleep so I can ride the rattlers. A guy can't be ridin' the rattlers if he needs sleep."

I lie up here and think. Here is a stiff who has lived his life, and now he is dying under these lousy blankets in a mission. Who is there to care whether he lives or dies? If all this stiff needed was a glass of water to save his life, he would croak anyway. Nobody in this mission would give him a drink of water. This stiff is dying, and this other stiff in the next bunk is raising hell because the rattles from his hollow chest keep him from sleeping. This stiff has not always been a stiff. Somewhere, some time, this stiff has had a home. Maybe he had a family. Where are they now? I do not know. The chances are he does not know himself. He is alone. The fritz has made him alone. He will die alone. He will die cooped up in a mission with a thousand stiffs who snore through the night, but he will die alone. The electric light outside will go on and off in the dark, "Jesus Saves," but that will not help this stiff. He will die alone.

I yell to this mission stiff who is the night man.

"What the hell are you yellin' about?" he says. "Don't you know you will wake these other stiffs up?"

"There is a man dying up here in this lousy bunk, and you ask me why am I yelling?" I say. "Are you going to let this poor bastard suffer all night?"

"What do you think I am goin' to do with him?" he says. "I am no wet-nurse for a bunch of lousy stiffs."

"You are a God-damn mission stiff," I say, "and mission stiffs are sons of bitches."

"You can't talk like that to me," he says. "I'll have you kicked out of the mission. Tomorrow I'll have you kicked out of the mission."

"You call an ambulance for this stiff," I say, "or I will call it myself, and beat the hell out of you besides."

"I will call the ambulance," he says, "but you will not be here tomorrow. I'll see that you are not here tomorrow."

He cusses and goes out to the office to call the ambulance.

Pretty soon the doctor is here. There are two guys with him. They are dressed in white. They carry a stretcher between them. This croaker climbs up on this three-decker bunk and looks at this guy. He feels his pulse and times it with his watch. He sticks a thermometer in his mouth. When he pulls it out, he shakes his head. He pulls out a piece of paper and a pencil.

"What is your name?" he says to this guy.

This stiff does not answer. He cannot answer. This stiff will soon be finished. There will be no more mission swill for this stiff. He walls his eyes and gurgles in his throat. He moves his claw-like hands. He wants to talk, but can't.

"Where do you live?" this croaker says.

This stiff does not answer him. He cannot tell him, but I can tell him. He lives wherever he can find a hole to get in out of the rain. He lives wherever he can find a couple of burlap sacks to cover up his bones. He cannot tell him this, because he is dying. I have seen a lot of old stiffs die. I can tell. His bloodless lips pull back over his yellow teeth. It looks as though this stiff is grinning at this croaker who asks him where he lives. I shiver in my blankets. This stiff is a ghost. A ghost of skin and bones. A bloodless ghost. I try not to look at him. A dead man's grin is a terrible thing. A mocking, shivery thing.

This croaker climbs down off the bunk.

"This guy has not got a chance," he says. "I can't do any-

126

thing for this guy. He is starved to death. He is skin and bones. He will be dead in an hour."

"What'll we do with him?" this mission stiff says.

This bastardly mission stiff does not want to be bothered with an old stiff who will be dead in an hour. He is afraid he might have to help carry him downstairs. All mission stiffs are the same. They are all bastards.

"Load him up," this croaker says to the guys with the stretcher; "we'll take him with us."

They load him on the stretcher and take him out. He does not move his face. Only the whites of his eyes show as he walls them around in his head. Only the sound of the rattle comes from his hollow chest.

There are not a thousand snores through the night now. There are none. These stiffs in the bunks raise up on their elbows and watch these two guys in white carry this stiff out. These stiffs know what they are watching. They are watching a funeral. This stiff is not dead yet, but they are watching a funeral. He will not come back. You will see them carry out plenty of stiffs in a mission on these stretchers. You will never see them again after they carry them out. We know that we are watching a funeral. When they carry you out of a mission, you are dead.

They thump down the stairs with this stiff. I lie up here and listen to them thump. These other stiffs lie back in their bunks. Some of them pull the covers up tight around their chins. They are cold. It is not so cold in this room. They are not cold because they are cold, but because they are afraid. I know what they are thinking. They think that that stiff on the stretcher they hear thumping down the stairs is not the stiff that is on it, but themselves. They can see themselves lying on this stretcher. They see the whiteness of their eyes walling through the darkness of the night. They hear the rattle that comes from a hollow chest. That is the way they will land up.

127

They know that that is the way. You cannot forever be eating slop and freezing to death at night. Some night you will not be able to get your breath for the rattle, and they will come and carry you out on a stretcher. There is no snoring now. We stare wide-eyed at the shadows that play across the ceiling. We watch the flickerings of the sign outside that says: "Jesus Saves."

Underneath me is this itch and crawl. I tell myself it is the stickiness of the dirty blankets. But it is not that. I know what it is. It is lice that itch and crawl beneath me. I lie here and feel them crawl. I do not scratch. It does no good to scratch. I lie here and grit my teeth until I can stand it no longer. I pull these blankets off me and strike a match. I cannot see them. They are too small to see. I brush these blankets off with my hands. I take these newspapers out of my pants pocket and spread them over the bed. I leave some of the paper hang over the sides. Maybe if they try to crawl out to the edge to get me, they will fall to the floor and break their necks. I lie back down and spread the rest of these papers over me.

It is better now. There is no itch to make me lie and grit my teeth. It is better to freeze to death than to be eaten alive by lice. The stiff under me snores again and scratches. The stiff under him snores and scratches. I lie here and try to think back. I try to think back over the years that I have lived. But I cannot think of years any more. I can think only of the drags I have rode, of the bulls that have sapped up on me, and the mission slop I have swilled. People I have known, I remember no more. They are gone. They are out of my life. I cannot remember them at all. Even my family, my mother, is dimmed by the strings of drags with their strings of cars that are always with me in my mind through the long, cold nights. Whatever is gone before is gone. I lie here and I think, and I know that whatever is before is the same as that which is gone. My life is spent before it is started. I peer into the blackness of the ceiling, and in its blackness I try to find the riddle

128

of why I lie here on top of this three-decker bunk with the snores of a thousand men around me.

I look over at this stiff's empty bunk. Dead in an hour. I shiver. Great Christ, I think, is this the way I will go out, too? It is hard enough to pass out in a nice feather bed with all your family gathered around and crying. It is no snap to die like that. But this way. Lying up on top of a three-decker bunk. No mattress under you. Only a dirty blanket. Lie here and rattle and groan. Lie here and feel the lice crawling all over you and under you. Lie here with only the whites of your eyes gleaming through the dark. To feel the bones sticking out of your skin. It will get me, too, like it got this guy. It is getting me. I can feel it. Twenty years before my time I will be like this guy. Maybe it will be in a mission like this, and they will come and carry me out on a stretcher. Maybe I will be lying in the corner of a box car with the roar of the wheels underneath me. Maybe it will come quick while I am shivering in a soup-line, a soup-line that stretches for a block and never starts moving. I lie up here on my three-decker bunk and shiver. I am not cold. I am afraid. What is a man to do? I know well enough what he can do. All he can do is to try to keep his belly full of enough slop so that he won't rattle when he breathes. All he can do is to try and find himself a lousy flop at night. Day after day, week after week, year after year, always the same—three hots and a flop.

MICHAEL KOHLER

An Unfinished Novel

SYNOPSIS

This synopsis of "Michael Kohler" was prepared by Kromer for a 1936 application for a Guggenheim Fellowship. The synopsis is followed by the six completed chapters of the novel, left in typescript by Kromer at his death. These chapters, together with a shorter version of the synopsis, were first published in the *West Virginia Heritage Encyclopedia*, supplementary series, volume 24 (1974).

PLANS FOR STUDY AND WORK   TOM KROMER

MICHAEL KOHLER, *the novel on which I am basing my application for a Fellowship, is a working class novel dealing, for the most part, with working class people. It is my belief that the industrial scene and the proletarian character, an almost untouched field, is fertile material for the novelist who approaches it with understanding and sincerity of purpose. In my work* WAITING FOR NOTHING *I attempted to paint one picture of this scene, the unemployed worker thrown adrift and no longer able to sell his only commodity, his labor. My reasons for confining myself to this one segment of the whole problem were two-fold. It was my belief I could better picture the misery, the futility, the disintegrative effects of this life by dealing with it alone. I feared to blur the effect for which I was striving by introducing the extraneous element of causes. My second reason was closely correlated with the first.* WAITING FOR NOTHING *was my first effort in the working class field and naturally I suffered from some timidity rela-*

133

tive to my ability. I no longer have that timidity. With one hundred pages of my present work, MICHAEL KOHLER, completed, and almost two years of study and research in the historical scene of which I write behind me, I am confident I can now deal with this industrial scene in its broader significance.

MICHAEL KOHLER has its beginnings during that muscle-feeling period on the part of labor of the early eighties which Selig Perlman calls the "Great Upheaval." The years following the Civil War had witnessed a refashioning of American society. While it is true the Industrial Revolution had appeared earlier, its implications were not fully apparent until the middle eighties when the factory extension and machine technique reached new heights. It was during this period that the worker began to realize the difficulty, or rather the impossibility, of having any voice in the price that was paid for his labor. While such statements of policy as that made by a prominent industrialist of the time to Samuel Gompers, "I regard my employees as I do a machine, to be used to my advantage, and when they are old and of no further use I cast them in the street," were no doubt rare, yet there is no doubt the gap separating employer and employee was widening at great speed. With this hammering down of wages, the filthy living conditions, the wretched tenements, there is little wonder that many workers began to display sullen discontent.

It is with such a background as Chicago was at that time, teeming with its growing militant labor movements, that my story begins. From the viewpoint of their own social development these sullen currents of borning class consciousness left no mark on the two characters with whom I deal at that time, old Michael Kohler and his wife Julia. But this new class consciousness, manifested all too often in the "propaganda of the deed," and the ferocious reaction against it by the owning class in the form of terroristic red baiting and *flagrant fascistic suppression which came to its climax following the Haymarket Affair, was to leave a fearful and bewildering impress on those who felt its fury solely because they were foreigners at a time when industrialists wished to direct the attention of the public away from the real issue. Already the attempt of the working class to organize itself into a collective body was being termed an "alien doctrine," and in periods of suppression an alien accent is tantamount to anarchy and the bomb. As I say, this experience of persecution resulted in no awakening of class consciousness. It did, however, leave its impress indelibly in the form of fear and bewilderment. It was into such an atmosphere of fear, bewilderment, and poverty that my principal character, Michael Kohler, is born in the coal mining community of Glen Ellum, Pennsylvania, in 1900.*

It is with thirty-six years of his life that I deal, and here I believe that I go firmly, for it is in such a family and in such an industrial section that both I and my father and grandfather before me have had their roots. My Michael Kohler, like my father, began work in a coal mine as a greaser and trapper boy at the age of eight. The death of old Michael Kohler in an explosion of black damp and the consequent responsibility of the support of his mother by Michael Kohler at the age of ten, and such like occurrences in thousands of other families, called up no flow of sentiment against the industrial set-up which fostered these abuses. Miners, ox-like, went to their deaths from the black damp or the miner's cough, accepting all these things as the natural hazards of a short and squalid life. Their children, too, were fed into the hopper with an equally stolid thoughtlessness.

I skim rapidly here the wave of militancy on the part of the workers at Glen Ellum during this period, the bloody labor war which followed, the influence of all this on Michael Kohler, a young but partisan participator, the conflagration which destroyed the whole mine property, the fleeing of

Michael Kohler on the rods of a freight train towards the mills in Pittsburgh where he had heard that "things were better." He winds up in Huntington, West Virginia, and the Judson Art Glass company. It is in this locale that he spends the next ten years of his life. Working the night shift in the sheeting heat of the glass factory, attending school in the daytime, he is goaded on always through the backbreaking work and poverty by the sustaining thought that education is the weapon with which to knock down the barriers that separate him from the good life of which he occasionally catches glimpses. We see him next alternately proofreading on newspapers, working his way through several years of college, school teaching in mountain schools, and with the coming of the depression and the bankrupting of the counties, the closing of the schools, the inability to get jobs for which he is trained, the vast journeys from one end of the country to the other, seeking always work of any type, attaining a job in a tunnel construction, and contracting silicosis.

From there with the resuming of his wanderings in a broken state of health we find him in California attempting at odd times to write the story of these wanderings and this piteous life. It is in San Francisco that he meets the girl he marries and through neglect and starvation, in pregnancy sees her die. With his son he wanders to Toledo, Chicago, New York and back to Toledo.

This is the bare plot of MICHAEL KOHLER. *The reader will appreciate the difficulty in which a writer finds himself when propounding the barest bones of his story. One line, one paragraph of apt characterization may have more power and sincerity of purpose than the entire skeleton structure would show. My aims are these: to write a novel dealing with the proletariat as I have known them from birth; to create a character who struggles for existence on an historically authentic scene; to have this character blindly plastic and passive to the compulsion of these economic and social forces in early* youth, an environmental philosophy of unquestionable acceptance; to have him accept bodily in his later youth that philosophy which is propagated and fostered by the owning class and which is so fortuitous to the perpetuation of the social and economic abuses and inequalities of his time, i.e., that the maladjustment, the inability to survive adequately under the system is not due to any flaw in that system but to a lack of ability or intelligence in the dispossessed one. My character, experiencing the first vague and intuitive proddings of an innate creative urge, experiencing a vague, but nonetheless compelling, unrest at the sterility of life as he lives it in the factory and in what squalid home life he is able to make for himself, takes steps to rectify his lack of education, to which lack, in his blind acceptance of the stereotypes of his time, he is certain he owes his present restricted existence.

Need I say that when this education has been won—at what hardship and sacrifice the reader may well know—that he found himself in the depression of 1929 oftentimes pleading for jobs that he would have disdained to take even during his enslaved childhood.

His wanderings over the country, his impregnation with an industrial disease, his eventual questioning of all these precepts and the social philosophy which he had accepted from childhood, all these things he but shared in common with millions of others like him who were so peremptorily cast off by society in those years and are still cast off. The education that he had won with such struggle, served only to heighten the frustration he felt at the stifling and abasement.

The last few years of Michael Kohler find him striking out against these forces with the publication of a book that points out some of them. Other than the feel of accomplishment and the sustaining belief in the existence of a talent within him, his position is no better. A dying man, he sees with infuriating clarity the path that he has missed; sees for the first time the *sloppy thinking, the jingoistic hodge-podge that has been his thinking; sees clearly a life lived in its entirety without one hard blow struck at the thing that has enslaved his every waking hour since birth and in the final exactment of tribute, has claimed its last full measure, his life. What self-condemnation, what retributive thoughts, what disease-crazed hallucinations of the eventual fate of his son,—it is with these things that I leave* MICHAEL KOHLER.

CHAPTER ONE

OLD MICHAEL KOHLER had arrived in America with Julia in the winter of 1885 with three plentifully patched but clean blankets that his mother had given him at great sacrifice when he had left the village in the old country, a great, black iron skillet, and a ticket from New York to Chicago, a loan, as was the passage money, from Paul, his cousin, who already had his own business in America. They were young then, the both of them, Michael twenty and Julia but sixteen, and there was so much happening to them, the long, multi-colored tickets arriving so unbelievably, the exhibiting of them unfolded to their very ends on the table, the marriage, the leavetaking, that at last, when Paul had met them at the great station in Chicago, it was like coming out of the stupor that Michael had got in from the vodka at the weddings sometimes. Paul had taken charge of them then and he had been so confident, so sure of where he was in all these people, naming each street with a detached casualness, giving the population, great strings of figures that had swirled the heads of the two of them but were reassuring and calming to listen to when Paul named them like that so casually and certainly. They had tagged desperately beside him, aweing at his assuredness as they picked their way three abreast down the crowded walks. Michael, not daring to walk single file so afraid was he of losing sight of Paul in all this crowd that jostled and scowled at them, clung relentlessly to his arm and Julia clutched his fearsomely, neither of them giving ground to the streams of people, but forcing all to flank them, timidly but stolidly. Paul was dressed in a shiny, blue serge suit that bulged in the back so from his big muscles that he was stooped from them. His fat cheeks, red to begin with, glowed redder from the cold blasts of wind that swept up the street till it would sometimes shove them backwards from its force. They turned corners, cut off to side streets, even once took a short cut through an alley, and they marveled that Paul could find his way so. Always, as they walked, he recited figures, pointed out the new construction, named streets, aware always of his own well creased suit and how well it looked beside the clothes of Michael whose yellow hair stuck out of his red toboggan, whose coarse pants bagged at the knees, his shoes made of canvas by himself with strips of rawhide sewed at the bottoms. Paul would dart looks at Julia through the reflection of the great store windows, and from the succession of windows, without looking directly at her at all, he had noted the large, black eyes, the thin face, pretty for its thinness though a little sad, the long, rusty black dress, and the black shawl that covered her head and was thrown so around her shoulders.

When at last they had reached the third floor room of the hotel that Paul had already rented for them on the floor above his own room, it was already far past the opening time for his locksmith shop and he had left them alone in the strange room. They were like two children, a little scared of all these things that confronted them in the room, but determined to explore them no matter the risk, examining this, picking up that, and the water. . . . It was the water that was the greatest mystery and the hardest to believe. In the village at home there had been long walks to the well, carrying great buckets that pulled their shoulders almost to the ground they were so heavy when full. Here you had but to walk to the white bowl in the corner, had but to turn so slightly one of the little handles and the water came, dripping at first and then at your will as you turned further and further the silver handle, in gushes so great that were you not so very, very careful in your turning of just the right amount, the water would splash clear to the yellow paper that covered the walls. Julia cooked dinner on a little iron box that was a stove which Paul had showed them how to light, but even then Michael would not get close to it as Paul had done so casually, but had turned the tap that made a hiss like a great snake and threw the match in from a safe distance. Before he could jump back farther, the room was filled with the sound of the puff and the fire leaped outside the box and almost burned him. But after that first great blast, the fire obeyed the turning of the tap this way and that like a child, coming up in strong blue columns from the little holes or dying down to flickering red smudges at his will as he turned.

When Paul came up that evening, Julia had already cooked potatoes for them, not daring to touch the other things that were on the shelves, thinking that perhaps Paul would want them saved for Sunday. Paul patiently explained that it was not only the potatoes that were eaten in America but many other things such as were on the shelves before them, many of them that they had never before seen. He had brought with him a bottle of red wine and when supper was over and the dishes were washed the talk grew and grew as the wine got lesser and lesser in the bottle till finally Michael, who had been timid with Paul at first, was slapping him on the back and telling him what a fine man and a good man he was for loaning them so many dollars to come to the new land, and that he would see to it that he never regretted his goodness, and that he would pay back even if he and Julia had to work the skin from their fingers to pay back. Paul would see that they would do good here and that they would soon have a business like Paul's, not as good as Paul's, but a good business nonetheless. And Paul, the red wine flushing his red, fat face, had got very dignified at these thanks and had bowed once slightly from the hips at Michael and once slightly at Julia who sat very stiff in her chair, a little dizzy from the glass of wine she had drunk. Paul cleared his throat and said that such was nothing for was not Michael his cousin and was not Julia now his cousin nonetheless if it was but marriage that made her so, and it was nothing. He got up from his chair and walked, not very steadily, to the shelf and brought forth a bottle of black ink and a pen and placed them on the table. From his pocket he drew a tiny, narrow book on which was written something in American which Michael and Julia could not read, knowing no American, and he cleared his throat then and said that it was nothing, but that since now that they were in America and that things were done such and so here (business was business) and here it was customary to sign the note on which was stated in black and white the amount and also the interest and, since it was done so in America, tomorrow they would go to the insurance company and get the life insurance policy which would be made over to him, Paul, in the event that Michael should get killed, not that he was expecting that, though, and he burst into a great fit of laughter at that, the thought of Michael getting killed, and Michael bellowed his great laugh, too, and they drank again to their mutual good health and Michael's and Julia's prosperity in the new land.

After a while when there was no more wine left in the bottle and Julia had once or twice already yawned in her hand, Paul sulked in his chair and became quarrelsome and talked moodily of a man that he had been good to once, that he had loaned money to, but who had never paid back and who had left Chicago without paying back. He said that for all he knew Michael, too, might forget who had been good to him and might forget to whom it was that he owed so much money. Michael shifted uneasily in his seat at this talk, not knowing what to say and surprised that the talk should have turned so when, as for him, he wished to slap Paul on the back, to pinch the cheek of Julia, and laugh from down in his belly he felt so good. Once, when he came back from the bathroom, Paul glowered down at his shoes and pointed derisively at them and laughed so at the canvas with the rawhide sewed to it that Michael stood in the middle of the floor ashamed of his shoes until a great rage came over him at Paul laughing at him so and in front of Julia, too, that he drew back his great hairy fist to smash the face in front of him that was jabbering at him. Julia jumped from her chair and grabbed hold of his arm and held it and Paul, scared now, stopped his laughing and said that he was but joking and what was there to be mad about. Paul had gone down to his room then and they had gone to bed in the bronze bed and they lay there with their heads rolling from the red wine till at last it was morning and the sun was shining through the cracks in the green window blind and it seemed a minute ago that they went to bed.

Paul had not been friendly with them after that. He no longer came up to see them and when they would go to his room, he would only sulk in the chair until they would leave with embarrassment. Because of this they moved from there to a three room house at the edge of town that they furnished little by little at the second hand stores. That winter Michael carried hod and it was as nothing to him. He would carry the hod loaded with brick to the bricklayers on their scaffolds and when the day was over he would be covered with the red brick dust and the powdery cement, but he would not be tired at all and he would come bellowing through the house for Julia and when he would find her he would swing her up on his shoulders and carry her while she screamed to be put down all over the house. When the winter was over the house was all furnished and the furnishings were paid for. Each week they sent to Paul some money and with the following winter he was paid and the insurance policy put in black and white in the name of Julia.

The carrying of hod was child's play to Michael with his wide shoulders and strong arms. While the other workers grumbled at the backbreaking work and the poor pay, he would pile up almost more bricks than the hod would hold if there were people around the railing watching the construction. He would carry them with ease up the steep ladder, not holding to the ladder at all but only slightly touching the rungs with his fingers to keep his balance. When one construction would be over he would go to another. To get a job in America was nothing. You had only to pack your lunch in the morning and follow the streets. Before you walked far you would see a job of construction. There would be men mixing cement in front and the sidewalk would be barricaded by railings so that the walkers must go out in the street to get by. Already in a year he had learned all there was needed to get jobs in America. He would walk up to the man with a tie or the blue prints in his hand who was always around the construction somewhere.

"Have the hod carry job?" he would ask.

If his broad shoulders and child's grin did not bring a job, he would pull up the sleeve of his shirt and flex the giant muscles of his arm until they quivered. Only once had he been turned down for a job when he asked.

"Got a card?" the foreman had asked.

"What's card?" Michael asked.

"Union card. Only union men work on this job."

"How you get this card?"

"You join a union."

"Where you go for that thing?"

The foreman sent him to Big Dan O'Brien at the Central Labor Union. Michael paid his dues and got his card. When he came back the foreman put him to work and on pay day there was more in his envelope than ever before.

"That sonofabitch union good thing," he told Julia that evening as they were eating supper in the kitchen. "I gonna work for that union all time. That Big Dan got me to work all time for him."

"Ask first before you work if Big Dan run that job before

you work," Julia cautioned him. "If no, ask other place. Work all the time for Big Dan."

After that when Michael was hunting a job of construction he would ask first if it was a union job and if it was not he would turn his big nose up in contempt.

"I carry the hod only for Big Dan," he would say proudly and walk on down the street.

In the spring they planted a garden in the large back yard and they would both go out there after supper, unless it were too dark, and weed it. Sometimes Mrs. Pera would be weeding her garden, too, and then Julia would go over to the fence and they would talk. Mrs. Pera's husband, Caesar, worked in the yards of the Harvester works. Julia would listen closely while Mrs. Pera talked and in the evenings she tried to teach Michael what she had learned. She borrowed a primer from one of Pera's little girls and when her housework was finished she would read it. Sometimes by the lamplight in the evenings she would go over and over a page with Michael till at last he would snatch the book away from her and make her dance with him all over the house while he bellowed a tune till she would be afraid Mrs. Pera would call the police.

"I got plenty words now to carry the hod," he would complain.

Once or twice a week they would drink beer in the evenings with Caesar Pera and his wife Anna. They would buy the beer in great buckets full and from the time she drank her first glass Anna Pera would talk and she would not stop even a little until it was time to go home. Caesar would sit in his chair with his big hands folded over his belly and stare at the fat, olive skinned Anna with an adoration that became greater as the beer dwindled in the bucket till Julia would look wisely at Michael and they would leave. Caesar, too, belonged to the Central Labor Union and twice the two families went to hear the speaking at the hall. Julia discarded her black clothes for some colored calico ones when Michael insisted that she would be prettier than all if she would but stop wearing the black dresses. She could not understand all that the speaker had said at the meeting but she could understand some. But Michael all through the speaking amused himself with the antics of a fly that was turning drunken somersaults on the floor by his feet. When Julia tried to talk with him that evening about what had been said, he did not know what she was talking about.

"Big Dan get you job so you ought to listen good when they talk there," she had complained to him. "You don't learn if you don't listen."

"This sonofabitchin' fly turn on his belly then flip flop all the time. Don't you see that fly?"

"Big Dan don't want you to watch flies. He want you to listen good. Next time you listen."

It was as they sat in the kitchen at supper one evening in May that they heard from the front yard the scream of Anna Pera. When they had jumped from the table and run to the porch they could see her there in the yard staggering and screaming. There were also two men there on the porch and on the face of one of them was blood spattered even into his hair and between the two of them they held this wide board. It was Caesar Pera who was stretched out upon it. His face was covered with blood and dirt and in his right temple there was to be seen a jagged hole. One of his eyes was closed but in the other only the white was to be seen. To Michael it was plain that Caesar Pera was dead.

First Anna Pera would run toward the porch and the body of Caesar Pera and then she would dart like one crazy back to the walk again. Those who were carrying Caesar Pera on the board lowered the board to the porch and began to run around the house and out towards the tracks of the railroad. Both Michael and Julia had then run across the yard, Julia to try to calm Anna Pera and Michael to carry Caesar Pera within the house. Julia would try to take hold of Anna Pera's hand and to hold her but she would not let her but would fight her and scratch her when she would try. Michael leaned over the body of Caesar and picked him up in his arms and when he did so he could feel the stiffness and the coldness of him. In his arms he carried him to the bedroom and placed him on the bed. Outside he could hear the screaming of Anna Pera and then he heard those loud voices, men's voices. He could hear them dragging her through the back door to the kitchen and he could hear her crying in there. He pulled the white bedspread out from under the body of Caesar and covered him with it.

When Michael looked up from the bed, his mouth dropped open. Two policemen stood in the door, a fat one and a short one. He did not know how long they had been standing there in the door watching him. He straightened up from the bed and walked slowly towards them. They did not move to come and get him but when he reached them they grabbed him and held him while they snapped the handcuffs on his wrists. They shoved him out into the hall and then he could see that the house was full of these police. In the kitchen he could hear them thundering questions at Mrs. Pera who was crying, and he could hear the trembling voice of Julia answering their questions as they asked them. In the living room they ransacked the drawers of the dresser and looked closely at each tiny piece of paper. One of them held up the end of the rug and another was on his hands and knees looking under it for something. They dragged him out to the front porch and when he would say to them that Caesar Pera was a friend and that it was only last night that his wife, Julia, and himself, had drunk beer with the Peras in the Peras' own house, they only shoved him the harder toward the black patrol wagon in the road. When he would tell them that they had but to ask Mrs. Pera if it was not two men, one big, one little, who had brought her husband home dead already on the board, and when he had said to them that it was the good God's truth that he had not killed Caesar Pera but it was another not known to him, something had struck him behind the ear and when he awoke they were dragging him through a door and into an office on whose walls there were pictures of many policemen.

They had sat him up in a chair and when he would slump over in the chair because of the dizziness that was in his head, they would jerk him back and point their fingers at him and jabber at him and ask him where was the hiding place of where August Spies had hid the dynamite, and where the hiding place of Parsons, and who were the names, and to name the whole list, and who was it that was next on the list for the bomb? For hours they had done this and at last he could stand their pointing and jabbering and their jerking of him no longer and he had lashed out at them with his handcuffed fists to smash the jabbering red faces in front of him. Then one of them, this big one, had swung back this stick, this blackjack, and had beat him across the Adam's Apple till he choked for breath. When he remembered more he was on the concrete floor of this little room with the iron bars around it and the door that was not bars but solid iron. On all sides of him there were others of these rooms and in each one was a man or many men. Even through the dizziness of his head he could see that many of them were covered with blood from their heads down and many of them were crying aloud. There was one beside him on the floor who raised up and asked if they had as yet caught Parsons and when he tried to tell this one, as he had the police who had not listened one word, that he did not know about this Parsons of whom all talked, he could not say the words for the throbbing in his throat from where they had beat him.

He did not know how long it was that he was in this room, but it was many days for they had brought the mush and the beans and the water many times before he came, one man with many keys on a ring, and he had told him to follow him to the office again. There he had sat down in the chair again expecting them to beat him but they did not beat him. They asked him his name, where it was that he lived, and again they asked him many times about this Parsons, but they had not beat him when he said that about that one he knew not one thing and that Caesar Pera was a friend and that he would not kill his friend. At last when they were through with their questions they had told him to go away from there, to go away from his job of the hod carrying, and to go many miles away from Chicago or when they saw him again they would kill him.

Julia was sitting by the door waiting when he got home and held to him and cried but they had not beat her but had only asked her so many questions over and over that at last she could answer them no longer. Together they made bundles of their clothes and the furniture they left there. They huddled up in the seat in the great station till a porter had stood in the door and called out the names of many cities and it was Julia who decided they would go to Pittsburgh when she heard that name for she knew it was a long ways away from Chicago. There Michael would get a job and they would save their money and when there was enough they would go back to the old country and away from this place. When Michael had asked the woman at the desk in the station at Pittsburgh about the job of hod carrying, she had written on a piece of paper a name and he and Julia had gone there to see. It was a big room filled with benches and many men, and in front was a blackboard on which a man wrote in chalk. They had sat there for a long time when a man had tapped Michael on the shoulder and asked him if it was a job in the mine that he was looking for. Michael had answered him that it was a job and as for him it did not matter if it was the hod carrying or the mine. He had flexed his muscles to show the man how big they were, and the man had smiled and took them again to the station and showed them where to stand on the platform till the train came in. There were others there already and

before the train came there were many more with their families and their mattresses and blankets.

It was but a short ride on the train and when they got off at
the little yellow station, they were at the mine. Michael did
not understand such as this for no sooner were their feet on
the station platform than there were many men surrounding
them and guiding them across the wooden bridge of the red
creek, and there were guns strapped to the hips of these men
but they were not policemen nonetheless. There were other
men there too, with their women and their children, a great
mob of them, and Julia held tight to Michael in fear as these
hooted at them and called them many names and threw rocks
at them as they crossed the bridge. Inside of the big yellow
company store, though, it was quiet. They gave them groceries there and oil and carbide lamps, and then they marched
them up to the road to the two very long rows of houses, a row
on each side of the muddy road. In front of each house there
were piled beds and mattresses and chairs and sitting by the
piles were women and children who hooted and screamed
sonofabitchin' scab at them as they entered the houses. The
house they gave them was not such a house as was theirs in
Chicago but dirty with the soot from the mine and with but
two tiny rooms. An enameled bed from which the white
enamel was all chipped was in one room, and in the other no
more than a stove, a table, and some dynamite boxes.

In the night when they were sleeping a rock came crashing
through the window, but the next day there were soldiers in
uniform who came on the train and it was quiet after that.
When it was evening some of these soldiers came to the house
and they took him and the others to the mine. They had lined
them up and given them powder and put them on the hoist.
The hoist had shot down into the blackness and Michael
could hardly get his breath when they went down so fast. It
was dark down there and even with the carbide lamp there
was not much light. Another had gone with him and showed

him the way to the big sloping room off the entry way far up
the narrow tracks down there, and it was this one who had
also showed him how to drill the hole into the narrow vein of
coal, how to pour in the powder, and how to tamp it down.
Those first days down there under the ground Michael had
not minded. There were no more rocks crashing through the
windows and it was many miles from those police in Chicago
who had beat him and asked him so many questions. It was
the shots that he liked. He would light the fuse till it would
hiss as a snake and then he would run out the door into the
entry till the blast would come that would shake the earth
and echo and echo many times against the walls. It was the
noise of the blasting that he liked best but it was not more than
a few times each day that he would get to light the hissing fuse
and run. All the rest of the day he would bend over the pile of
coal on the floor that his powder had torn down, and throw it
into the car with his big shovel. It was only when he would fill
the car and bellow down the entry for the man with the mule to
take it away that he would see anyone. The rest of the time, all
the rest of those hours in the dark, there was no one to see how
fast he loaded the cars and how easy. When it was a year that
had passed since he had started down there he no longer even
liked to hear the blast anymore or listen to the crunch of the
coal as it came tumbling from the vein. He was sick of this
dark. Many times he and Julia would talk as they ate of the
good times they had had with the Peras and of their house as it
had been in Chicago and the good roof that was on it and how
they did not have to catch the water in cans when it rained as
now they did. But it was the hod carrying job that Michael most
liked to talk of and of the time when he could get that job once
again.

As a year passed and then more years and there was no
money to be saved for them to go away on to another place
away from here, they no longer talked anymore of going away
and they no longer talked of saving money that could not be

saved. They hardly talked at all anymore. When Michael would come home he would eat and go to bed from the tiredness in his back and Julia no longer rubbed his back from where it hurt but would sit in the rocking chair by the window and listen to him snore in there. When Paul was born, the neighbors had come in that night and they had danced all over the floor and drank wine and sang songs but the next morning he had had to go to work in the mine again and his head was splitting from the ache that was in it. When Michael was born the neighbors had not come in that time and he had not gotten drunk. When Mrs. Brodeski had carried him in squealing to the kitchen to show him, he had hardly looked up from the carbide lamp he was cleaning. He had thought how many more mouths were there going to be to feed with his sweat?

CHAPTER TWO

THE FOOT OF SNOW covering the mud that was the red sulphur clay when the first sleet came could not transfigure it, nor was the flurry of white fuzz in the air opaque enough to hide its sooty ugliness; Glen Ellum was a Pennsylvania mining town. From the far end of the two long rows of company houses that faced each other across the road, to the black tipple that reared up out of the top of the hill across the red sulphur creek, the soot matched flake with flake and layer with layer with the snow as it fell. Only up the slopes of the opposite hill, and that far up, were the trees and thick sassafras clumps heavy and gleaming-free from the greyness below. All day a white disk of a sun had slid obstinately through the murk towards the tipple to the west, but now a rusty scale was jutting out from the water's edge of the creek and the shawled women plowed through the snow to the pumps with kettles of boiling water to prime them with. It was almost breakfast time and supper time (it was two shifts that were worked at Glen Ellum) and from the hundred chimneys the black coal smoke curled upward a few feet and then hung flattened in the grey sky. The road passing between the rows of houses was threaded with a slushy black path that ran as far as the yellow company store, but across the wooden bridge and up the hill to the workings only a shadowy indentation showed where the path was. It was only when the whistle shrieked in the engine room up there that the path would be beaten to an oozy black ditch by the miners on their way home from the black stopes a mile underground, and by the night shift who would go up an hour afterward.

From the workings on the flat top of the hill Glen Ellum was no more than a dirty black cloud of smoke down there, and the heavy smoke belching from the engine room stacks sank ponderously down there to make it blacker and dirtier. Only the top of the tipple jutting up over the smokeline was white with the heavy snow. The rest, the square, unpainted office, the powder shack, the long rows of pot bellied mine cars on the narrow, rolling tracks, lay subdued in the dismal grey cover that thickened by the minute.

Little Michael Kohler lay flat on his back in the slush beneath the empty mine car. He finished the rusty wheel he was working on and scooted up farther between the narrow track, pulling the steaming bucket of axle grease along with him. With a lump of coal he pounded on the axle to loosen up the rust around the wheel and swabbed a fistful of the grease at the crack. The warmth of the thick, black stuff made his hands feel good but his face was drawn from the icy wind that whipped a swirl of fine snow beneath the car. The wooden cars stretched as far up in front as he could see, and the string of them that Ed Chenzko was greasing on the next track was just as long. He stuck his head against the wheel and let the grease drip slowly onto his face. The black stuff that smeared him from his red toboggan to his mackinaw made him look older than his ten years and that was as he wanted it. The faces of the miners coming up from the stopes below at the end of the shift were no blacker than his.

He finished the front wheels and wiggled up to the next car. Through the couplings of the cars on the opposite track he could see the fat, lazy figure of Johnson, the bookkeeper, standing in the office doorway smoking and Michael watched him hawk-like. The wind beat the grease fire smouldering between the two strings of cars till the sparks flew in all directions.

"Watch that fire," Johnson called authoritatively. He knocked his pipe against the clapboards of the office and the tobacco coals raced each other across the snow.

"Watch your own sonofabitchin' fire," Michael muttered. He did not like Johnson, not because the officious bookkeeper had ever done anything to him but because no one else at the mine liked him. Steve Brodeski was always saying that because Johnson sat on his fat ass on a stool in the office that he thought he owned the goddamn place. With the slam of the office door Michael darted his grimy face out from under the end of the car.

"I'm gonna take your old rooster neck and twist it in a bow knot," he hissed menacingly and pantomimed with his hands how he was going to twist Ed Chenzko's thin neck. "You're a old yellowbelly and your old man Pearl Chenzko is a old yellowbelly, too. Pearl! Pearl! Pearl!," he taunted sing-songily. "Ed Chenzko's old man's got a sissy name. Sissy name! Sissy name!"

"I'll show you!" Ed Chenzko stuck his warty face out from under the car on the other track. He was fourteen years old and big for his age. With his wrinkled, rickett head he looked like an old man. "Soon's that whistle blows I'm gonna take your old neck and stretch it all the way down the hill and walk rope on it."

Michael made a menacing gesture as though to start over after Ed and slammed his head on the coupling. He picked up the piece of coal and pounded on the coupling with it.

"You hear that? That's me bangin' on your old hard head with my fists when that whistle blows. I'm gonna make you scream for your old woman. I'm gonna knock you down on your dirty old prat and step right on your dirty old neck."

"I know what you'll do when the whistle blows." Ed shook his grimy fist. "You're gonna run your ass off when the whistle blows. Whyn't you lay over on this side of the car if you ain't gettin' ready to run your dirty tail off?"

Michael tensed his ear for the shriek of the whistle in the engine room. "I already greased that wheel on that side. Whatta I wanta grease it again for? Ed Chenzko's a dirty stinkpot and he's so dumb and yellowbellowy he greases the wheels twicet. Oh, sissy name! Sissy name! Sissy name! You dirty—" The blast of the whistle cut off his words. With one twist of his body he rolled out from under the car. His head banged the edge of the car and knocked his toboggan off. He did not stop long enough to pick it up. He scooped up his dinner pail from the pile of ties without lessening his speed and pounded into the drifts of the unbroken path over the hill, his shirt tail and yellow hair flying in the wind. Ed Chenzko tore around the short cut by the office, screaming as he ran. His big head, far in advance of his body, plowed straight into Johnson's belly as he stepped off the porch. Johnson gasped and sank to the snow, fighting to free his neck from Ed's legs.

"Goddam you!" he gasped, "goddam you."

Ed clawed at Johnson's stomach and fought his way to his feet. Michael was already down the hill and tearing across the bridge but Ed plowed down the hill after him. By the time he panted across the bridge Michael was out of sight around the end of the company store and sprinting up the road. As he leaped the ditch at the side of the road his three decker dinner pail came apart and scattered in all directions over the road. He paid no attention to it but dashed through the yard and up to the sagging porch. Ed was coming up the road screaming curses as he came and pounding his big feet duckfooted on the snow. Michael moved across the porch till he was square in front of the window. He reached mechanically behind him for the rocks that he had piled there in the morning. As Ed started to leap the ditch he whizzed a rock at him and barely missed his ear. Ed stopped at the edge of the ditch and panted for breath.

"You dirty sonofabitchin' coward," he screamed. "You dirty stinky coward. I'm gonna beat you to death." He reached down and clawed at the snow for a rock but he couldn't find any.

Michael whizzed another rock across the ditch and knocked the snow up against Ed's legs.

"Yah! Yah! Yah!" he taunted. "Whyn't you come up on the porch and fight if you wanta fight so much. Whatta you rootin' around out there in the snow for if you wanta fight so much?" He threw two rocks in quick succession and reached back on the window sill for some more. There was only one left. A cunning look came into Ed's usually ox-like eyes.

"Throw that rock," he jeered. "I dare you to throw it." He moved slowly up to the ditch again, ducking from side to side as Michael made false swings with the rock. Michael was aware of his dangerous position once he was out of rocks and continued to make false swings with the rock without letting go of it. He knew the front door was locked. Julia kept it locked so he and old Michael wouldn't track mud through the house. If he dashed around the house for the rear door Ed would be sure to catch him before he reached it. Ed was bigger than he and his legs were longer.

Ed caught sight of the sections of dinner pail on the ground. He reached down in the snow and picked up the bottom section.

"See this?" He held it aloft. "Now see it." He dropped it in the snow and jumped up and down on it. He walked over to the other two pieces and jumped up and down on them till they were nothing but twisted tin. "I dare you to throw that rock." Ed advanced stolidly down the edge of the bank and up the other side. Not twenty feet now separated him from Michael who was jumping up and down on the rotten boards of the porch and excitedly throwing his arm toward Ed without letting go of the rock. Michael banged on the window.

"Jute!" he yelled, "you better come out here quick. Ed Chenzko's gonna break the window."

"Yellin' for your old woman!" Ed jeered. He came forward, warily watching the rock in Michael's hand.

"Jute! You're not gonna have any window. Ed Chenzko swears to Christ he's gonna break the window."

He could hear the footsteps of Julia hurrying through the

bedroom. He stopped his frantic dancing and advanced several steps toward Ed. "You'll try to break our window, will you, you dirty long rubberneck. I'll pound this rock on your head. You're not gonna break our window while I'm around here." Michael was talking loudly enough so that Julia could hear every word he said as she fumbled at the key in the lock.

Ed heard the scraping in the lock and backed slowly up the road. "Sissy, yellin' for his old woman," he taunted.

Michael whizzed his last rock. Julia opened the door and stuck her head out. She had a red handkerchief tied around her head and the grey hair stuck out unruly in front.

"Who's trying to break the window?" she said irritably.

Ed was running duckfooted up the road as fast as he could go.

"That dirty Ed Chenzko said he was gonna break every window in the house. I'm gonna pound his old head with a rock if he don't stay away from here." As Michael went through the door, Julia cracked him on the head with her knuckles.

"I want you to quit this fighting every night."

Old Michael was sprawled out on the sunken springs of the iron bed with one hairy leg stretched out from under the grey blanket. His big features were almost hidden by the two-week growth of grey beard. He was snoring raucously with his mouth wide open.

"Ain't he goin' to work?" Michael pointed at him.

Julia shrugged her shoulders helplessly.

"I've been calling him for an hour. He just won't get up."

Michael walked over to the bed and yanked the blanket off. Old Michael hugged his yellow underwear to his chest and continued snoring.

"Hey, get up." Michael shook him. "You're late for work. Whistle's gonna blow pretty soon."

Old Michael groaned and opened his eyes sleepily.

"Whassa matter?" he asked querulously.

"You're late for work. You're gonna get the can tied to you if you keep on bein' late all the time."

Old Michael shivered and slammed his red feet on the cold floor. He swung his open palm at Michael half heartedly and Michael ducked.

"Don't talk so big," he growled.

Michael went into the kitchen and warmed his hands over the coal stove.

"Is he up yet?" Julia asked irritably.

"I got him up. I pulled the blanket off him."

"I don't know what's got into him. He don't even want to go to work anymore."

"He's gonna get the can tied to him if he don't watch out."

Julia took the big, black skillet off the stove and set it down on the table. She pushed the coffee pot back on the stove to heat it and walked to the bedroom door.

"Hurry. Potatoes get cold."

Michael took his mackinaw off and hung it up behind the stove.

"This old shirt's tore up the back, Jute," he said.

"Sew it up when you go to bed. Go wash."

Old Michael slouched into the kitchen shivering and putting his shirt tail in. He walked over to the window and looked out.

"Snow," he grumbled. "Walk up to your ass in snow. No snow walk up to your ass in rain. Always some goddam something." He strode disgustedly out the kitchen door to the pump. Michael followed him out. The wind tore across the yard making tiny drifts and then sweeping them fiercely around the side of the house. The pump was a mass of snow and ice. Old Michael lunged viciously at the handle but it wouldn't give. His hand stuck to the frozen handle and he burned it when he yanked it loose. He kicked the pump angrily with his brogan and strode back into the house. Michael followed him in.

"Always some goddam something," he swore as he pulled a dynamite box up to the table. Michael dabbed at his face from a saucepan of water Julia had on the edge of the stove and wiped the grime off on the towel. He pulled up another box and sat down at the table.

"You better hurry," Julia said. "You're late."

"Plenty time," Old Michael grunted.

Julia went over to the rocking chair by the window and sat down.

"Steve Brodeski say he hear have to take cut now pretty damn quick. No orders," Old Michael said without looking up from his plate of potatoes. "Cut! Sonofabitch," he banged his hairy fist down on the table so hard the dishes jumped. "Belly empty now. Now sonofabitch talk cut!" He raised his shaggy eyebrows belligerently at Michael and when he didn't look up from his plate, he shifted his stare to Julia in the rocking chair. She shrugged her shoulders.

"Go to Pittsburgh. Maybe you can get a job in the mills and little Michael can go to school. I've always tried to get you to try the mills."

Old Michael stopped his glaring and slammed his fist down on the table again. Michael's coffee cup toppled over and spilled the coffee into his lap.

"Hey! Whatta you think you're doin?" He reached over and poured half of old Michael's coffee into his own cup. "Whatta you have to bang the table for when you talk?"

"I do it by sonofabitch hell," Old Michael bellowed. "They cut. I leave. Get job in mill. Little Michael get job in office, wear collar tie. How you like that, hey?" He slammed Michael on the back and knocked him up against the table. "You get collar tie, you big muckitymuck. Maybe you get old man job clean out office, hey?"

Michael sucked his coffee from his saucer without saying anything.

"You get job in office. Get education. Make lotsa money. Old man sweep out office."

"I'm gonna be a train engineer," Michael said.

"You be what I say. Work in office. Give old man job sweepin'." Old Michael glared through his eyebrows again.

"I'm gonna be a train engineer," Michael persisted.

Old Michael pulled back his hand, and Michael ducked down.

"You do what I say," old Michael said emphatically. "You get job in office. I sweep out goddam place." He got up from the table and got his coat and hat from behind the stove.

"Dinner pail behind the stove," Julia said without turning around in her rocking chair.

Old Michael picked up the bucket and strode out the door without saying goodbye.

Julia got up out of the chair.

"Go to bed when I make it. I'll sew your shirt, then."

CHAPTER THREE

AT SEVEN-THIRTY old Michael's picture, the one with the new miner's cap, fell off the nail on the wall and shattered the splinters of glass all over the floor. One sliver of glass pierced the new miner's cap and came up from the other side through his Adam's Apple.

Julia was ironing clothes over by the window when the picture fell. She walked slowly over to the picture on the floor and her eyes rested on the splinter of glass through old Michael's Adam's Apple. The glare of the fire from the coal stove made a rainbow all over his face, but she didn't pay any attention to the rainbow but only to the funny look it gave to old Michael's eyes. She wet her finger with her tongue and held it up in the air. There wasn't a breath of breeze. It was sweltering hot in the kitchen and the steam from the pot of water on the stove made creamy clouds on the window. She picked up the lamp and held it up to the nail that the picture had hung to. It was bent back ceilingward and she tried to pull it out with her fingers but it wouldn't come out. She put the lamp back on the table and leaned down and picked the frame up from the floor. She held it between her hands and stared a long time at the wire that was nailed to each side of it. That was what she had been afraid of. The wire was not even broken. It was just as good and as strong as that day three years before when it was hung on the wall. It had been a small picture but the man who had come around and asked for pictures of dead relatives to enlarge had enlarged it. Julia did not keep pictures of her dead. She burned them and buried the ashes by the red sulphur creek in the rear of the house. When Paul, her oldest, had been blown to bits on the dayshift, there had been no pictures to burn. He had never had his picture taken. So she burned his overalls and buried the ashes. Sometimes, when she thought of it, she crossed herself when she passed her picture graveyard.

She put the picture down on the table and swept up the splinters of glass from the floor. This was bad business and she still had that funny feeling in the top of her head when she went back to her ironing. She had just finished the blue denim shirts when the blast shook the house and rattled the windows and lasted for several seconds. There was another one right after that but it was shorter than the first. Julia did not look up from the suit of yellow underwear she was ironing. She sprinkled on some more water but she forgot to pick up the iron and scorched the leg. It was old Michael's underwear and the thought flashed through her head that she could cut them down for little Michael. When the iron got cold she put it back on the stove. She sat down in the rocking chair and rocked back and forth slowly. She could hear little Michael scrambling into his clothes in the bedroom. The first blast had awakened him. Julia tightened her shawl around her throat for although the room was warm she was cold. She stared through the drifts of snow on the window sill and watched the lamp in the Brodeskis' across the road move backward and forward in the room. Steve Brodeski would be hurrying over to the mine about now. Michael ran in from the bedroom. He grabbed his coat off the nail in back of the stove and dashed out the door still carrying it. After she had sat there for a long time the snow turned to rain. It had drizzled the night Paul got his head blown off on the dayshift and it had drizzled when they buried him. She sat there and rocked back and forth in the chair that old Michael had made from the weeping willows and hoped that it wouldn't be drizzling when they buried him.

After a while Mrs. Saltis came in and hung her dripping green shawl over the stove to dry. She pulled up a dynamite box by the window and sat down. Both of them sat there for a long time and listened to the rain coming down. It was coming down harder than ever now and it looked as though it might rain all night.

"Any news from the mine yet?" Julia asked.

"Sonia just come back. They let down a canary but it come up dead."

"They always come up dead. What they want to kill canaries like that for?"

"They're all down there, August and the three boys. I got supper on the table. Sweet potatoes. August and the boys is crazy about sweet potatoes. They're all cold now. The sirup gets sticky when they get cold like that. They was only goin' to work a couple hours over down there tonight to get a lot of bone cleaned out but they was down there when it happened. Sonia said they was down there."

"Anybody get out?"

"John Arbannis got out. His light went out on him and he was on the hoist when it happened. The gas got him on the hoist but he come to when he got in the air. He says there's forty-three down there. He says they wouldn't have a chance to block the tunnel for he passed out on the hoist it was that bad."

"Little Michael is over there now."

"Sonia seen little Michael. He said to tell you he wouldn't be home tonight. That's why I come over, to tell you he said he wouldn't be home tonight."

Mrs. Saltis walked over to the stove and wrapped her shawl carefully around her head.

"It's rainin' so hard or I'd go up there but I guess there's not much use to go up there. Sonia was up there. She said the canary come up dead. I don't see how they'd have time to block the tunnel with John Arbannis passin' out on the hoist

164

like that." She walked over to the door. "Don't you think its rainin' too hard to go up there?"

"There's no use to go up there," Julia said. "You'd just be in the road up there."

Mrs. Saltis went out and closed the door.

Julia walked over to the stove and picked up the iron. She wet her finger and dabbed it against the bottom of it and when it sizzled she carried it over to the ironing board.

Little Michael was only ten but he could remember other blasts before this one. Old Michael had not got caught with his pants down in the other ones though.

He stood on the knoll by the tipple as close to his fire as he could get. They were lowering canaries in green cages every hour. They'd lower them down the shaft and leave them for several minutes and when they'd pull them up they'd be stretched out on their backs dead. The whole top of the hill was swarming with people. Fires were flaring up by the tipple, around the office, and between the tracks. A stream of women and children filed over to the pile of ties and lugged them over to the fires. Some of the fires had whole families huddled around them but except for a few babies crying there was no noise save for the muffled sound of tramping feet on the slush. Michael could not understand the quiet. In the daytime he could hardly hear anything for the chugging in the engine room behind the office and the rattle of the coal going over the chutes to the cars. Now everyone seemed to be walking on their toes in the slush. It was only when he passed near one of the fires that he could occasionally hear the moan of some woman with her head buried in her shawl. It was so quiet that he could hear the miners talking in low voices over the tipple. Varner, the superintendent, was hurrying back and forth from the engine room and finally the chug of the air pumps started. Down at the bottom of the hill and across the creek to the road Michael could see a solid file of bobbing lanterns but the houses except for two lone lights that he could see down

there, were all dark. He stared over at the shaft that loomed
big and tall in the dark and tried to imagine where old
Michael was down there and whether he was alive or dead. He
tried to imagine how it would be if he was dead but he
couldn't imagine him any way but shovelling coal into a car
down there in the dark room or snoring loudly with his
mouth wide open. He couldn't imagine old Michael dead like
Paul was that time. Paul hadn't had any head when they carried him into the house and he never had any head when they
buried him, either. They couldn't find his head.

When they had lowered four canaries down the shaft,
Michael saw Julia slopping across the tracks. She had her red
shawl pinned tight around her head but the water was running down her face and off her chin. She passed Mrs. Chenzko's fire in the space between the two tracks and stopped.
Mrs. Chenzko stared blankly into the fire and did not even
look up when she stopped. Julia shook her by the shoulders
and half lifted her to her feet.

"What are you squatting here in the rain for?" she asked.

"Waiting," Mrs. Chenzko said uncertainly.

"What you waiting for?"

"Just waiting to see."

"Go home," Julia ordered, "no use to freeze your brats to
death because your man is dead."

She walked over to where Michael was hunched on the
ground by his fire scooping out a hole in the yellow clay. Beside his knee in the snow was one of the yellow canaries they
had lowered down the shaft.

"Put your coat collar up around your neck before you get
the croup." She pulled Michael's toboggan down further over
his ears and fumbled at his wet coat collar.

"They sent four canaries down but they all been dead so
far," Michael said. "There's forty-three down there."

"You better go home. You're wet," Julia said.

"You better go home yourself, Jute," he said. "I'm gonna

stay here and go down with the first bunch if they'll let me."
He called her Jute. He had always called her Jute just the same
as he had always called old Michael Michael. He picked up
the canary and Julia handed him her handkerchief without
saying anything. He wrapped the canary up in the purple
handkerchief and put it down in the hole. He scooped mud
over it and crossed himself and his muddy fingers made the
imprint of a cross on his dripping coat. Julia looked at his
skinny body hunched on the ground and the muddy cross
across his coat. She turned her eyes over towards the shadow
of the tipple and crossed herself.

"You'd better go home, Jute," Michael said, "you're soakin'
wet."

"You go down with the first bunch and find him," she said.
"If you can't tell, he's got a grey shirt on. The collar's turned
and sewed with blue thread. Make them bring him up right
away no matter. We'll bury him tomorrow and go away."

"Where to, Jute? Where we goin'?"

"I don't know. Anyway we'll go away from here."

Julia turned and slipped over the hill. In the quiet Michael
could hear her hacking cough almost at the bottom of the hill.
He walked over to the next fire and sat down on a tie by Steve
Brodeski. Steve was squatting astraddle a tie whittling at a
board. The rocks embedded in his face from an explosion
made black raised scars all over his face.

"Me lucky sonofabitch," Steve said, "maybe nex' time
won't be lucky sonofabitch. Ever' bastard get it some day. All
the time work ass off for nothin' then, poof, finish."

Michael warmed his muddy hands over the blazing ties.

"Me and Jute's goin' away from here tomorrow. Maybe I'm
gonna get me a job in the mills in Pittsburgh."

Steve shook his head disapprovingly.

"I work in sonofabitch mills. They no good, either. Maybe
they better than the mines, though. Better to get ass knocked
off with crane than buried in hole."

"Maybe I'm gonna get a job in the office."

"You get job in office and be like that horse ass mucklehead Johnson."

The crowd suddenly surged away from the fires and over by the shaft. They were getting ready to lower another canary over there. There were only the sleeping children left by the fires.

"No use," Steve said. "Have to wait till morning. They all dead down there. If John Arbannis pass out on hoist what chance they got down there?"

Michael could tell by the rumbling of the crowd that they were bringing up the cage and the concerted groan that followed told him that the canary was stretched on its back. He got up off the tie and walked over there but he couldn't get near the cage for the press of the crowd. He could see the head of Ed Varner, gaunt and worried looking, pushing his way out through the crowd.

"You people might as well go home and get some sleep," Varner called out. "Maybe they had time to block the tunnel. Anyway you might as well go home till morning."

Johnson, the bookkeeper, climbed up on the wheel of a coal car.

"The boss says you people might as well go home," he yelled through his cupped hands. "He thinks the gas won't let up till morning."

"A hell of a lot he's worried if it never lets up," a surly voice called from the crowd. "There's plenty more that forty come from."

The crowd stiffened and Varner stood stock still in the path he had cleared. He turned sharply around.

"Who said that?" he snapped angrily. "Where is the man that said that?"

"I said it," a squat, swarthy miner called out and the crowd magically cleared a space around him. "I say it again. A hell of a lot you care about that forty down there. How long since anybody went down there lookin' for gas? I been workin'

down in that hole a month and I ain't seen anybody lookin'
for gas. I got a brother down there—" he halted, "but a hell of
a lot you care about that."

"What's your name?" Varner bit the words out.

"Anderson's my name," the miner said belligerently.
"H. Anderson and if you wanta tie the can to me for callin'
you, go ahead and spread the ink."

Varner stared hard at him for several seconds and then
dropped his eyes.

"Hell, Anderson," he said, "I'm not gonna fire you for sayin'
what you think. You think I'm responsible for this blast and
tell me in Christ's name what I had to do with this blast? If
there happens to be black damp down in that shaft, do you
think I put it there? If they don't send a man over here to
inspect, can I help that? Don't you think I like to see you boys
work in as much safety and make as much as possible? I'm no
slave driver. For Christ's sakes get it out of your heads that
because I happen to be the boss of this outfit that I own it.
Goddam it, get this through your thick skulls," Varner's voice
rose to an enraged shout, "I don't own this goddam mine. I
only work here. Do you think I'd live in this hole and stay
here and see my men blown to hell every year if I didn't have
to? Do you think I like to stand here and know there's forty of
my men blown to hell down there?" Varner took a threatening
step towards the unimpressed Anderson who was meeting his
eyes steadily. "I told you maybe they had time to block the
tunnel. Well, I'm tellin' you now that every bastard down in
that hole is blown to hell. I don't give a goddam what you
think about me. A goddam hell of a lot of difference it makes
to me what you think." Varner swung around and walked
rapidly towards the office. There was hardly a sound till the
door slammed and then the crowd shifted restlessly but no
one made a move to go over the hill.

"The old man is right some," Steve said. "He don't own
goddam mine."

"Then why in hell don't he put in a kick if he thinks so

goddam much of his men like he says," Anderson spoke up. "If they don't send the inspector why don't he write and tell them to get his ass over here?"

Johnson straightened up on the wheel of the car and cupped his hands to his mouth again.

"Boys," he called out, "I know goddam well you boys don't like me and won't believe anything I say because I happen to be in the office, but it's the godalmighty's Christ truth that the old man fights for your interests more than you think. There ain't a week goes by he ain't writin' for that gas inspector. He can only go so far. You boys know that. He's got a good job and you boys can't blame him for wantin' to hang on to it. But I'm tellin' you you're harder on the old man than he deserves."

"Bull shit," Anderson spit out. "You're just like the rest of them. Squat your fat ass on a stool and you think you're partners in the goddam business."

The crowd mumbled agreement.

"I know what you think, boys," Johnson said weakly, "but just the same I'm with you boys. Don't think I think I'm any better than you boys just because I happen to hand out the checks on pay day. Hell, I know I'm just a working stiff like any of you."

The crowd started moving impatiently back to their fires and Johnson climbed down off the wheel and slouched over to the office.

Michael went over to the pile and brought back two ties and laid them down by the fire near Steve. He was so sleepy he could hardly hold his head up. He took his coat off and wrapped it around his head and lay down on the ties.

"That Johnson horse ass," Steve grumbled.

He nudged Michael to see if he were listening but he was already asleep. The next thing Michael knew Steve was shoving him in the belly and when he pulled the coat off his face it was getting light.

"You wanta go down?" Steve asked. "Gas gone. Goin' down in a minute."

Michael got stiffly up off the ties. He was so numb all over from the cold he could hardly move. His bones ached in every joint. The rain had stopped but part of his clothes were still clammy.

"When they goin'?" he asked sleepily.

"Now. Old woman over there by the fire got light. Better get it."

Michael limped over to the fire by the mine cars. Mrs. Brodeski was stretched out on some ties and sound asleep. Her mouth was gaping open and Michael could see her yellow teeth stained brown from the snuff. The two kids had rolled off their ties and were sound asleep in the slush. He picked the carbide lamp up off the ground and joined Steve at the hoist. Johnson was standing in the doorway detailing the men to go down. Steve pushed past him brusquely and Michael hung to Steve's coat tail and tried not to let Johnson see him. He was half way on the hoist when Johnson caught sight of him and pulled him off.

"No kids on there," he snapped. "Outside with you."

"Horse ass," Steve muttered and pulled Michael back on the hoist.

"Look here, Brodeski," Johnson said angrily, "I want you to stop that talk to me. If you don't stop it, you're goin' to land up some day without a job around here." He reached out his pudgy hand after Michael again and Steve shoved his hand away. Johnson shrugged his shoulders helplessly. "Toller, Kramer, Garoffolo, Erskine. All right that's a load." He pushed the other men away from the gate and closed it. "Let 'er go. Load!" he called to the hoist man.

The hoist shot downward into the darkness and Michael caught his breath at the speed they were descending. The air was thick and heavy and the whole load was choking for breath before they got to the bottom.

"You know where your old man work?" Steve asked as they went through the gate.

"Twenty-three," Michael said. "I know where it is good. I been down here lotsa times."

"You watch out for rocks fallin'," Steve cautioned.

The miners spread rapidly through the entries, their lights dipping up and down in front of Michael. He tried to keep up with Steve but the pools of red water between the tracks caused him to slip and slide when he tried to run. In a little while he couldn't even see Steve's light anymore. He didn't know if he had turned into one of the rooms off the entry or whether the entry had curved so that he couldn't see him. His own flickering carbide lamp was making grotesque shadows on the facing and on the roof that danced up and down as he stumbled forward in the dark and he wished he could see a light somewhere. There was a strong powdery smell in the air and before he had stumbled a half mile down the entry his head was splitting. A black mound lunged up before him as he tried to leap a pool of water and he fell over it on his face. His lamp sputtered out and it was pitch dark. He sprawled between the tracks for several seconds before he dared to move. His breath was coming in quick gasps and his heart was banging inside him. He jabbed frantically at his lamp before he could get the blue flame to sizzle up. He was lying directly across a mule. Its lips were pulled back away from its teeth as though it was ninnying without making any noise and two of its legs were sticking stiffly up in the air. Michael scrambled to his feet and started trotting through the water that was several inches deep. There wasn't a light in sight. At the entrance to No. 18 he gasped and jumped backward. Just outside the entrance a miner was propped up in a sitting posture with his head thrown back against the facing. Another miner was lying across his legs. Before he could jerk his eyes away he recognized August Saltis and one of his boys. Michael knew the other two boys must be in the room.

Up in front he could hear a rumbling and banging as though a mine car were hitting rocks on the track. He strained his eyes to see a light but even when the rumbling was almost upon him he couldn't see one.

"Who that with light?" Michael recognized Steve's voice.

"Me," Michael called out. Already he felt better. He was no longer afraid. He hurried forward and the rays of his lamp picked up Steve straining behind a mine car. His face was dripping with sweat.

"I push this sonofabitch mile in dark. Light go out back there. Rocks all over track. Sonofabitch hard work."

Michael climbed up on the wheel and looked over the side of the car. There were two miners sprawled out in the bottom. One of them had one eye open and looked as though he were winking at Michael.

"Who's in there?" he asked.

"Benny Zionchek one. That other one I don't know his name. He live about five houses from me, though. There plenty more back there. I see plenty more but two a load for me. Your old man back there in corner of twenty-three. I look through door and see him in there." Steve starting shoving on the car again and Michael stood still and listened to the rumbling till he couldn't hear it anymore. Then he reluctantly splashed through the water again. At the entrance to twenty-three he stubbed his toe on a pile of coal and fell face down on top of it. He could feel his face burn from where the coal cut into it. He crawled over the pile and stood uncertainly in the sloping room. At first he couldn't see old Michael for the coal that was littered all over the floor but in a little while his eyes picked him out over in the corner against the facing. He stepped over the slate and broken timbers till he was standing directly over him. Old Michael was lying on the floor with a six inch beam choking across his throat and a huge hunk of coal lying across his legs. Michael slid the beam off him and tried to lift the coal but he couldn't budge it. It was a solid piece. Old Michael's tongue was sticking far out of his mouth. It was swollen up to twice its size and purply in the carbide light. There was a long thick splinter from the beam clear through his throat and sticking out both sides. Michael tried to pull it out but it broke off. Old Michael's eyes were popped out like a couple of big marbles and even with them popping out like that Michael wasn't afraid. When he had seen August Saltis and his boy out there he had been scared but now in here with old Michael for some reason or other he wasn't scared a bit. He thought, "Old Michael looks funnier than hell with his eyes popped out like that."

He sat down on a hunk of coal and waited for some one to come and take old Michael out. After he had sat there for more than an hour and no one came, he went out to the entry. He could see four or five lights bobbing up and down. From the rumbling he knew they were shoving a car in front of them. He sat down on the pile of coal in the doorway and waited.

CHAPTER FOUR

THERE WERE forty-three down there, but they never found but forty. They found old man Sigmun's belt buckle so they didn't look for him anymore. They looked for the other two, though, but they couldn't find them. The company sent in an investigating committee from New York. They said it was these two that caused the blast. They didn't say how but they said it was undoubtedly these two. Old man Sigmun had something to do with it, too, but not as much as these two. They found old man Sigmun's belt buckle but they didn't find anything of these two.

The opening was all cleared by Monday and the dead from the dayshift buried. They buried them in the rain. Frank Darby the engineer said he could hear the women moaning clear to the engine house and the cemetery was a mile away. The night shift went back in on Monday night. The company was bringing in forty more men on the local from Corning. They paid their fares and took it out of their pay at so much a week. Some of the families of the dead miners went away from there to relatives and some moved over with friends. Old man Sigmun's widow, Mary, leaned a shot gun near the door and waited for the sheriff. She said she had had a husband and now all she had was a belt buckle and she'd be goddamed if they'd evict her. They let her stay there all winter, but by spring she was pretty well starved out and went to her sister's down the creek.

When Julia came back from the cemetery, she got her and Michael's clothes all packed up. She went up to the office that night to get old Michael's pay but there wasn't any pay. Old Michael still owed the company. He had bought some carbide and powder the day before the blast and he owed the company for that. She came back to the shack and sat down in the rocking chair and stayed there till late that night. When Michael came back from the company store there wasn't any blanket on the bed and she had to undo the bundle and get out the bed clothes. The next day she had to take the pots and pans out to cook with and when she got through using them she just left them out.

They got along that winter with Michael's three dollars and the company not saying anything about the rent and when spring came she had the misery in her side so bad she couldn't think of anything else. At first she swabbed on mustard poultices. They blistered the skin outside but the misery was on the inside. By summer she could just barely make it across the floor if she held on to something and by winter Michael was cooking the meals. She told him she believed old Granny Plum's yarbs would help her. Mrs. Saltis had said they had helped a misery in the side that she had had.

The next noon Michael was greasing cars and he stole a dollar out of Tony Zignego's coat that was hanging on a pole. Joe Sirventi was moving some timbers behind the tipple and saw him take it. There were four dollars in the coat but he only took one. He hid it in the toe of his shoe. When Joe and Tony faced him with it at quitting time, Michael said that Joe Sirventi was a goddam liar and probably took the dollar himself. Joe slapped him across the face and made his nose bleed. Michael dived for a hunk of coal but they drug him into the tool shed that was dug into the side of the hill. Tony said to either come across with the dollar or he would beat him to death. Michael said that Joe Sirventi was a no-good lying sonofabitch and that if anyone was going to beat him to death they better do a good job of it.

They knocked him down and tied his feet together with some rope that was in there. They searched his pockets but they couldn't find anything and then they tied him head down from the rafters. They swung his head back and forth against the slate walls of the tool shed. The blood from his head and nose dripped down the walls and made a red pool on the floor. There were pieces of his hair and skin sticking to the slate. Every few swings and Tony would tell him to come across. His head from his nose down was soaked with blood and there were big blue knots on his forehead where it had hit the slate.

He called them sonsofbitches.

After a while they broke the ice on the barrel of water outside and doused him with buckets of it. It froze on his clothes almost as it hit and made white frost all over them. He passed out after a while and Tony and Joe got scared and cut him down. Tony said maybe, by God, he had only had three dollars in his pocket in the first place. He said maybe the old lady rifled his pockets. She did rifle his pockets sometimes. They struck matches and looked at his bloody face but they couldn't tell if he was dead or not. He didn't move and he looked as though he were dead. They covered him up with a burlap sack and slipped out. They were both scared and they promised each other to keep their mouths shut.

When Michael came to he was stiff from the cold. His head was throbbing so that he could hardly see and there were white lights dancing in front of his eyes. He didn't go home right away but stumbled down the five miles in the dark to old Granny Plum's and gave her the dollar for the yarbs. Julia was sitting up in the chair by the window when he came in. He told her he had found the dollar for the yarbs and when she didn't say anything he repeated that he had found the dollar in front of the company store. He said he got hit on the head with a lump of coal but he didn't say how he got wet. He ate supper wrapped in a quilt while she dried his clothes out behind the stove. She didn't thank him for the yarbs but when he was in bed and breathing heavily, she pulled herself over to his pile of rags in the corner and kissed him lightly.

Her legs kept swelling till they were twice the size they should have been. The company doctor said it was the dropsy and she'd better get to her relatives if she had any relatives. Her side broke out with running sores and she was only a skeleton except for her water-logged legs. When she dragged herself across the room to her bed, Michael used to sit in the rocking chair and imagine he could hear the gurgle of the water in her legs.

She was stretched out on the bed when it started to rain on Sunday. When she reached her bony hand up to brush away this lace curtain that was brushing against her face in the breeze and saw it disappear and there was her hand in the air and no curtain, she called Michael over to the bed and told him to always be a good boy. Michael didn't know what she was talking about but he said he would. She lived three days after that. When Michael came home from work, she was sitting up in the rocking chair with her eyes wide open and her head tipped over to one side as though she had been listening for his footsteps. The lamp was lit on the table. He spoke to her several times and when she didn't answer him he walked over and touched her on the shoulder and her head fell stiffly down on her chest. Michael hadn't been scared when he found old Michael with his eyes popped out in twenty-three but he was scared when he saw Julia. Old Michael had had a hunk of coal across his legs and there was a splinter clear through his neck. There wasn't any coal across Julia's legs or splinter through her neck either. He backed out of the door and ran over to the Brodeskis'. Mrs. Brodeski got a couple of neighbors and they laid her out. They washed her and found her rusty old black dress that she had been married to old Michael in and they laid her out in that.

They buried her in the rain on Friday. It rained hard all day

Friday but it rained harder during the burying. They wanted to wait and bury her on Sunday but because of the sores on her side that smelled even before she died, she wouldn't keep till Sunday. It had rained when they buried Paul and it had rained when they buried old Michael. After that Michael always felt uneasy when it rained. He got a funny feeling in the top of his head when it rained.

While Julia was laying out for the burying, Michael had stayed with the Brodeskis' across the road. After the burying was over and Julia was in the ground, he just kept on staying there. Nobody said anything about not staying there and Michael never thought anything about it. On pay day Steve met him at the door and took his three dollars away from him and gave him back fifty cents. That evening Michael went down to the company store and bought a quarter's worth of licorice and spit off the porch of the company store like old Michael used to spit amber juice. He bought a gilt framed mirror with the other quarter and the next day, Sunday, he went out to the graveyard. He lugged bronze colored slate from the side of the hill and piled it up neatly till it was almost as high as his head. He piled it about where he thought Jute's head would be. Not right on her head but about a foot from there. When the rocks were all piled he wedged the mirror between the two top ones. The sun caught the gilt like gold. He took out his barlow and cut off a yellow forelock of his hair and put that beneath a rock at the base of the tombstone. Jute would like that. In her big Bible that he was now using for a pillow there were strands of old Michael's hair and Paul's hair that she had cut off before the burying. When Jute had died Michael had wanted a piece of her hair to keep but he was ashamed to ask anyone to cut it off for him. But the day before the burying he had seen Mrs. Brodeski cut off a piece and put it in her Bible. Later that evening he stole it and put it in his own Bible.

When the tombstone was all finished, he stepped back a few

steps and squinted at it with his head tipped a little to one side. He had inherited one weak eye from old Michael and he always carried his head a little to one side.

"Jute," he said out loud, "you've got yourself as fine a tombstone as you'll find in this whole sonofabitchin' graveyard."

Mrs. Brodeski had thrown a quilt in the corner of the bedroom and he slept there. Jan and the baby slept in the other corner and she and Steve slept on a pair of old rusty springs on the other side of the room. They had as much to eat as he and Julia had had and besides he was hardly ever there except at meals and bedtime. In the evenings he sat in the company store listening to the miners talk. He never got to know Mrs. Brodeski very well, but Steve never did either for that matter and he had been married to her for seven years. When she wasn't cooking or washing clothes she was sitting on the kitchen floor paring her corns with Steve's razor if he wasn't in the house or with the paring knife if he was. Steve had long ago stopped telling her what happened at the mine during the day for she only grunted when he got through talking. When Steve would swear at her for not paying any attention to him when he was talking to her, she would only grunt again. Now Steve stayed away from the house as much as he could.

Sometimes in the evenings before he went to bed Michael would go over to the creek and sit on a rock by it. He liked to watch the red sulphur water whirl by and imagine where it went to. He had always wanted to go to the end of the creek and one Sunday he had followed it for miles and when the dark came it looked just the same as it did when he started. When he got home Jan had already gobbled up the spuds that Mrs. Brodeski had shoved to one side of the stove. He pinched Jan when no one was looking and didn't follow the creek anymore. Sometimes, if there were a lot of stars, he would watch the sky for falling ones and he knew that someone had just died when he saw one. He used to try to imagine himself down in a hole with dirt on top of him like Jute and Paul and old Michael, but he couldn't do it. Sometimes he'd imagine himself going towards the stars a million miles and then another million and another and no matter how far he went he could always go another million and he'd finally get dizzy from trying to figure it out and go to bed.

He always kissed the Bible before he put it under his head for a pillow.

"God have mercy on old Michael," he always prayed.

He never prayed for Jute. Jute was in heaven but old Michael was in hell. He didn't know where Paul was for he didn't remember him very well. Old Michael used always to say that when you were dead you were dead and if there was a God why did he let people starve to death and work their prats off in a coal mine. Once he said a God like that was a sonofabitch and Julia had crossed herself when he said this and even old Michael felt scared after he'd said it, but he wouldn't let Julia know it. But after a while he went in the bedroom and Michael had seen him cross himself. Julia always said that old Michael never wanted to do anything but dance in his young days and now he was cussing God in his old days and he would surely go to hell when he died. Michael believed in God. He believed he sat up in heaven on a red plush seat like he could see in the passenger coaches that passed below the tipple every day. He believed He had big handle bar mustaches like the polak in number seventeen. The polak could shovel more coal than anybody and he had patted Michael on the head once.

He never had much time to play with the other boys in Glen Ellum. Sometimes on Sunday he and Ed Chenzko would hunt for frogs but most of the time they were fighting and Michael had to always be ready to run to keep Ed from beating him up. He didn't know the rest of the boys in Glen Ellum very well and didn't like or dislike them except for Elmer Varner, the superintendent's son. Michael wouldn't even speak to him when he passed him on the road. One day Michael had been standing in the middle of the railroad tracks throwing rocks at a bottle that he had placed on top of a pile of ties. If he didn't hit the bottle in five minutes he would drop dead. Elmer Varner came out of the store with an armload of groceries and passed Michael throwing at the bottle. He put his groceries down on the track and starting throwing, too. He had a white shirt on and it was clean. Michael noticed that it was clean and thought that he would wash his overalls when he got home. He didn't have but one pair and Mrs. Brodeski never said anything about washing them when he went to bed so he'd walk down the creek and wash them in the sulphur water. Mrs. Varner came out of the store while Elmer was throwing at the bottle. She was a red faced woman and had on a black waist with a high collar that was pinned tight at the throat. Michael thought she had better loosen up a little on the collar or she would choke to death.

"Elmer Varner!" she screamed.

Elmer disgustedly picked his groceries up off the ground.

"Heck," he said, "caint ever do nothin'."

Mrs. Varner shoved him down the cinder path in front of her.

"Just wait till your father hears about this, young man, playing with a bohunk."

Michael stopped throwing at the bottle. He didn't know what a bohunk was but he didn't want to be one. He watched them from the tracks till they went through the gate of the white house and then went over to the bottle and knocked it off. He sat down behind the pile of ties and started to cry. It was the first time he had cried since they had buried Jute. After a while he got up and started home.

"Old sonofabitchin' red faced bohunk, herself," he said out loud.

The next time he saw Elmer Varner he didn't speak to him. At first he didn't remember about his overalls but after a while he remembered about them and walked down the creek and washed them. He put them on wet and the next morning his chest hurt him when he breathed but it hurt him sometimes whether he washed his overalls or not so he didn't pay any attention to it.

Michael was twelve the winter that Vito Kiroff came to live at the Brodeskis'. Steve had known Vito in the old country so they had put a couple of quilts on the kitchen floor and he slept there. Vito's face was pale and his eyes were coal black and there were dark shadows under his eyes. He had been working in the Red Rooster mine in the southern part of the state and when he told that first night how the miner had starved there when they had closed the mine down for a week and had not opened it up for three months his black eyes flashed and he shook his head so that the long hair flew up and down on his head. He had a low deep voice and he had been to universities in the old country.

"A smart one, that Vito," Steve would say. "You watch, they kill him sometime."

In the evenings he would talk. He talked always of starvation wages, lousy living conditions, and the time that was coming when the proletariat would begin to feel their muscles and begin to use them. He had belonged to the Black International and to the Knights of Labor and he had been in strikes. Once in a strike a bomb had exploded and a man's bloody arm had flown through the air and hit him in the face. Michael used to crouch behind the stove and shiver when Vito would describe how the blood had smeared across his face from the arm.

"A worker's arm," Vito would almost whisper. "Not a policeman's arm. A worker's arm."

Miners would drop into Steve's in the evenings and sit by the lamplight and listen to Vito talk. Sometimes they would ask questions and sometimes they would talk themselves. Most of the time they talked about how they worked their asses off for the owners of the Glen Ellum mine for nothing. When the talk would start like that Vito would tip his chair back against the wall, puff slowly on his pipe, and say nothing. Sometimes, if he especially liked what was being said, he would smile and flash his white teeth in a half snarl half smile.

"Yes," he would say. "Yes."

Michael always sat behind the stove with his knees cocked up under his chin and listened to every word that was said. He didn't understand all the words but he liked to listen to them talk and especially to Vito talk. He never knew Vito very well till he came out on the back porch one night when Michael was there watching the sky for falling stars. He leaned up against the railing beside Michael.

"You like the stars. Every night I see you watching the stars."

Michael shook his head yes.

"You go ahead and like the stars and you will go a long ways." He looked down at Michael. "How old are you?"

"Twelve," Michael said. "Goin' on thirteen."

"How long is it that you work in the mines?"

"A long time," he said. "I forget how long."

"You forget how long. Yes, I know. So long you forget how long. I know. I forget myself. Maybe we raise plenty of hell if we remember how long."

Michael noticed that he frowned when he talked and flashed his teeth.

"I'm goin' away from here sometime, though," Michael said. "I ain't aimin' to stay here so awful long now."

"Where?"

"To the mills. I'm gonna get me a job in the mills in Pittsburgh."

"They're bad, too, but they're better than the mines." He held his narrow chest till the spasm of coughing was over.

"That is what you get in the mines. You starve to death in the mills, too, but you stay away from the miner's cough."

"I'm gonna go to school, too, and get me a education," Michael said.

"You read books?"

"Not now. I caint read now, but I know the letters. Jute learned me the letters before she died." He had never cared before whether he could read or not but tonight in front of Vito who could read the books so well, he was ashamed he couldn't read.

"We will fix that," Vito said. "Tomorrow we will start to fix that. Maybe that is the reason. He can't read," he half muttered to himself. He went back in the house but Michael stayed out on the porch for a long time but he didn't watch the stars anymore. He could hardly wait till tomorrow so he could learn to read.

That night Michael dreamed of God. He was sitting on the red plush seat like in the passenger coaches but he did not have handle bar mustaches like the polak but his face was like the face of Vito and Michael was reading to him from a great black book like the timekeeper's book and Vito was listening to him read.

CHAPTER FIVE

THEY TACKED the notice up on Saturday. The day shift milled around the white slip of paper nailed on the side of the office. Most of them couldn't read and they were straining their ears listening to several miners up in front laboriously spelling out the words. Some of them were laughing nervously but most of them listened with blank looks on their faces.

"Maybe they close the sonofabitch down," Steve Brodeski said, craning his neck towards Vito Kiroff who was coming towards the office from the hoist.

Vito pushed through the opening they made for him.

"What's the news?"

"What she say, wise fellah?" Steve asked. "We all canned maybe."

Vito read the notice through.

"They can our prats out, hey?" Steve asked nervously. "Maybe they close the sonofabitch down?"

"Cut," Vito said. "Ten percent cut starting Monday."

"What she mean, ten cent cut?" Steve asked. The miners all around the office were swearing and muttering to themselves.

"It means they're going to take a dime out of every dollar you make," Vito snapped.

Without a word Steve drew back his hairy fist and smashed it through the notice. His arm went through the office wall up to his elbow. He licked his bleeding knuckles. "That's what Steve Brodeski say to ten cent cut," he said.

Johnson the bookkeeper came running to the door.

"What the hell's goin' on out there? Tryin' to tear the damn

place down?" He tried to look stern. "Who smashed that
wall?" He caught the belligerent glare of the miners bunched
in front of the office and grinned weakly. "No use to tear the
damn place down."

Old man Youngblood bristled up to him in the door.

"You tryin' to starve us to death around here?" He looked as
though he might swing at Johnson. "We ain't makin' enough
to feed us around here now."

"I ain't got a thing to do with it." Johnson retreated back a
step. "Them's orders and orders is orders."

"Maybe," Vito said coldly, "maybe we don't take this cut.
Maybe we raise plenty hell around here."

"Come on, boys, there's no use to talk like that," Johnson
said placatingly. "When the company gets back on its feet
you'll get your pay boosted again. I got letters in here. The
company's losin' money and they gotta cut right now but it's
just temperary that's all, just a temperary cut."

Vito was flashing his smile at Johnson.

"You believe what you are talking, Johnson? You believe
that?"

"Well, when the company makes more money, you make
more money. That's sense, ain't it?"

"Damn nonsense," Vito said.

"Well, there's no use to beef with me. I only work here.
You'll have to talk it over with Varner when he comes back
from Pittsburgh tomorrow. Orders is orders as far as I'm concerned. I just work here the same as you guys." Johnson went
back in the office and closed the door.

The miners slouched over the hill swearing among themselves. Michael fell in step beside Vito.

"You know about beating an old horse to death, Michael?"
Vito asked without looking up from the ground.

"Huh?" Michael asked. "What's that?"

"When you are older and read the books more you will
know about beating an old horse to death."

"What is it?"

"You're going to see plenty hell around here. You ever see a strike?"

"No."

"You're going to see a good one. I see plenty of strikes in my time. I wait. Sometimes the white notices go up all at one time everywhere. Then will be hell. That will be a big strike. You know what they will call that strike?"

"What?"

"Revolution. When all the ten cent cut notices go up at one time, revolution."

Michael didn't know what a revolution was but he hoped he got to see one.

"How long till that happens?"

"Soon. Maybe not in my time but you will see it. In your time you will see it."

When they got home and had eaten supper Michael listened to Steve and Vito talk about the strike till he got tired of it and walked down the road. Elmer Varner was walking home with an armload of groceries.

"Sonofabitch bohunk," Michael yelled as loud as he could. He didn't care if Elmer told his old man or not. His old man was a sonofabitch bohunk himself.

The miners met over in the woods by the cemetery on Sunday afternoon. From his perch on the limb of the tree Michael could look over into the graveyard and see the tombstone that he had made for Jute with his own hands. All of the miners were there but four or five. They squatted on the ground and smoked. They took turns about getting up and talking, most of them stuttering and fumbling for words, but Michael noticed that when Vito got up he did not stutter and they all sat up straight and listened when he talked. They called the strike for Monday and appointed Vito and Steve to go talk it over with Varner when he came back from Pittsburgh. Steve stood up.

"I been in lotsa strike," he said. "Some strike we win but most strike we lose. We lose strike because sonofabitch won't stick together. If stick together we win all strike. I wanta know if there is sonofabitch that won't stick, stand up and say he won't stick."

Nobody stood up and Steve shrugged his shoulders.

"We'll meet here again Monday at three o'clock," Vito said.

On Monday morning Michael woke up at daylight. He could hear Mrs. Brodeski banging pots around on the stove in the kitchen and he knew it must be pretty nearly time to get up. He put on his clothes but he couldn't find his shoes. He fumbled around in the dark room feeling for them and finally had to strike a match. Jan had them under his head for a pillow. He gave them an angry jerk and Jan's head hit the floor with a loud thump. Steve groaned in his sleep on the springs at the noise but Jan didn't even wake up.

He went out to the pump through the kitchen. Mrs. Brodeski was waddling around on the floor in her bare feet. She never wore shoes in the house because of her corns that were always bothering her. He filled the washpan full of cold water and had already splashed it on his face before he remembered about the strike. He felt funny when he thought of it and couldn't realize he didn't have to go to work today. Today was Monday but he wasn't going to work today but it was Monday. He went back in the house feeling good at not having to go to work. It was just like Sunday only better because maybe he wouldn't have to go to work tomorrow, either.

"I forgot about there ain't no work today," he said to Mrs. Brodeski.

She was squatting in the floor paring her corns with Steve's razor and only grunted when he spoke to her.

He went back to the bedroom and crawled in bed with his clothes on. He pulled the ragged blanket up around his chin and felt good lying there and knowing he could lie there as long as he wanted. He thought of Vito lying out there on the kitchen floor and he wished he'd hurry up and be as big and as smart as Vito. He would be if he kept on growing as fast as he was. The strike was because of Vito. Vito had shut the sonofa-bitch down. If it was not for Vito he would be getting up and going to work and greasing cars today instead of lying here warm in bed. The mine was big. It was a big thing to shut the mine down but it wasn't too big for Vito. He lay there and felt big himself because he knew Vito and because he lived in the same house with Vito and because he, too, was in the strike the same as Vito or the polak and anybody else. He saw him-self walking up to a white notice on the wall and saw himself smashing his fist through it till his fist went clear through to the office inside. He saw himself making a speech to a bunch of black faced miners and when he was through they patted him on the back. Vito had told him about the big universities where you could go if you had the money and learn things and be somebody and he saw himself coming home to the mine after he had been there and the men would meet him when he got off the train with the red plush seats and he would lead them to old man Varner's house.

"Old man Varner, you scabby sonofabitch," he muttered out loud, "what are you gonna do about that ten cent cut?"

No more licorice. He would stop chewing licorice and save his money. Vito said you couldn't get to the universities un-less you had the money. He would get the money. On pay day he would keep a dollar out of his pay instead of fifty cents like before. Steve would not like that and would swear at him but to hell with Steve. Steve did not have any more sense than to think you could go to the universities for nothing. Vito knew more about it than Steve for Vito himself had been to univer-sities in the old country.

The afternoon train on Wednesday brought in fifty men. Seven or eight of them were carrying rifles and shot guns and they had revolvers strapped to their hips. The strikers had been looking for them and most of them were around the station to meet them when the train pulled in. Vito tried to get up on the platform to talk to them but two or three of the guards shoved him away. The strikers hooted them as they marched across the bridge and up the hill and a few of them threw rocks at them but nobody was hit. The scabs didn't say anything but walked stolidly along trying to act as though nothing were going on. They started putting up the barbed wire fence around the mine buildings at once, working at night by flares and in the morning it was all finished. They started working the mine that evening.

The next morning Ed Varner sent word that he would like to see Steve Brodeski and when Steve went up there he told him to tell the strikers to be at work in the morning or get out of the houses. He said Vito Kiroff needn't come back no matter what. The company store had not opened on Monday so by Wednesday there weren't any more beans in Steve's house and by Thursday the potatoes were all gone. They had saved the peelings from the potatoes and they started eating them. Mrs. Brodeski boiled them and then fried them. Her baby caught the croup and would choke for breath when it coughed till it was blue in the face. A lot of the miners began to get sick but the company doctor wouldn't come to see them. Ed Varner said they weren't working for him any more so they hadn't any right to the doctor. He said he'd give them a week to get out of the company houses or he'd get the militia and put them out.

On Friday morning Michael woke up with a pain gnawing at his stomach and a dizzy feeling in his head. He fell down twice when he raised up his leg to put it through his overalls, and he finally had to sit down to put them on. There was nothing to eat in the house and no one said anything about anything to eat. Jan began crying because he was hungry and Steve said he would whip him if he didn't stop whining. Jan kept on crying and Steve pulled back his hand to slap him. Mrs. Brodeski jerked Jan away and they were still quarreling when Michael went outside. It was the first time he had ever heard her quarrel or even talk much. He started walking down the creek to get his mind off his stomach. After he had gone about a half a mile, he heard a splash in the water. He picked up a large rock and the next time he saw a frog on the bank he squashed it. After an hour he had three frogs. He cut their heads off and cleaned them with his barlow and started home. He was sick in the stomach from the ache that was in there and every time he coughed, he gagged. He saw a rusty lard bucket floating in the creek and he waded out and got it. He thought that three small frogs wouldn't go very far at the house. He washed the can out and filled it half full of the red water and built a fire. When the water was simmering, he threw in the frogs. He ate two of them. They tasted bitter but he wasn't so hungry when he had eaten them. The gnawing in his stomach was gone. He wrapped the other one up in some leaves and stuck it in his pocket for Vito. When he was almost home he got to thinking that maybe Vito wouldn't eat it but give it to Jan so he ate it himself and then he felt ashamed of himself for having eaten it.

They were all standing around the table eating dandelion greens when he got home. There was no grease left so Mrs. Brodeski had boiled them in water without seasoning. His share was set over to one side of the stove and he felt more guilty than ever about eating the frog so he gave Jan his greens. Mrs. Brodeski thought he was sick and made him go to bed. When she came in later and put a wet rag over his head he felt so guilty about the frog he started crying when she got out of the room.

He went out in the kitchen at supper time. Even Vito was drooping around the house. He looked haggard around the eyes and kept pacing up and down the room. Mrs. Brodeski had borrowed a piece of bacon rind from somewhere and she had cooked up the last of the potato peelings. Michael sprinkled a lot of salt on his and they didn't taste so bad that way.

"We can't keep up like this," Vito said without looking up from the dynamite box he was sitting on. "Tonight is as good as any other night. No use waiting. If we wait, some of the men will back down and go back."

"Tonight is good with me," Steve said. "I think ever' body say tonight. Some don't have potato peel now."

Vito got up and raked what potato peelings he had left into Michael's plate.

"Here, eat till you bust," he grinned wearily. He went over and put his coat on. "I'll go and see what they all say. Myself, I think tonight is as good as any other night."

CHAPTER SIX

THEY passed Michael's dead in the graveyard. As he swung around the curve in the dark, he could have reached over and touched Jute's headstone that he had made with the bronze slate and the gilt mirror. He waved his butcher knife high in the air so old Michael could see it and then he felt foolish for fear Vito might have seen him, too, but Vito was stumbling through the brush at his side and not paying any attention to him. They tramped through the woods for a mile before they came out into the clearing. Down the slope below them they could see the fires that the scabs had made inside the wire enclosure. They were too far away to make out the scabs but once in a while the fires would be dimmed by shadows passing in front of them and Michael knew it must be the scabs warming in front of them. The strikers stopped at the grove of sassafras and gathered around in a bunch. Most of them were clutching clubs and pick axes in their hands but a few of them had guns. Old man Dazzo was swinging a cane knife. He could hardly walk now for the rheumatism but he had told Michael that in his young days he had cut off a scab's head with one sweep of a cane knife. Vito pushed himself to the center of the crowd. Michael strained his eyes to see him up there but it was too dark and there were too many in front of him.

"We'll rush them from here," he could hear Vito's voice and he imagined he could see his white teeth flashing in the dark. "There's no use fooling ourselves. The guards are waiting for us down there and we won't be able to surprise them. Down

there are your houses. There's no use of me telling you about
your kids' empty bellies and your women's empty bellies. You
got empty bellies yourselves. Remember this. All you've got
to remember is this when you get down there. There never
was a scab that wasn't a son of a bitch. You all know what to
do when you get down there so let's go."

They started trotting down the slope. Michael managed to
catch up with Vito and dogged his heels. The path was covered with the fine sleet and he slipped as he went. As they got
closer they could see the scabs huddled in the enclosure as far
away from the fires as they could get. The guns started to bark
behind the piles of ties and behind barrels in the enclosure
and the strikers dropped to their bellies and started crawling
the last hundred yards. Michael crawled through the weeds,
holding his butcher knife high in the air so as not to cut himself on the sharp blade. The weeds were so high here he
couldn't see the other strikers but from the glare of the fires
he could see the weeds moving in front and on all sides of
him. When they were within twenty-five yards of the wire
fence, Vito yelled and leaped to his feet. The rest of them
jumped to their feet and thundered behind him towards the
fence. The guns began to bark louder from the inside and two
or three miners in front fell forward. Michael could see one of
them get to his feet and limp forward but the one near him
was thrashing around in the weeds. When he was half way to
the fence Michael felt a stab and a burn in the calf of his leg.
He flopped down in the weeds and put his hand down there.
He knew he was shot because when he took his hand away it
was sticky and wet. It didn't hurt much but only burned a
little like the time he had stepped on a pin and it had gone
clear up to the head in his heel. Old man Dazzo hobbled up
from behind him screeching slavic oaths as he came.

"I'm shot," Michael yelled at him, but he didn't pay any
attention but kept hobbling towards the fence. He could hear
the crash as the strikers jumped bodily into the fence and

trampled over it. He felt peeved at old man Dazzo for not stopping. It was not every sonofabitch got shot by a scab. He felt big and grown up and he wished Vito was there so he could show him the hole. "What does a sonofabitch do around here when he gets shot?" he said out loud. He could hear the screaming curses of the strikers and scabs as they clashed in there. He tore off the sleeve of his shirt and tied his leg up and started crawling on his hands and knees towards the fence. He crawled through the hole that the strikers had made and limped over behind a pile of lumber. Over behind the string of mine cars at the right he could hear a man crying piteously.

Most of the hits were being made by a guard perched behind a beam at the top of the tipple. He was firing both a rifle and a shot gun up there. Sam Gerlach crouched between the two rows of mine cars watching him and then methodically rested his gun on the edge of a car and drew a bead. He pulled the trigger. The shadow up there straightened stiffly up on the beam and then slowly toppled through the air like a fancy diver. Sam cocked his ear but he couldn't hear him hit bottom on account of all the noise.

Jim McCoy staggered behind the pile of lumber and sat down. He was holding his head with both hands and Michael could see the blood dripping from between his fingers. Over by the office scabs and strikers were piled on top of each other fighting at close range with whatever they could get their hands on. At the sound of a pick handle on skull a miner would grope blindly out of the mass of thrashing arms and legs and either lie quiet on the ground or start crawling slowly away. Most of the guards had stopped firing for fear of shooting their own men.

John Arbannis and his boy, George, crawled on their hands and knees past the engine room towards the guard crouched down in the shadows behind a barrel to the right of the tipple. A stream of flame shot out from the hole in the wall near the top of the engine room. The guard up there was firing from the rafters. George got the full blast of the shot gun in his face. The right side was blown away and the left side was pock-marked with buckshot. Tiny streams of blood spurted from each one and converged in a pool at his shirt collar. His right eye was shot entirely away but the left one was only punc-tured. His hand was pressed up against his left eye and the creamy fluid from the eyeball seeped through his bloody fin-gers. John squatted dumb on the ground beside him till the motion of the scab caught in the barbed wire fence attracted his attention. The scab had on a red woolen shirt and was panting and swearing as he tried to free himself from the barbs. John snatched up his pitchfork and dashed towards the trapped scab, the prongs of the fork thrust out and gleaming in the half light from the embers of the fires.

"Baby killer, sonofabitch scab," he panted as he ran.

The scab jerked his head around and gasped unbelievingly at the tines of the fork. The white froth of slobber was run-ning out of John's mouth. Two prongs grazed each side of the scab's throat and the middle one went through his windpipe. He screamed once and thrashed his arms up and down and tore the flesh from his fingers on the barbs. John let go of the pitchfork without pulling it out. He stood and shook his fist in the dead scab's face.

"Sonofabitch, baby killer scab," he slobbered.

He staggered back to George's body on the ground. He sat down beside him and sobbed in his hands.

"What I gonna tell Maria?" he kept repeating, "what I gonna tell Maria?"

The scabs were backing off down the hill but some of the guards were holding out behind their barricades. Every little while the guard that got George Arbannis would stick his gun out through the hole in the engine room and shoot. Ugly Sudski limped behind the pile of lumber and sat down beside Michael. He had a knife jab in his side and the blood was running down his pants leg.

"You got a chew?" he asked Jim. "What hit you?"

"A freight train it feels like." He handed over a package of tobacco. "It's splittin'."

Ugly chewed on the tobacco till it was soggy and then slapped it into the hole in his side. He tore off his shirt and girded it around the wound to hold the cud of tobacco in place. "This is what comes of friggin' around," he said. "I let three of them ketch me out there by myself."

"One of 'em got me," Michael said. "I'm shot in the leg."

"I'd like to go back out there," Jim said, "but I caint see two steps in front of me."

"Most of them are runnin' their asses off down the tracks. I seen John Arbannis get one of them through the throat with a pitchfork. He's hangin' over there on the fence with the fork through his neck."

"I can still hear the guards shootin' out there, though," Jim said.

"There's four or five of them still left out there shootin' from behind some ties." Ugly stuck his head out from around the lumber and watched the little dabs of flame that were coming from the top of the engine room. "It's that bastard over in the top of the engine room that got George Arbannis. He's got a shot gun."

"What we need is some guns ourselves," Jim said. "How you gonna fight them guys with guns when you ain't got any guns yourself?"

Most of the yelling was coming from down the side of the hill now. Michael knew the strikers must be backing off the scabs over the hill but the fires were going down and he couldn't see.

"I'm gonna send that guy where he belongs without any gun," Ugly said. He pulled a wad of oil soaked waste out of his pocket and tied it around a flat rock with a string he tore from his shirt.

"If you're gonna try to brain that guy with a rock biscuit what do you want to cover it up for?" Jim asked.

"I got a plan. If you wanta see something pretty just watch."

"You're gonna get your ass shot off if you go friggin' around out there."

"I know what I'm doin'." Ugly crawled around the side of the lumber. Ugly was sliding on his belly around to the side of the engine room and when he slid beyond the glow of the dying embers of the fire, Michael lost him in the dark. He watched till the sputtering ball of flame arched through the air and crashed through the engine room window. The sound of the dull puff came almost with the sound of crashing glass. The black smoke belched from the window and licking out of it, the flames. Even from behind the lumber pile Michael could feel the earth tremble as the explosion came. Pieces of wood and metal skyrocketed into the air and he could hear them smashing to the ground all over the enclosure. The guard came crashing out the door through the clouds of smoke with the flames from his oil soaked clothes beating around his head. He ran a few steps and then stumbled and fell. His head moved up and down for a little while and then he lay still on the ground. Michael could smell the smell of burned meat in the air.

"Christ Almighty!" Jim muttered.

The fire from the engine room leaped high in the air and comets of it jumped across the intervening space and licked at the tipple. In a minute the coal dusty timbers were roaring clear down the shaft. Smoke began sifting up through the roof of the office. Strikers and scabs ran together down the hill to get away from the searing heat.

"Somebody'll get his ass sent to the pen for this," Jim yelled at Michael as they sped side by side down to the tracks.

Jim kept running and crossed the bridge. Michael stopped in the weeds by the railroad tracks and lay down. Up on the hill the fire was shooting high into the air. Strikers were stampeding in every direction and he could hear their feet pounding on the wooden bridge as they made for their houses.

When the freight pulled in at midnight he crawled out of the weeds and ran up and down the tracks trying to find an empty boxcar but he couldn't find any. They were all filled and sealed. He tore a loose board off the station platform and pushed it across the rods of a boxcar. When the train jerked forward the board slipped and he thought for sure he would fall under the wheels. He held tight to the rods and scooted the board back in place. He wrapped his arms around the board and held tight. All around him was the whine of the wind and the roar of the wheels on the rails. The wind shifted and began lashing at him harder than ever. He could feel the cold sleet in it. After a while his hands no longer burned from its lashings. They had no feeling in them. It was pitch dark under there. His clothes were soggy from the dew that the weeds had been covered with. He could feel them freeze and stiffen from the sharp wind that blasted up dust and gravel from the roadbed. He could hear the heavy gravel banging up against the bottom of the car and once a large piece hit the bottom of the board he was lying on. He was numb all over. After a while the cars began to buckle up as the train slowed down. He was so cold he didn't know if he could crawl out from under the car or not. When the train came to a stop he lowered himself off the board to the roadbed and slid out off the track. It wasn't so dark out there as it had been under the car. The moon was a large yellow ball up there. Up in front he could hear the engine panting and he could hear the hiss of steam. He could see the glare of the cinders in the firebox. He jumped up and down and swung his arms to warm himself.

He couldn't see any houses anywhere. There was nothing but underbrush and scraggly trees. The engine whistled three times and the cars jerked forward. He grabbed hold of the steps of a boxcar and ran along beside it. The train gathered speed as it went and jerked him from his feet. His feet slid along in the cinders till he pulled himself up with his hands. When he pulled himself up the last step to the top he lay still for a while to get his breath and then crawled slowly over to the middle of the car. The wind tore over the tops and cut through his wet clothes. He sprawled flat on his stomach and rode the roll of the top with outstretched arms on the sleety roof. He was sleepy. He closed his eyes and then opened them again quickly. Down below he could hear the pound and the sing of the wheels on the rails. Up in front the sparks flew from the engine and he could feel the swish of the smoke that flattened back over the tops and struck him in the face. It was warm up there in the engine cab. If he was to crawl over the tops to the engine cab where the fire was and say to them up there that he was freezing to death back there on the tops and couldn't stand it any longer, what could they do? They couldn't throw him off at fifty miles an hour. That was murder. They had to hack that tramp off with hatchets at the mine that time. The rain had froze him to the tops and when they pulled into Glen Ellum they had to hack him off with hatchets. They had carried him over to the company store like a board—that's how stiff he was. His feet were numb and he couldn't feel his legs back there. He could feel a tingle in his hair as though his hair were standing on end but he wasn't afraid. He was cold. He had seen with his own eyes when they had chopped that tramp off with hatchets at the mine that time. That's how cold it was. The rain had frozen him there just like a block of ice.

He stretched his hands out in front of him and slid towards the sparks of the engine up there in front. He stopped when he reached the end of the car. He reached his hands back to his legs and started rubbing them. There was no feeling in them and no feeling in his hands either, but he knew that he was rubbing them. He'd have to jump the gap to the next car. A few jumps like that and he could leap down into the tender and crawl around to the cab. He kept rubbing his legs till they were tingling a little. He got up on his hands and knees and tried to stand up. He started to tumble over the side of the car and he sat down. The roadbed was rough here and the cars were lurching from side to side. He rubbed his legs till the car stopped wobbling so much. He raised up on his hands and knees again and pulled his feet flat on the top. Up in front the sparks of the engine flattened out instead of shooting up in the air and the smoke swished back in clouds. He raised tremblingly to his feet. The top of a mountain was shooting fifty miles an hour straight at his head. He fell flat on his belly and the pounding of his heart choked him. He held his breath as long as he could in the tunnel and then let it out and held it. The tunnel was choking with the black smoke and his ears hurt from the noise reverberating from the walls. By the time they roared out into the air he had forgotten that he was cold. The train jerked and buckled as it slowed down. Up in front he could see the glaring light of another engine and he knew they were pulling into a siding. When they came to a stop he crawled down to the ground as fast as his frozen legs would let him. He stumbled over to the door of the boxcar and tried to reach up and rip the seal off but he was too short to reach it. He lugged rocks from the side of the bank and piled them in front of the door. He reached the seal from the rocks but he couldn't pull it off. He got out his barlow and cut the wire. At first the door stuck. He kept pushing as hard as he could and in a little while it budged and then slid open. He pulled himself up into the car and then slid the door shut before anybody saw him.

He struck a match. The car was half full of baled straw and smelled good. He stretched out on top of a bale and was sound asleep before he knew it. When he awoke the train was no longer moving. He felt warm and dry in the car but when he slid open the door the wind outside slashed him in the face and made him shiver. The car was standing alone on a siding.

Over to the right of the tracks was a large brick factory. He could see the flare of furnaces inside and hear the rattle of pipes. Even in the doorway of the boxcar he could feel the warm heat waves coming from the furnaces. He jumped to the ground and walked over across the tracks. The yard in front of the factory was strewn with dots and pieces of glass and in the center of it was a high yellow water tank standing on four iron legs. It was warm under there and he was shielded from the wind that was roaring up the tracks.

The voices of the night shift woke him up as they came out to eat their lunch under the tank. He sat up and rubbed his eyes and when he remembered where he was, he was scared they would run him away but nobody paid any attention to him. The workers, both men and women, sat around on the ground alone and in groups and Michael noticed that their dresses and shirts were streaked white from the salt of the dried sweat. His eyes darted from one lunch box to another and the sight of the thick sandwiches they were munching made him think of the twitching frog legs that he had eaten. He had had nothing to eat since Mrs. Brodeski had cooked up the last of the potato peelings. That was two days ago now. His eyes unconsciously followed each movement of their hands as they lifted the sandwiches from the lunch boxes to their mouths.

"There's a kid ain't never seen a piece of bread or he's forgot what a piece looks like." The peroxide blonde with the blue apron around her waist was looking at Michael and talking to everyone. All of them squatting on that side of the tank looked over at him, and he dropped his eyes down to the ground.

"Hungry, kid?" the fat man next to the blonde asked.

Michael shook his head yes without speaking.

The fat one reached down in his lunch box and handed him a sandwich. The blonde handed him a banana wrapped up in a pink doily.

"That ain't my pink underwear," she said, "that's a doily."

All the girls giggled and the men laughed explosively. Everyone began digging down in their lunch boxes till he had a pile of fruit and sandwiches stacked up in front of him.

"You down all that, kid," the blonde said, "and you will take the Judson Art Glass Company record away from Hypo McGinnis here." She reached over and slapped Hypo's pot gut resoundingly and he smirked and slapped her across the hips.

"When we goin' to get married Gertie?" he said.

"Say, when I sleep with that lard barrel you got tied to you, you'll know it." Gertie stuck her snubbed nose up in the air.

Hypo crossed his yellow underwear covered belly. Michael could see the bristling black hairs that penetrated through to the outside. Hypo took hold of one with his fingers and pulled it out with a yank, making a terrible face and bellowing as he did it.

"It takes a man to carry that around," he grinned.

Michael was stuffing the food into his mouth as fast as he could cram it in. He didn't want to eat so fast but he was afraid they would think he wasn't hungry if he didn't. Every once in a while he would dart furtive glances at Gertie. Her hair shone golden in the flickering light of the furnaces. In the daylight it was streaked at the roots and shone brown. She did not pay much attention to it because she figured that if nothing turned up by July she would go ahead and marry Hypo McGinnis.

When the whistle blew from the inside of the factory, they all pulled themselves to their feet and went back in. Gertie slapped Hypo over the head with a paper sack she had blown up and ran as fast as she could towards the box department in the rear of the building with Hypo wobbling after her as fast as he could go. Michael relaxed against the tank and began to eat more slowly. A man with a pencil and a piece of paper in his hand came out of the factory door and walked over to where he was under the tank.

"You wanta work, kid?" he said.

"Sure," Michael said. He raised up to his feet. His leg hurt him bad but he tried not to wince.

"All right. Tell Madden in shop eight to show you how to carry in. What's your name?"

"Michael Kohler."

"How old are you?"

"Twelve."

"You're fourteen from now on. Don't forget it if anybody asks you."

SHORT FICTION

THREE CAMEOS

WHEN the little blonde with the pipestem legs and the little bronze crucifix next to her heart on a red string keeled over in front of the 5 & 10, and the reporter wrote the article about how she was starving to death on her feet because she was too proud to beg, there was an awful rumpus raised. They kept the hospital phone busy offering her homes in decent respectable families, but no money, though, because it is not right to give money, for don't all the blind beggars on the street skulk into a Rolls or a Pierce in the evenings and go home to their apartments and Christ only knows how many apartments they own besides the one they live in. So they didn't offer any money but someone must have took her in for she didn't keel over in front of any more reporters, and I never heard any more about her so I guess someone must have taken her in.

But when this other one keeled over later, there wasn't any reporter there, so they took her to the can and locked her up and charged her with vagrancy. It could easily be seen that she read the papers and was just taking advantage of a good thing. That's what the cops thought, and that's what any right thinking person would think, for you know, people just don't go around on the streets keeling over from starvation. They gave her a meal of the jail fare of beans, grits and molasses, and when they came in to take her to court the next morning, she was sprawled out on the floor, dead, and the fellow who was up for running through a red light got his case tried first, and he sure was glad to get his case tried first for everyone knew that this old judge used to get in a terrible humor after he had been trying cases for two hours, and was as apt as not to give this guy life for running through a red light after he'd been trying cases for two hours.

RUTHIE had dark hair and Jim had dark hair which was kind of funny for you'd expect unlike to attract each other, but there's no getting around the fact that they were crazy about each other, and when you stay crazy about a man when he hasn't had a steady job in three years, you sure must be crazy about him. The baby sort of took after Jim, had his eyes, blue eyes grey eyes, but Ruthie hadn't minded that for the baby was a boy, and you kind of expect a boy to take after his father. They got a couple of dollars from the County Relief every week, and paid a dollar a week to live in the stuffy attic room with no light and all the light they ever had was when they had enough over to blow on a candle sometimes. They got along pretty good on carrots and beets and lettuce that you could pick up for a penny a bunch in the market and sometimes Jim got a job mowing a lawn, and then they'd blow themselves to a piece of meat, but that was only sometimes and not very often. Whenever Jim saw an ad in the paper he answered it, and he'd been doing that for three years, but he'd never got run over and killed by a truck before like he did this time. When this reporter got hold of this, he wrote an awfully sweet story of how Jim had been out of work for three years and can you believe it, poor Jim was killed while he was starting to work for the first time after he'd been out of work for three years. Everyone said it sure was tough to get knocked off just when you were getting off the County Relief rolls, and they said it sure was a tough break for poor Ruthie and the baby but nobody brought anything to eat for you just don't feel like eating when you are facing tragedy like that and anyway a lot of people are awfully proud and you can't tell if they're going to be touchy or not when you bring them something to eat and the only safe way is not to take a chance.

SHE rented No. 6 on the third floor, back, and she hardly spoke to anyone all the time she was there. She used to go out job hunting in the mornings and stay until almost night, and you could tell by the fagged-out look on her mannish face when she came back that she never had any luck. But then how could she with that outlandish costume she wore, blue serge business suit, a man's blue dress shirt, tie and a pair of brown, low-cut shoes. You've got to wear something soft and womanish if you want to get a job clerking in a store. They like them soft and womanish. She never seemed to eat, and Christ knows what she ate for no one had ever thought to ask if she was hungry. She didn't own anything, excepting of course that frame made out of the strips of copper and bronze, and it was pretty and so was the girl's picture in it for that matter. Mrs. Pink and the hired girl used to go in her room when she was job hunting and look at the picture, and Mrs. Pink used to shake her head for she had read a book once and those mannish clothes and that mannish walk meant something and you can bet your life Mrs. Pink knew what it meant, too.

After they drug her out of the lake and took her to the morgue, it wasn't ten minutes till the picture was gone, and Mrs. Pink didn't waste any time in looking in the hired girl's room and sure enough there it was under the mattress. They had a terrible fight for Mrs. Pink wanted that frame herself and it was her house and you'd think that she had more claim to it than the hired girl, anyway. They were both scratched up pretty bad when the cops got there and they dragged both of them off in the Black Maria. They got five and costs and I don't know who got the frame, but anyway Mrs. Pink or the hired girl didn't get it. It was an awfully pretty frame made out of strips of copper and bronze.

Originally published in the *Pacific Weekly*, May 31, June 7, and August 26, 1935.

HUNGRY MEN

IT WAS 1930. The UP, SP, Sante Fe, B&O, and a hundred other lines stretched their tracks across the country that stank with the stench of overflowing silos and warehouses and granaries rotting with food and with feed that no one had the money to buy. Long rows of box cars sweated in the railroad yards and rotted on the rusty tracks and the big black mallays that puffed thru the night with their strings of cars, half loaded, held more men in the reefers and on the tops and under the rods than there were pounds of freight in the cars.

Passenger trains screamed and bellowed in mock impatience through the night, and on the blinds and clutching to the steps under the doors and on the tops were more gaunt faced men who held in the emptiness of their guts with their hands than rode the cushions. It was 1930 and the depression was on. Rust grew on the locks of the factories and the machines grew grimy with the heavy oil that no one wiped off from their backs anymore, and in the nights the rats came and sniffed the stillness of these machines that hummed so and shook so before 1930. Men came to the factory doors and looked at the rust that grew more daily on the locks of the doors and looked angry for they wanted to go and take their coats off and stand by their machines and run them and watch the yards of cloth that spewed out from their mouths and see the long orangy strips of metal that poured out from the guts of others. Sometimes, they that were locked out of their factories and chained away from their machines by the barred doors, gathered in front of the doors and talked and swore but not at the machines that they couldn't see because of the barred doors and the barred windows but at the men who owned the factories who wouldn't open up the doors and let the air in through the windows.

Men lived in attics and barns and cellars and tents and on the ground. And carpenters and bricklayers there were in 1930 who did not even have a tent and who squatted and snored of nights beside acres of lumber in the mill yards and the lumber became warped and crinkled in the sun.

It is 1930 and Los Angeles.

We stand in front of this mission a long time and after a while the line starts moving. We shuffle through the door and sit down at the tables. Two hundred of us sit down at the tables and in front of each of us is a bowl of lima beans that smell like scorched hair and a stale hunk of bread. We go after the bread and the beans. This hunchback across the table from me fishes this piece of meat out of his beans with his spoon. It is two inches long and has black fuzz all over it. It is not often you get a piece of meat two inches long in the missions, black fuzz or not. It is the leg of an animal and the foot is still on it with the spreaded toes.

"Why in hell don't they skin the seasonin'?" this stiff says.

"Rabbit?" I says. "I see a black rabbit once. Squirrel, maybe."

This hunchback does not like a piece of meat with black fuzz and toes on it in his lima beans.

"Rabbit or squirrel, they oughta cut the feet off the seasonin'," he says.

We gulp down our beans.

Pretty soon this stiff next to the hunchback grabs his mouth with both hands and hits down the aisle for the door. This hunchback looks down into the bottom of this stiff's bowl. He takes his spoon and digs down into the bottom of the bowl. He holds the spoon over his head.

"Not rabbit and not squirrel, by God, they're seasonin' the

beans with," he screams, "but rats. Look at the head of this goddam rat and layin' here by my plate is a leg and where in the hell is the other three legs is what I want to know? Who eat the other three legs?"

The rat head wobbles on the spoon. The lips snarl back from the sharp white teeth. There are no whiskers on it. I notice that the whiskers have all been scorched away.

"Hey, looky what they done to Oscar!" yells this stiff next to me. "Looky, they have deecapitchulated Oscar!"

Some of us make the curb outside and some of us make a privy out of the floor. Fruitity-Toot, the hatchet faced pansy with the lisp, turns green under the rouge on his cheeks and squeals to the floor in a dead faint. After a while we pour water on Fruitity-Toot and go back to our beans and eat them and go up and beg for seconds on the scorched lima beans.

We go outside where the mission stiffs can't hear us and where the head guys can't hear us and we ask ourselves what the goddam hell they are seasonin' the beans with rats for and ask ourselves if they think we fell for that cock and bull yarn about that rat gettin' in them beans by accident, they are crazy as hell.

No one tipped any tables over.

No one threw a bowl of lima beans at the life sized picture of the "Lost Sheep" that hung on the wall.

The *Times* got no "Cops Bang Red Skulls" headline.

We are the *lumpenproletariat* . . . of whom you can expect nothing.

It was 1931 and when you walked down the streets you would occasionally hear a man with the ass out of his pants humming "How Can We Work When There's No Work To Do?"

We griped on the curb and asked ourselves what are the bastards seasonin' the beans with rats for?

President Hoover screeched out from the headlines and screeched out from the magazines that hell there wasn't any depression and the neighbors would come through in a pinch for sure. The Red Cross squatted on their emergency rations and waited anxiously for an act of God that they might bustle and rustle to the rescue. Miners with their scrawny, hungry white-faced women and croupy pellagra-ridden brats with the coal dust from the mines of West Virginia and Illinois and Pennsylvania in the creases of their aching bellies combed the rusty sulphur water for rusty frogs and crawfish and scoured the bare sassafras hills for dandelion greens that they boiled in water without seasoning. After the rusty frogs and the crawfish and the dandelions were all gone the miners from West Virginia and Illinois and Pennsylvania thought that if they could come to the Capitol and show the Big Sticks and the High Muckity-mucks what they looked like they would maybe do something about their empty guts and keep the company elected and owned and paid sheriffs from kicking their ragged blankets and beds out into the mud that was the yellow sulphur clay when the rains came. And so they came and they couldn't talk very well to the Great so they made posters and the ones who could write printed on the posters what their grievances were and what they needed. Some of them demanded relief for they were starving in their rags and some prayed for it. The ones who demanded were singled out by the sheriffs for future action for it was plain that they were Reds. When they reached the White House the cops took their posters away from them and said they could march by the White House but to stay off the grounds. They sent a committee of three to see the President. The secretary led them back out the door and off the varnished floors and explained that the President would sure do something about the condition of the miners from West Virginia and Illinois and Pennsylvania.

The cops escorted them to the edge of town and when they got back to their shacks days after some of them found that their ragged blankets and beds were piled high by the sulphur creek when they got back and the doors to their shacks were barred and there were white notices on the doors that they couldn't read. Some of them left their beds there for they had no way of carrying them and started tramping down the road with their women and their kids and their scrawny shanked dogs fatter than their masters. Most of them had no dogs for the dogs had long ago left by instinct this place where there were no bones for the kids to suck on let alone bones for the dogs. And there was rumor that some of the miners had eaten their dogs and then went down in front of the company store and asked had any one seen hide or hair of their dog?

It was 1931. *Night and we are twenty men that moan and hock and spit and groan on the splintery floor of this box car and listen to the sing of the wheels on the rails and the roar of the wind underneath us. We are mechanics and school teachers and bricklayers and lawyers and street sweepers from Iowa and Texas, Rhode Island and Utah and Maine. A black boy in the corner sings bass and low*

"Ahm weary totin' sech a load,
Tredgin' down that lonesome road."
We raise up on our elbows and sing with him,
"True love, true love, what have I done,
That you should treat me so."

This white faced kid in the green sweater holds his belly with both hands and moans. His skinny legs are cramped up in a knot to his chest and the sweat drips down his face and off his chin and sprinkles on the floor. We stick our heads out the box car door and wait for a flash of the white mile posts that fly past us.

"Fifty more miles," *we tell this kid.*
"Forty-nine more miles."
"Only forty-eight more miles now," *we tell this kid.*

After a while he passes out and we don't tell him how many more miles anymore. Pretty soon we hear this stiff walking over the tops. We lean far out the door and nail his legs as he dangles down from the tops. We pull him into the car and he takes this ice that he has stole from the reefers out of his shirt. We pull this sick kid's legs down from his chest and pack his belly with ice and watch the mile posts.

He stops sweating after a while and we know we got that ice too late and we know the appendix is busted.

This darky from South Carolina hums Lonesome Road Blues and the stiff next to me mutters he wishes to Jesus Christ he could get his fingers on a gat.

We do not expect the revolution from the Proletariat.

It was 1932.

Wise men scratched their heads and said the depression was the result of speculation and boom and what the country needed was a planned economy. Hungry-faced men with flashing black eyes and white teeth that snarled in the sun got up on soap boxes in the parks and on the street corners and spoke in whispers in shrieks in supplication and told their grimacing hungry gutted listeners that Morgan and Rockefeller and Ford and Mellon and the Dupont de Nemours and the others owned 80 per cent of the country and the cops would come about that time and take their blackjacks and bang them against the heads of the men on the soap boxes until they crumpled in a heap so that the cops could more easily drag them to the Black Maria that waited on them at the curb. And the hungry gutted listeners that ate a bowl of mush for breakfast and would borrow a little coffee for lunch smirked and giggled nervously as they watched the cops give it to the Reds and then crept off down an alley to hunt in the rear of the restaurants for a snipe.

It was 1932 and St. Louis and me and the guy from Harvard and the guy from Columbia hopped off of this freight and started dinging the backdoors for a handout. It was night and no one gave us anything to eat and we went to the restaurants and they wouldn't give us anything to eat either. After a while me and this guy from Harvard and this guy from Columbia started foraging in the garbage cans in the

*rear of the restaurants for pieces of bread and half eaten
grapefruit and I found a piece of bread already spread with
butter for I was better at this than these guys for they had
never done that at Harvard and Columbia. After a while the
manager of a restaurant called a cop and he came back there
in the alley and pinched us and said we were nothing but
goddam swine and he oughta shoot a bunch of slop swillers
like us.*

*They charged us with vagrancy but you don't want to ex-
pect too much help in the revolution from the* lumpenproletariat.

It was 1933.

Men stretched in the long undulating soup lines down the
blocks of the city streets in the rain, and as they shifted from
one blistered foot to the other the line rose and fell and
breathed like a gigantic tapeworm that passed through and
wallowed for a little while in the swill that the missions were
passing out for the glory of Jesus Christ. Their sunken eyes
glared venomously at the "Jesus Saves" sign that mocked
their misery in neon lights that flashed on and off as the dark
came. They shuffled nearer and nearer to the barrels of slop
that waited steaming and vomity in the oveny kitchens of the
missions. Once in they caught the stale bread and the slopped
over pie pan with the stenchy stew that the missions gave for
the glory of Jesus Christ. They listened vacant faced to the
sermon that droned incessantly from the platform in front of
the tables and heard no word of it. They came outside again
after a little while and tightened their belts over their aching
guts and searched the gutters among the horse dung and the
spit for a cigarette butt. They sat in the doorways and on the
curbs in the evenings debating in fanatic fervor with themselves whether to listen long hours to the sermon in the missions for a flop or to take a chance on the cold splintery floors
of the box cars in the railroad yards. Some of them, dreamers,
sat on the curb and on the park benches and dreamed and saw

themselves standing at their machines in their factories and saw themselves lined up at the office window on pay day for the yellow pay envelope filled with green money. Some of them way-laid passersby on the street, in their over-wrought minds, and banged them on the heads with clubs and pulled them over in the shadows. And when they searched them, their pockets were filled with green bills that would keep them the rest of their lives in plenty. Some of them saw the armored cars with their treasure from the banks drop one of those white sacks filled to bulging with green money and no one saw them drop it but them and they picked it up and hid it under their coats and went down to the railroad station and bought a ticket a long ways away from there and woke up from their riches with the slap of a policeman's billy against their feet. They get up from there and sulk down the street without looking back and the mission doors will be locked by this time.

It is 1934.

Beside the tracks of the UP, SP, Santa Fe, and B&O are towns built by the unemployed of tin cans from the garbage dumps and old pieces of sheet metal, and scraps of boxes. There are smokestacks in the houses and in the evenings you can see the flickering fires from their furnaces as they cook up the green baloney butts and the split peas and beans that they bum from the warehouses and the soggy potatoes that they pick up alongside the tracks. And every town has one of these sores on its outskirts and some have two or three and men hop off of incoming freights cold and hungry and desperate and they cook up a cup of coffee from the old grounds that they find stuck hard and dry to the edges of the old coffee pots that sit by the fire places. They hulk around these fires in the night like hollow eyed ghosts in the night and the people in the town do not know they are there except sometimes comes a knock on the door and a whining voice asks can it mow the lawn for a piece of bread spread with butter. But sometimes too many whining voices ask can they mow the lawn for some bread spread with butter and then the cops of the town and the firemen go down to these jungles by the tracks with their 45's and their axes and shoot and cut holes in the skillets the coffee cans the boiling up cans and set fire to the shacks and the townspeople come for miles around for they think the planing mill is on fire. But it is only a bunch of cops making fires and a bunch of firemen playing firemen.

No one fights the cops and the firemen for they have gats and axes and the law and they are afraid to fight them. They pack up their bindles and trudge down the tracks and when they get out of sight they lay in the shadows and wait for a train out of there and cuss the cops and firemen for lousy sons of bitches and hope for the time when they can catch one of them in a dark box car alone and see themselves pulling his guts out with their bare hands.

Armies of men in 1934 and millions of men moving West and East and North and South. Two hundred on a train coming this way and two hundred on a train going that way and what the hell difference does it make which way you go? There is no work anywhere and no food anywhere if you have no money but you can smell the rotten smell of rotting food in the silos in the warehouses in the granaries.

It is 1934 and Los Angeles, California.

We are a hundred stiffs that sprawl in this flophouse. The Yellow Car strike is on. Day before the conductors and motormen walk out the company hangs a notice up on the board.

Any employee not appearing at his post of duty tomorrow will have his job filled with a scab. It will be taken for granted that that employee has resigned and he will not be rehired by this company.

They said it nicer but it was a lock-out. The Yellow cars ran with scabs. Cops rode the Yellow cars. Cops rode the Yellow cars to protect the scabs. It's hard to get union recognition

when the cops ride the cars and protect the scabs and protect
the dividends of the Yellow car company. Strikers can't live
forever on solidarity. They had to stop the Yellow cars. They
put pegs under their wheels when they stopped. They told the
passengers and the scabs to get off and they turned the cars
over on their bellies. They rocked the cars and after a while
they turned over on their bellies. A street car is a futile and
desolate looking machine with its wheels kicking up in the
air like that.

We are a hundred stiffs in this flophouse. Twenty-five
strikers put a peg under a car in front of this flophouse. They
rock and groan and sweat but they can't turn it over. We line
the curb and watch them shove. We hear the sirens of the cops
that are coming with their gats and their saps and their tear
gas bombs.

This bug guy on the curb with the scar slashed across his
face rolls up his sleeves and grins.

"I used to be a Wobbly," he says. "I'm pretty strong yet. Any
you other stiffs used to be Wobblies?"

He strides across the street. The old ones follow him and we
young ones follow the old ones. We lean on that car and you
can hear the glass smashing for a mile. A car looks funny with
its wheels kicking in the air like that and we walk back to the
curb just as the squad cars skid to a stop. The cops chase the
strikers with clubs but they don't pay attention to us stiffs on
the curb who are goddam no-good *lumpenproletariat.*

There were 22,000,000 people on relief in 1935 and the National Debt was 34,000,000,000 dollars and not even the wise
men knew how much money that was and threw up their
hands and asked where is any more money going to come
from and Bugs Baer said that there was plenty more where
that went to but wise men do not listen to such talk as that.
People were going crazy every day and the booby-hatches were
chocked with people that had gone crazy and you could see
them staring at you through the iron bars and they'd take

these beans, red beans, one at a time and string them on a lavender wire and hide them under the rug, and when they'd come back a long time after they were not there for someone had eaten them while they were away and they cried because someone had eaten them. And the man with the patent leather shoes and the gold fob said it wouldn't do a damn bit of good to cry because there wasn't another bean in the house and hardly a bean in the world for that matter, and it wouldn't do a damn bit of good to cry. And then they'd go to the closet and hunt and there were angels there. Seven angels not counting the one that spilled black shoe polish all over her red carpet slippers and black cats omenin' around the house and the moan of babies left to die in the rocks of the mountains.

Strikes in Detroit and Milwaukee and Seattle, and Portland, and Frisco and L.A. and Walla Walla and Bad Axe, Michigan. The masses feeling their muscles and the cops would come and the militia would come and some of the strikers they'd beat and some of them they'd kill. And hungry faced men with flashing black eyes and teeth that snarled in the sun got up on soap boxes in the parks and on the street corners and spoke in whispers in shrieks in supplication and told the hungry workers they used to sweat with in the factories in the fields in the offices that Morgan and Rockefeller and Ford and Mellon and the Dupont de Nemours gouged and fatted on 80 per cent of the country and the cops would come and bang their heads with blackjacks till they crumpled in a heap so that they could more easily drag them to the Black Maria. And when they were gone another got on the box and the cops slashed at him with their blackjacks and shot at him with their 45's and their blackjacks made no marks and their 45's no bloody hole and the cops were afraid for they never saw a one like this and they were afraid. The black eyes flashed and the white teeth flashed in the sun and starving men with their rags white from the salt of their own sweat listened in Frisco and L.A. and Detroit and Chi and New York and Mis-

sissippi as they stood before the barred windows and the
barred doors of their own factories:
"There is—a way out!
Our riveting guns built the skyscrapers and bridges,
Our shovels dug the mines and highways, laid the rails,
Our muscles and blood went into the ships,
Went into the fields and all that's here—
We'll take it now—STAND ASIDE!"

Originally published in three parts in the *Pacific Weekly*, July 13, September
28, and October 26, 1936.

THE CONSEQUENCES
TAKEN

SHE was having a baby. You called the doctor, DElmar-395. He said,

—Is the money waiting—you said,

—For Christ's sake, doc, my wife is dying—he said

—Will the money be there—you said,

—In God's name, doc, WE ARE EXPECTING THE BABY MOMENTARILY—the slush-iced voice wheezed—the money—the receiver clicked. Mrs. Pink, stinking drunk at your elbow, staggered up the stairs.

—They won't ever come lessen you got the money. I guess I better go up and ketch the brat afore it falls out on the floor—you thought,

—But one fatality in 7,000,000 miles which is safer than Ford, which is safer than Sikorsky, which is even safer than most things you can mention—you thought,

—Shall it be said that there are two sides to the C&O tracks, or shall we measure to a gnat's eye equidistance between the rails and let the abortion take place, but always acting cautiously in removing cinders and creosoted splinters from the ties that might cause infection—

When there were no more towels to catch the blood, you called EMergency-777. You forgot all the hours that you waited and they didn't come. The hemorrhage stopped itself. You slid the rotogravure on top the soddened mattress and Barbara-Hutton-Mdvani-Ish-Gebibble was washed, all unbeknownst, in the precious blood of Jesus. She slept. When you

224

awoke in the night and placed your palm over her forehead and there was no sweat there but it was dry, without placing your ear to her breast for her heart beats, YOU KNEW SHE WAS DEAD. You lay there and watched the curtain blow to and fro gently from the breeze off Ivy street and thought,

—The soul goes trippingly through hemorrhage clots, through curtains, through sash, and off up Ivy street—you thought,

—Cocktail glasses don't break themselves except in Tia Juana, and the Foreign Club is burned and Kay and Bill are fused and locked in arm and arm in bulbous glass—you thought,

—The majority of deaths in abortion cases are caused by infected instruments. Imminent Domain? The legal gentleman poses the question dare we cut the cord, twist the scalpel on cinders, between rails, without first consulting John W. Davis, who will consult the Van Swerigens, who will send a letter, a telegram, call us local or long distance to carry on for Humanity, or postpone the miscarriage till No. 6 gets through, or carry the patient 30 feet off the right of way, P.S.ing that in the opinion of the directors of C&O, John W. Davis assenting, that the baby should be had, the consequences taken—You carried the white porcelain bowl to the kitchen and emptied it down the sink. You watched the red maelstrom of the suck till the last gurgle and rinsed the sink from the faucet. You brushed the cockroach from the drain board and mechanically sprinkled from the box of Twenty Mule Team borax. You spread the overcoat over her and lifted the baby from her outstretched arm. You pulled the lid back on the trunk and laid the baby down on the clothes that were in there. You covered it cautiously so as not to awaken it with the blue dungarees and the denin shirt from the closet. Somewhere you had read, you had heard, it was bandied, that hogs have eaten babies. You knew for a fact that they fed them coal for worms. You closed the door softly behind you and creaked down the stairs to the street. You walked and you were distinctly unaware of all the hours that you walked. You passed Pete's and you were cold by that time and you went in there. You glazed over the rows of bottles in Pete's—Crab Orchard—3 Star—Seagram's—5&7—all poured from the same barrel behind the bar. Your frozen fingers trembled over the nickels in your pocket. You said,

—Shot of bar—Pete said,

—Fine evening—you answered,

—Lovely—and thought,

Oh, that lady in red,

oh, that lady in red—

The skinny drunk hunched over the marble topped table banged on the table with his fist and said,

—What thish country needsh ish a good war—

He stared belligerently at you, but you did not pay him any attention. He stuck his nose down into his beer and drooled into the glass,

—War over ol' Polish Corr-ee-dor,

Corr-ee-dor,

Corr-ee-dor—

Suddenly, trepidatiously, you recollect, that you may not forget to remember, you are the father of a son to be reared to the YMCA cut to the jaw, NO BATHING SUITS ALLOWED . . . old man . . . talk like a coupla the fellows . . . man-to-man . . . girls . . . gentlemen . . . your sister . . . terrible diseases . . . hard and soft chancres . . . last, but not least, blueballs . . . they say in the South Sea Islands THEY WHEEL THEM AROUND IN WHEELBARROWS . . . fathers have eaten sour grapes and the children's teeth are set on edge. You thought,

—Blood lost 30 feet from the right of way may ooze slowly down the grade towards the creosoted ties of the C&O, ooze into the ties, drawing termites, piss ants, black widow spiders who will eat into the ties to get at the clots, causing grave danger, grave accidents, loss of dividends, loss of confidence in the Road—you thought, mechanically but with such clarity the words pounded three-dimensioned on your brain,

—We advise . . . the baby should be had . . . the consequences taken—Pete said,

—Have one on the house—you said,

—Thanks—and thought,

—The cortege moved, a magnificently sombre procession, through the blocks of the city's streets—you said out loud,

—Would you notify the health department, the police, or the commissioner of streets and sewers—Pete said,

—They sure are. The bastards are gettin' crookeder ever' day—you distinctly said to yourself,

—IT WILL BE DAYLIGHT IN ANOTHER HOUR—

Originally published in the *Pacific Weekly,* September 7, 1936.

A GLASS WORKER DIES

JUDSON ART GLASS CO., Makers of Fine Glass . . . and he'd
pick up this pipe that lay on the rack and sprint with it to
this tank that had in it the glass. These other working stiffs
would circle the tank the same as my old man and you'd
think this was a Merry-Go-Round in a circus when you'd see
them around the tank like this. He'd stick the end of this
hollow pipe down in the hole that was in the side of the tank
and down into the orangy glass and the heat would sheet out
and scorch his face and clear back to the stooping shoulders.

Pay attention only to me.

It's my old man Michael I am telling you about. He sits
there now and looks in at the embers of the fire and thinks of
nothing but the belching factory chimneys and the pot of
glass that he will see no more for his sweat will drench their
goddam floor no more and come up in hot steam from their
floor no more. The bugs have got him at last and he sits by the
fire and hardly speaks all day. Gas on the stomach he thinks
and he will be all right in a week. Gas on the stomach, hey, old
man? And what are those pussy sores on your side and on
your belly if it is not the cancer that had worked clear through
you and clear through to the outside? Look at your legs that
are swollen up like a couple of telegraph poles. Bloated up like
a couple of telegraph poles your legs are and if you got up out
of that chair and walked, you would gurgle when you walked.
That is not you sitting in that chair, old man. You are in the
factory. You are molded up in the tumblers that people drink

highballs out of and get drunk and throw them on the floor, and I know that it is not a tumbler that is on the floor, but my old man, broken and splintered and crumbled.

He'd pull this wad of glass out of the pot and hurry over to the marble, this shiny, steel, flat marble, and he'd roll it around on the marble till it was as round and as smooth as the pipe it hung to. Then my old man would blow through this pipe that was a hollow pipe, and the glass on the end would come out like a balloon, a red balloon, a carnival balloon. But where the hell was the carnival there? The pink lemonade, the hoocha-koocha dancer, and the red lemonade?

And now it's the lake. The old man thinks the lake will help his indigestion. He thinks the lake will help the sores that cover his side and spread to his belly that I can see as I wrap the thin gauzy bandages around his side and his belly. Well, I hope he is right but I know he is dead and as good as dead. For don't I know the lake won't do him a bit of good and nothing will do him a bit of good for when he laid his pipe down on the rack and keeled over on the floor that was wet with the sweat of a million bottles, wasn't he dead then? He is only a shell that sits by the fire and now he wants to go to the lake and he is like a peevish child that wants to go to the lake. A broken tumbler thrown on the floor by a drunk who asks for another and says he will pay for the tumbler and what's a tumbler that's broke when you're feeling good? Hock the family furniture and send the old tumbler to the lake. Three-and-a-half per cent a month and aint that forty-two per cent a year and pay it and like it. On to your sister, old man, who lives on the lake in Lorain and for Christ's sake stop grinning like that with the skin of your lips stretched across your teeth like that.

And my old man would hand this pipe up to the blower who stood on the dummy, this boxy platform with a mold that they called a dummy, and that blower had the bugs and

*he knew he had the bugs. He knew it. Cancer? Hell, not can-
cer. He blew all the cancer out into the pipes and my old man
caught the cancer. It was T.B. for the blower and at that he
was better off than my old man for he knew he had the bugs
and he knew he wouldn't have to blow his guts out on top of
that dummy forever. But my old man didn't know he had the
cancer, though, and wasn't that a good joke on my old man
for there he was a'slavin' his ass for them shoes for the three
four five beautiful smart kids and he couldn't ever get them
shoes and wasn't that a good joke on my old man? And
wasn't that a good joke on the Metropolitan for there was a
thousand with the Metropolitan and the old Metropolitan
would screech out from the magazines and screech out from
the newspapers for my old man to get his ass away from there
to the milk and to the sunshine and to the milk and wasn't
that a good joke on the Metropolitan?*

And we met him at the station when he came back and
what's the black hearse backed up against the curb for and
can't you guess? Not on the cushions tonight and not on the
tops and not under the rods. He's riding the express car
tonight in a pine box for what's the use to buy a coffin away
up there in Lorain, Ohio, for don't you pay by the pound, or do
you pay by the pound?

Walk along the street of sorrows oh,
Walk along the street of dreams.

Sit up in the driver's seat, old lady, and let's take the old
tumbler home from the lake for he's

The old man of the mountain.
The old man of the mountain.

Put him there in the parlour and lay him on the couch for
that's what the silk covering on the couch is for, so the old
man can lay on silk. Wake up, old man, wake up! You would
get a kick out of this, laying on silk! Eat your fried spuds in
the kitchen and can't make it go down very well for it sticks
in your throat with the old man laying in there. Have a spud,

old man. You oughta have the habit. You oughta miss your spuds. And who is screeching in there and what are you yelping for, Billie? Black cat on the old man's chest and he won't get off! A sign that is and my old lady thinks that is a goddam bad sign and aint we got troubles enough in this house without black cats omen' on my old man's chest and him as dead as four o'clock?

On to the church and hello old horse-face-man-close-to God. Like hell you got my old man on the mind. You got a slew of juicy, lump-bringing words on the mind. Working stiffs in stiff starchy collars and shiny blue serge suits sit and squirm in their seats and working stiffs' wives sit beside them and squirm with them. And just listen to that goddam kid in the back a'squawkin' his head off and get that kid out of there for he's ruinin' the funeral. It's not often you have a good funeral. And never, never squawk loud at a funeral but so soft and low and get the vulgar kid out of here.

ROCK OF AGES

That's the one and sing'er out loud for that's the one he wanted. My old man always said he had gas on the stomach but he was no fool, my old man wasn't. He told us what he wanted and first the

ROCK OF AGES

and then

THE OLD RUGGED CROSS

and after that just start shoveling the mud in. But don't you forget the cross and put it in the outside pocket of the coat next to his heart. He asked for it so put it here just to humor the old man, but, hell, and it aint no secret among the working stiffs that my old man's heart is over there in the cracks of the concrete floor of the glass factory where he sweated his life away and sweated his heart away. But what's the use to mention that here for aint old horse-face gettin' ready to turn on the water works?

> Look up, look up
> And seek your Maker
> Before you travel on,
> A hey nonny-nonny
> And a hot cha-cha.

And the send-off! Great Christ, was there ever such a send-off as my old man is getting? Bellowing, rolling, tumbling clouds, dark and black and mad, and I do not blame you for getting sore up there for this show they are throwing for my old man. Pall-bearers and grave-diggers chanting and weeping and singing and who gives a good goddam about my old man? Throw my old man in the mud and cover him up with the mud. And the rain pours down in watery sheets and plasters the blue silk dresses of the working stiffs' wives to their scrawny necks and plasters to their breasts till you can see the nipples of their breasts. The thunder rolling and you can bet, by God, somebody up there is goddam mad up there for all this foolishness for a working stiff that blew his heart out throwing the end of a hollow pipe.

Stawmy weathah and, oh, ahm suh loneleh.

Big black straps and I wanta creamy casket when I die. Fifteen men on a dead man's chest. Lower the mainsails. Lower the jibs.

And the sands on the desert grow cold.

Splash she goes. Plump in the amber water in the bottom of the hole. Pull out the straps for you gotta save the straps for more working stiffs. Quintuplets coming up and twins and triplets.

Stawmy weathah and, oh, ahm suh loneleh.

232

Here's mud in your eye, old man, and mud in your face, and mud in the sores on the old man's belly. Mumble the prayer and jibber the chant and moan the song and throw in the mud. Clunk the first shovelful and clunk the second and third. Five beautiful smart kids stand around the hole and watch the water eddy in the bottom of the hole. Clunk the fourth shovelful and I will not wait till they cover you clear up, old man, for I am getting goddam soaked and the old lady is getting goddam soaked, too.

Originally published in the *Pacific Weekly*, November 16, 1936.

BOOK REVIEWS

A VERY SAD BLURB

HUNGRY MEN, by Edward Anderson. Doubleday, Doran and Company, 1935.

You will see no Jesus Christ looks in the eyes of Edward Anderson's *Hungry Men*, no working stiffs dying of malnutrition on lice-infested blankets of three-decker bunks in the missions, no soup-lines that stretch for blocks in the city streets and never start moving. In a word, you find no Hungry Men. When one of Mr. Anderson's puppets gets a gnawing in his guts, he takes him up to a backdoor or a restaurant and feeds him. When Mr. Anderson's hero, one Acel Stecker, is mooning on the waterfront over a respectable two-bit whore he has fallen in love with, you will never guess what happens so I might as well tell you. The Communist in the book hands him fifty bucks and says here, take this dough for I will not be needing it, and make a home for the gal. In "this land of plenty where nobody starves," Mr. Anderson would get thrown off a freight train if he pulled some of these yarns on the two or three hundred stiffs with no more notches in their belts.

The blurb on *Hungry Men* is very sad, and at first you will be very sad, too, when you read it. But after a while you will not be very sad for at the end Edward says, "But the American isn't going to turn Socialist or Communist, at least not in this generation. I wanted to write something to explain it. America is rich. There is plenty and nobody is actually going to die of hunger. In *Hungry Men* I have tried to show what I mean." It is to be hoped that with the publishing of *Hungry Men*

Edward is safe back at the family hearthstone. He should not be traipsing around the country. He might get run over by a train. Only once in the book do you think he is maybe too smart to go to sleep on the track. That is when his hero, Acel, "starts wanting to know why this man has a chauffeured Packard, and he can't get his three-dollar shoes half-soled." But you will see in the last chapter that Edward is only joshing when he has Acel say this. For Acel, through rugged individualism, makes himself the head of a three-piece band. They are sauntering down the street ready to toot their horns for an honest penny when they are invited to play the "Internationale." Horror of horrors! Acel bloodies the nose of the one-eyed drunk who suggested it, lands in court, and instead of being tossed into the hoosegow, is complimented by the judge for refusing to hold any truck "with this hymn or song or whatever it is of a corrupt foreign government." Acel's little band renames itself the "Three Americans" on the spot, gets its picture in the paper, and a job to play at a forthcoming American Legion ball. Acel always knew "there was a survival of the fittest law. The strong are always going to have more than the weak. I'm sittin' in this dump here and the reason for it is because I'm not strong enough to be sittin' in Childs. However, I'll be eatin' in Childs before it ends."

We are not told how long the author of *Hungry Men* was on the fritz, but we are told he was on it long enough to make his book a human and authentic document. We are told the book contains no propaganda, and it is true that *Hungry Men* could run serially next to the "Thank God For Our Supreme Court" editorial in the San Francisco *Examiner*.

The book is without objective, rambling, the characters wooden and unnatural. It is the story of Acel Stecker, an unemployed musician, who finds himself one night in a mission, one night flopping on the benches in a seamen's hall. He gets a job pearl diving on an excursion boat, quits, meets a

238

girl, sleeps with her a while and leaves. He meets a Communist. The Communist is appropriately enough disposed of by being shot by the cops while trying to get better conditions at the Seamen's Hall.

He meets two other musicians, brothers, and they sprawl long hours on the grass in the parks and waste long paragraphs accusing each other of having "female trouble." They finally, much to the reader's satisfaction, get some instruments and start their band. They are getting along all right and only waiting for the big break to come and it does come in the guise of the American Legion as the aftermath of the "Internationale" episode. You leave the book with the glad assurance that though the depression go on forever, Acel remains a beacon light for impoverished musicians who have a yen to eat at Childs.

If you thumbed your nose at Arthur Brisbane and sold the country short in 1929, and want to see all the wonderful things that happen to Acel Stecker "from gutter to orchestra leader," you should read *Hungry Men*. If you are one of the 22,000,000 in Mr. Hopkins' little Christian Endeavor group who have landed big time jobs for refusing to play the "hymn of a corrupt foreign government," you will enjoy the book and the coincidence. If you have read all the Horatio Alger books and would like to get the same story with a depression slant, you will not be able to put it down until the "Three Americans" get their last encore at this gala ball the American Legion is putting on.

On the other hand, it you are one of the 22,000,000 who is not musically inclined, if perhaps you are one of Hughie Johnston's "cry babies," who "can't take it" after six years on the tail-end of Mr. Babson's business Cycle "which will begin to show an upward trend in July," if after six years of soggy potatoes and red beans, every time you spit, you're spitting pink, there will be no stopping you from ramming *Hungry Men* down the privy, and no stopping you from disrupting a lot of good bands at American Legion balls in a mad yen to get your hands on Edward Anderson, screaming all the while that lusty yell with which he ends the book, "I got some ideas, by God."

Originally published in the *Pacific Weekly*, June 21, 1935. Another version was published in *New Masses*, June 25, 1935.

MODERN MAN

MODERN MAN, by Harvey Fergusson. Knopf, 1936.

In *Modern Man*, Mr. Fergusson elaborates a complete theory
of individual and group behavior, and in his own words says,
"My purpose is to discover and define the underlying assump-
tions upon which modern behavior in the Western World is
based." It is a thought-provoking book. The disintegration of
consciousness in modern man, as evidenced in wide-spread
neurosis, suicides, insanity, and general stagnation, taking
the form of fanatical clinging to the conventions and supersti-
tions of the past, is lucidly accounted for in the light of Mr.
Fergusson's research. He formulates a hypothesis as to the de-
terminants of human behavior which is both consistent with
contemporary knowledge and applicable to contemporary experience, and in doing so points out the fallaciousness of that
most universally accepted illusion, free will, or what Mr. Fergusson terms, the illusion of choice. He finds this assumption
of Western man neither usable nor workable in the modern
world because knowledge constantly contradicts it, and modern man is forever in conflict with it. Thus, man, clinging to
the outmoded taboos of the past and at the same time living
in the complexities of the present, whose situations can no
longer be harmonized with these primitive precepts of action,
finds himself with no adequate guide to conduct. This unbal-
ance of consciousness can lead nowhere but to complete disintegration.

The serenity, dignity, and calm of the Indian, mysticized by so many romantic writers, is intelligently explained by Mr. Fergusson in the light of his own theories. The constant, ever-present conflict of intrinsic and extrinsic necessity, which ever harasses the modern man, is lacking in almost its entirety in the savage. His conduct from the time of birth is proscribed by the taboo, the tribal custom, the fantasies of the medicine man. No disintegrative, conflicting impulses fight for recognition in his consciousness. If the impulse conflicts with the taboo, the impulse, no matter how powerful, is discarded. His behavior pattern saves him from the illusion of choice and, consequently, from the turmoil of frustration, guilt, and remorse, which are always involved in the illusion of choice. Civilization begins, says Mr. Fergusson, when life becomes so complex that the rigid taboos of the primitive state no longer automatically decide the action of the individual in society. It is then, when man is forced to harmonize two or more conflicting impulses without recourse to authority, that the process of disintegration begins.

This frantic fear of facing his own impulses and harmonizing them, is the factor which shackles man to convention, makes him the slave of ridiculous cults, long after the outer necessity of these authorities has ceased to exist. Man lives in terror of change, while orally screaming for it. He is afraid to face the necessity of thought, and does so only when compelled, and then only in the light of the illusion of choice. Spontaneity and balanced consciousness, the only salvation of man's consciousness, in the opinion of Mr. Fergusson, are foreign things to modern man. Instead of obeying the impulses, harmonizing the conflicting impulses, and attaining a balanced consciousness through spontaneity, modern man struggles with a disintegrating consciousness to solve the chaos wreaked by the illusion of choice.

Originally published in the *New Mexico Quarterly*, May 1936. This review is a contribution to a symposium on Fergusson's book.

TOO PRETTY

PRETTY BOY, by William Cunningham. Vanguard Press, 1936.

Cunningham's objective is worthy. He has attempted to show in this novelized life of "Pretty Boy" Floyd the conditioning of a mind to crime by the rottenness and inequality innate in the capitalist system. Had he concerned himself only with the exploits of this slain bank robber and "Public Enemy No. 1," the result would undoubtedly have been a very well written, if sentimental, thriller, and there would be no reason for taking up the space of this column with it. But in view of the fact that Cunningham has endeavored to hinge this sociological factor onto the story, we are very much concerned with it, how he does it, the convincingness of his attempt.

Convincing it is not. At no time does this explanatory factor more than hinge loosely to the body of the story. "Pretty Boy's" opining that he and his stripe are no worse than the bankers, finds hearty acquiescence in the reader, not because of the sympathy the author has engendered in us for "Pretty Boy," but because the reader has watched the plundering since long before "Pretty Boy" looted his first till.

The "Pretty Boys," the Dillingers, the "Baby Faces," in real life were tough babies, and what sentiment was dammed up in their psychopathic heads and hearts was usually drooled out to flinty Ladies in Red who eventually turned them over to the G-men. *True Detective Story* readers who like their "cop-killers" straight will not like Cunningham's wax-work "Pretty Boy," who did not kill ten cops, as the original was supposed to have done, but no more than one or two and then more or less accidentally.

Cunningham's portrayal of "Pretty Boy's" home life in the Oklahoma hills is well done and harks back to the old fire he registered in *Green Corn Rebellion*. The squalor, the poverty, the hand-to-mouth existence is a fit prelude to a career of bank robbing. When "Pretty Boy" thinks of marrying and bringing his bride home to the clapboard shack his family lives in, and sees her "pouring cold, greasy dishwater, with nasty little hunks of stuff floating in it, into a black slop bucket and then rubbing her finger around the pan to collect a snotty ring of grease and wipe it off on the edge of the slop bucket," Cunningham sees his course clearly and follows it. And when "Pretty Boy" holds up his first payroll, gets caught, does his stretch, Cunningham is convincing for he is following the tried and true course of the actual flesh-and-blood "Pretty Boy."

It is when his character becomes motivated by instincts that would do credit to a Robin Hood or a Claude Duval that the book disintegrates into fake melodrama. At one time "Pretty Boy" is robbing banks and supporting fifty poor Oklahoma hill families on the proceeds. The harried life of the hunted makes for generosity. His need for hideouts makes it necessary for him to make himself worth more alive than dead. Perhaps "Pretty Boy" was generous beyond this need, but for "Pretty Boy" to take upon his shoulders the responsibility of feeding these people by the hazardous occupation of bank robbing seems a story a little too tall.

William Cunningham has manifestly created a character in "Pretty Boy" who is a blend of the real and the unbelievable. Were it Cunningham's intention to throw together a thriller for the pulps, it would be a useless gesture to knock any chips from his shoulder. It is his right to create all the rattle-brained characters the market will bear. But it is perfectly obvious that Cunningham is sincere in his attempt to show the influ-

ence of the system on the "Public Enemy" type. He has attempted a serious work and failed, not because of a lack of
sincerity or craftsmanship, but because he created a character
in the first place who did not belong on the stage on which he
was forced to act. A "Pretty Boy," to have any validity in what
Cunningham is trying to show, must have qualities that iden-
tify him with his class. Bank robbers run to type, and to show
the evolution of this type through the example of one character, that character must approximate his type even while
retaining his own personal traits. This has been Cunningham's failure, and while it is a great failure with regard to this
one book, it in no wise lessens the belief that this author will
write better books.

Originally published in the *New Masses*, November 10, 1936.

OTHER WRITINGS

PITY THE POOR PANHANDLER;
$2 AN HOUR IS ALL HE GETS

A MAN dressed in the seedy garb of a "down and outer," possessing a sallow, hungry look, a glib tongue, and a limp, needs to have no fear of the wolf howling at the door as long as he stays in Huntington. By touching an occasional passerby for a "nickel for a cup of coffee," he can make at least five thousand dollars a year by merely sauntering up and down Fourth avenue between Ninth and Tenth streets from 6 to 11 o'clock at night.

In a city-wide investigation of begging conditions carried on by the Marshall College Department of Journalism, I was given the "coffee and soup racket" with the privilege of working the streets anywhere in Huntington. However, I found the window shoppers on Fourth avenue between Ninth and Tenth streets to be a gold mine among themselves. Working from 10 to 11:30 o'clock on Saturday night, I wheedled three dollars from soft-hearted prospects, making 15 round trips between the two streets, and averaging 20 cents a trip. At no time was I referred to the Community Chest or any of its agencies.

I have ample proof of the adage that "love makes the whole world kin." Young fellows with girls who stopped in front of store windows to look at a dress or a coat were sure fire for a dime to a quarter. On only two occasions did I fail to get a touch from this group. One man refused me outright, and the other searched his pockets carefully, but couldn't find any change. I almost offered to change a dollar for him, but caught myself just in time. Many of these gave me money for fear of letting their girls think they were tight, and others took it as an opportunity to "show off."

I found it almost impossible to get money from men who had reached the "age of discretion." Most of them were wise to the tricks of the hand-out artists. They either said "sorry I'm broke" or gave me a hard look and walked on. Elderly men and women were ready to listen to my sad tale of hard luck, but I never got more than a few pennies or a nickel from them. I did not dare accost unescorted women for fear of being taken for a "masher."

KEEPS EYE ON COPS

The chief difficulty was in eluding the police. It was necessary to change to the other side of the street on several occasions, because they are sure on the job and you have to keep a "weather eye" out for a cop every minute of the time. In my role of the sickly young man who had not eaten for three days, I was no fit subject for rough handling or a visit to the Bull Pen of the city jail.

Another difficulty was competition. A short, fat fellow whose shoes were invisible under a pair of ragged trouser legs that swished the pavement was circumnavigating the square holding aloft a lone buffalo nickel. His recitation was simple and to the point. "Mister I need a dime to get a bowl of soup and I only got a nickel. Can you help me out?" He generally got his nickel or more. I followed him around the square four times and he must have collected at least a dollar in that time. Despite the fact that I looked hungrier than he did, he pounced down on me on Fourth avenue, holding up his solitary five cent piece for my inspection. "Mister, I only got . . ."

I cut in on him with "Boy, you oughta have a whole tub of soup by this time."

He gave me a fishy look and in accents subdued but emphatic invited me to "go to hell."

A "DUPER" IS DUPED

My belief that there is "honor among thieves" got a severe shock when I was "hijacked" out of 85 cents of my ill-gotten gains by an unscrupulous fellow who smelled as though he had drunk deep of perfume or canned heat. Such fumes were never generated in a distillery. I met him on the corner of Ninth street and Third avenue. Being after local color, I started the ball rolling by remarking that the poor man had no place in the oppressive atmosphere of this capitalistic age. He replied in kind and waxed into an eloquent tirade of seditious treason against all organized societies, and remarked as an after-thought that he had not eaten but one sandwich in three days.

With three dollars clinking in my pockets I royally escorted him to a restaurant. The quarter which I intended to plunge on this unhappy man was a pigmy in comparison to his appetite. The depths of his stomach had probably never been plumbed. When the last piece of pie had been consumed the bill was 85 cents, which I paid. Espying a piece of pie which he had dropped on his coat, he pulled out his handkerchief to wipe it off and from its folds dropped a five dollar bill! It suddenly dawned on me that I had been gypped, taken advantage of, and robbed. The man did not even have the good grace to blush. He simply grinned. I immediately gave him the air. He was no fit companion for a young man who wished to keep his amateur standing.

In my opinion the only solution to the deplorable begging conditions found in the city is the Community Chest and its agencies. By referring all requests for charity to the chest, we can be sure that each case will be carefully investigated, the needy taken care of, and the fakers exposed. My investigation alone shows that the city of Huntington can save a hundred thousand dollars a year on a conservative estimate. Twenty professional beggars, working the city for a year, can make more than the Community Chest has in its entire yearly budget.

Originally published in the *Huntington Herald-Dispatch*, March 1, 1929.

MURDER IN STOCKTON

THE Stockton Warehouse and Cereal Company workers strike is over, mediated by the Federal Labor Board at San Francisco. It was a great victory for labor, shrieks out the local press, and editorializes to the effect that "life is a serious business of give and take," and "you know there is an employers' side to this thing, too." Striking warehousemen, who have been earning from $16 to $18 a week for 48 hours' work, asked for approximately $25. The mediation board just couldn't see this, but magnanimously countered with shorter hours and a common hiring hall for all warehouses so the workers wouldn't have to walk so far when they were hunting a job. It was a typical Labor Victory as doled out by the average mediation board.

The strike was called on April 12 with a few of the 350 workers peacefully picketing the plants. On the 15th the City Council, one of whose members, R. J. Wheeler, is fortuitously secretary to the Merchants, Manufacturers and Employers Association, gravely decided that "there now exists a situation engendered by certain trade disputes which threatens to interfere seriously with the orderly conduct of business of all kinds, and which threatens to cause great disorder and many breaches of the peace." With this threat of a breach of the public peace by a handful of pickets, the council mobilized the entire city police force around the threatened warehouses, and in order more fully to cope with the menace, hired fourteen special deputies, later augmented to forty, to aid the police. Probably to heighten the feeling of camaraderie between the two protecting factions, the salaries of the deputies, amounting to more than $200 a day, were taken from the Firemen's and Policemen's pension fund.

There was no stopping the City Council in the face of a breach of the city peace. On the same day they passed the notorious anti-picketing ordinance, "prohibiting assembly for the purpose of preventing workers from going to work, prohibiting the preventing of any person patronizing any business place by means of compulsion, coercion, threats, intimidation, acts of violence or fear, use of gestures or loud and unusual noises." This measure was passed unanimously to "protect the strikers as well as the employers."

On the following day scabs were escorted in from Lodi by the police and escorted back again in the evening. This was kept up as long as the strike lasted, no doubt to protect the strikers. The menace at this time consisted of some carpet tacks strewn on the road which were the cause of several punctures to police tires. It is to be hoped the special deputies helped the police change these tires in appreciation of the pension fund.

Within 24 hours organized labor had 1700 signatures to a petition for a referendum on the anti-picketing ordinance. The City Council, backed by City Attorney Quinn, piously informed the voters that a referendum could not be invoked in the face of such a menace to the public peace. Labor clamored for the resignation of Wheeler from the Council, claiming his association with the M. M. and E. tended to prejudice his actions on the council. Mr. Wheeler refused to resign and implied that labor itself must be prejudiced even to hint such a thing. He is still on the City Council.

On April 27, Ray Morency, vice-president of the Warehouse Union, walked toward a car halted in front of a warehouse. It was driven by Charles Gray, son of the owner of the Gray Trucking Company, and it was Morency's intention to ask

Gray to cooperate with the strikers and stop hauling produce from the plants involved in the strike. When Morency was still five feet from the car Gray pulled out a pistol and killed him. At the time the strike started Gray already had two permits to carry Colt revolvers. He applied for another permit to carry a Mauser after the strike started and got it. Officials absolved themselves of all blame, showing they had canceled his other permits when they permitted him to carry the Mauser. With the entire police force and forty deputies to "protect the strikers," Morency had not thought it necessary to apply for a gun permit.

There was no police escort at Morency's funeral, the biggest in the history of Stockton. Three thousand members of local unions and sympathizers, augmented by additional numbers from the bay area, deciding that Stockton police protection was a dangerous thing—for strikers—marched through the street with Morency's body at their own risk.

The local press in the form of the Stockton *Independent*, had this to say editorially on the same day the entire city was in mourning for Morency's murder:

> *The quiet of Sunday morning can be utilized no better than in forgetting the unpleasant things of the week and recalling those that have been good.*
>
> *Speaking from a barrel top in a New York street the night after President Lincoln's assassination had plunged the country into despair, James A. Garfield told his hearers, "God reigns, and the Government at Washington still lives."*
>
> *Even so. There are so many fine people in the world, that we can well afford to forget those who annoy us. Times could be so much worse, that by comparison, we are in the midst of prosperity.*
>
> *In spite of the Depressionists, the clouds are rimmed with silver; there are rainbows everywhere if we will adjust our mental "specks" to see them, there are friends and neighbors and patriotic folk all around.*

255

*And every personal problem may be solved by patience,
effort and faith in one's self.*

No doubt this was a great spiritual blessing for Morency's
widow and two children.

Originally published in the *Pacific Weekly,* May 10, 1935.

AUTOBIOGRAPHY

I AM twenty-eight years old, and was born and attended school in Huntington, W. Va. My people were working people. My father started to work in a coal-mine when he was eight years old. Later, he became a glass blower, and unable to afford medical treatment, died of cancer at the age of forty-four. There were five children and I was the oldest. My mother took my father's place in the factory. My father's father was crushed to death in a coal-mine. My father never hoped for anything better in this life than a job, and never worried about anything else but losing it. My mother never wanted anything else than that the kids get an education so that they wouldn't have to worry about the factory closing down.

I worked in glass factories and proof-read on newspapers at nights while going through three years of college. I remember that the Art Appreciation book was pink, and the Biology book was green. Other than that, I do not remember very much about my college education. I taught for two years in mountain schools in West Virginia. I do not remember anything memorable about that except that Emil, one of my star pupils, who invariably made six on the Intelligence Tests, and who wanted to do nothing in school or in life but catch flies and pull their wings out, caught fifty-four flies in one day without ever having completely left the edge of his seat. At the end of nine months I had taught him to count to sixty, which, I felt, left a wide margin of safety in Emil's life for any emergency which might come up. Since the best that he had ever done under any other teacher was forty-three flies, and as far as I know he never beat fifty-four, I feel that I was a passing success as a school teacher.

At twenty-three I started out for Kansas to make the wheat harvest. My intentions were to hitch-hike, and after hiking all day without a lift, a freight train pulled to a stop beside the road. I crawled into a box car. I never again voluntarily took up the responsibilities of hitch-hiking, but I always aligned my interests with the interests of the railroad companies. They generally got me where I wanted to go, which was never more definite than "east" or "west."

There were no jobs in Kansas. The Combine had come, and I got my first taste of men trying to buck a machine. I got my first taste of going three days without food, and walking up to a back door and dinging a woman for a hand-out. It was a yellow house, but not too yellow, and I made it. Since then I have hit a thousand such yellow houses and have never been turned down. Women who live in green houses will not even open the door for me.

I remained on the fritz for five months and came home. There was no work at home. I bummed to California and then back again to New York and Washington, D.C. I was sentenced to sixty days in Occoquam Prison in Washington for sleeping in an empty building during a storm. Some friends got me out in eight days. I did not like Washington after that and came home and hunted for work for three months. There wasn't any work, and it was about that time that people started laughing at you for asking for work. After a while I stopped asking for work. I started out again and have been on the road almost constantly since then, except for fifteen months I spent in a CCC camp. This last time has been four years. Sometimes I would stay in a town for four or five months doing odd jobs for a room and something to eat. Most of the time I slept and ate in missions, dinged the streets and houses, and used every other racket known to stiffs to get by.

I had no idea of getting *Waiting for Nothing* published,

therefore, I wrote it just as I felt it, and used the language that stiffs use even when it wasn't always the nicest language in the world.

Parts of the book were scrawled on Bull Durham papers in box cars, margins of religious tracts in a hundred missions, jails, one prison, railroad sand-houses, flop-houses, and on a few memorable occasions actually pecked out with my two index fingers on an honest-to-God typewriter.

Save for four or five incidents, it is strictly autobiographical. Some of the events portrayed did not occur in the same sequence as I gave them, for I have juggled them in order to better develop the story. The "Stiff" idiom is, of course, authentic.

Originally published in the British edition of *Waiting for Nothing* (Constable, 1935).

AFTERWORD

IN SEARCH OF TOM KROMER

RELATIVELY LITTLE is known about Tom Kromer's life, but that is just as well, since the important thing about his book *Waiting for Nothing* is not how closely it is based on the facts but how close it comes to the truth. The facts are that Thomas Michael Kromer was born on October 20, 1906, in Huntington, West Virginia. His father, Allbert Kromer, had come to America from Czechoslovakia in 1885 at the age of two and six years later had begun working beside his own father in the coal mines near Pittsburgh. Allbert's father was later crushed to death in a mining accident. Around the turn of the century, Allbert left Pittsburgh for Huntington, where he took a job as a glass blower. There he met Grace Thornburg, a Huntington native who worked in the glass factory with him, and they were married in 1905. Tom was their first child; he was followed by Emogene, Katherine, Allbert, and Wilma. Tom was known within the family as "Bus," a nickname derived from a Buster Brown hat he wore as a child.

In 1912 the Kromers moved to Fairmont, West Virginia, and in 1917 they relocated in Kingwood. Tom attended elementary school there and was a bright student—quiet, self-reliant, and sometimes stubborn with his teachers. In 1919 the Kromers moved again, this time to Williamstown, a community in Wood County, West Virginia. They stayed there for four years, then returned to Huntington, where the father resumed work at the glass factory. Two years later Allbert Kromer discovered that he had cancer; a trip to a clinic in

Cleveland revealed that the malignancy was inoperable. He died in 1924, when his eldest son was eighteen.[1]

Tom Kromer graduated from high school in the spring of 1925 and the following fall enrolled at Marshall College, a small, conservative institution in Huntington. He remained a student there for the next two years, living at home and working part-time in the glass factory and as a proofreader for the local newspaper. The professors with whom Kromer was most friendly were Watson Selvage, head of philosophy and psychology, Arthur S. White, a member of the economics and political science department, and W. Page Pitt, who established a Department of Journalism at Marshall during Kromer's second year there.

In the spring semester of that year, Marshall became involved in the backwash of a controversy that had made headlines elsewhere in the country a year before—the famous "Hatrack" case involving H. L. Mencken, the *American Mercury*, and the Boston Watch and Ward Society. The April 1926 issue of the *Mercury* had carried a reminiscence by Herbert Asbury entitled "Hatrack"—a humorous piece about a small-town prostitute. When the issue was banned from public sale in Boston, Mencken decided to test the ban in court. On April 4 he traveled to Boston and at 2:00 P.M. that day sold a copy of the *Mercury* issue containing "Hatrack" to J. Frank Chase, secretary of the city's Watch and Ward Society. The sale had been prearranged, and Chase had brought along officers of the law. Mencken allowed himself to be arrested, booked, and arraigned for selling obscene literature. The case went to court, and on April 6 Mencken was exonerated. It was a signal victory for the Baltimore Sage and for liberal-thinking Americans, but in towns and cities throughout the country, files of the *Mercury* were removed from library shelves and destroyed.[2] In the spring of 1927, a year after Mencken's victory in Boston, files of both the *American Mercury* and the *New Republic* were taken out of the library of Marshall College, an act which polarized fundamentalists and free-thinkers on campus. Watson Selvage and Arthur White both protested the removal of the magazines, and as a result both men were fired from the faculty.

Perhaps discouraged by the departure of two of his favorite teachers and almost certainly short of funds, Kromer left college at the conclusion of the 1926–27 term and spent the following year teaching in backwoods elementary schools in order to earn enough money to return to Marshall. He reentered in the fall of 1928 and the following spring enrolled in Professor Pitt's course in feature writing. One of Kromer's assignments for this class had a significant effect on the next several years of his life. He was sent out to pose as a panhandler in downtown Huntington in order to see how much money he could collect. The purpose of the exercise was to show how easily people could be duped by fraudulent vagrants. Kromer was successful in the ruse and collected three dollars in an hour and a half. He turned the money over to the local Community Chest and wrote up the experience for the *Huntington Herald-Dispatch,* which printed the account on its front page for March 1, 1929, under the headline "Pity the Poor Panhandler; $2 An Hour is All He Gets." To Kromer it must have seemed a lark, a caper. Going on the bum probably looked like an easy way to get by.

Kromer must have regretted his naiveté many times during the next five years. His funds were exhausted at the conclusion of the 1929 academic year, and there was no work in Huntington, so he decided to hit the road in earnest and hobo to Kansas for the wheat harvest. "My intentions were to hitch-hike," he later recalled, "and after hiking all day without a lift, a freight train pulled to a stop beside the road. I crawled into a box car. I never again voluntarily took up the responsibilities of hitch-hiking, but I always aligned my in-

Photograph from "Pity the Poor Panhandler," *Huntington Herald-Dispatch*, 1929.

terests with the interests of the railroad companies. They generally got me where I wanted to go, which was never more definite than 'east' or 'west.' "[3]

There was no work in Kansas once Kromer got there, so he stayed on the bum for five months before returning to Huntington. Still unable to find employment in his home city, Kromer went back on the road and lived the brutal life of a vagrant during the earliest and worst years of the Great Depression. In 1931 he was in Santa Rosa, California, where he worked tending and harvesting grapes; the following summer and fall he labored in the hops fields in Napa.[4] Between these jobs he stayed on the move. At some point he drifted into Washington, D.C., where he was jailed for sleeping in an empty building. And somewhere else—no one knows where—Kromer played out his string and attempted to take his own life but was stopped by a woman. *Waiting for Nothing* is dedicated to her—"To Jolene, Who Turned Off the Gas."

On May 30, 1933, Kromer enrolled in the California branch of Roosevelt's Civilian Conservation Corps. He stayed for fifteen months, working at Fort Macarthur, Camp Halls Flat, Camp Murphys, and Camp Skull Creek. Most of *Waiting for Nothing* was written during his stay at Camp Murphys, and he began the novel with the working title "Michael Kohler" during this same period—probably while he was at Camp Skull Creek. Kromer sent the manuscript of *Waiting for Nothing*, then entitled "Three Hots and a Flop," to several publishers without success. He therefore had a friend, Mrs. Marcy Woods, send the manuscript to Lincoln Steffens, who was then living in Carmel, California. On July 5, 1934, the famous journalist returned the manuscript with this cover letter:

Dear Mrs. Woods—

This story, this portrait of a "stiff" is important. I sat up late nights reading it and I knew I was getting something I had never "got" before: realism to the nth degree. I can't imagine a publisher grabbing for it, but it might, and it should be read by a million people.

All I can suggest is that you try it on publishers, one after the other, til you find one that will publish it; it isn't enough to print this story. It must be published. And there are not many publishers.

Steffens[5]

Encouraged, Kromer sent the manuscript out again, but again was unsuccessful. He decided that he needed a literary agent and wrote to Steffens on August 28 for advice:

Dear Mr. Steffens:

I wish to take this opportunity to thank you for your kindness in reading the MS of my book "Three Hots and a Flop," which my friend, Mrs. Marcy Woods, sent you.

As you suggested, owing to the style and subject matter, it will be hard to get a publisher to touch it. I have just gotten it back from Covici-Friede.

Knowing your long experience as a successful writer, I thought perhaps you could give me the name of a reputable literary agent who would handle it. Picking an agent from the myriad of advertisements in writers magazines has just about got me stumped as they all seem to want from five to a hundred dollars for reading it. I am at present working in one of these Government Reforestation Camps and only making five dollars a month for myself and cannot stand the drain. Could you help me in this matter of an agent?

Thos. M. Kromer[6]

Steffens's recommendation was to employ Maxim Lieber, who would prove to be a good choice for Kromer. Lieber was then handling numerous prominent writers, several of whom had leftist sympathies. His authors included Josephine Herbst, Jack Conroy, Louis Adamic, Langston Hughes, Robert Coates, Erskine Caldwell, and Carson McCullers. He had also been Thomas Wolfe's first literary agent.

Lieber submitted Kromer's manuscript to Alfred A. Knopf,

Inc., one of the most distinguished trade houses in America at that time, and in our own time as well. Although Alfred Knopf had initially built his reputation by publishing major European writers, he was by now also issuing hard-boiled fiction by Dashiell Hammett, James M. Cain, B. Traven, and Michael Fessier. Kromer's book, with its clipped, direct style and its reliance on the vagrant idiom, fit well on Knopf's list. Its subject matter also was appropriate. Knopf was planning to publish, in the spring of 1935, a translation of Michel Malveev's *Weep Not for the Dead*, a book about homeless wanderers in Europe after the Great War. Kromer's book paired well with Malveev's account. Though not an activist, Knopf had a strong social conscience, and he must have been impressed and moved by Kromer's book. William A. Koshland, then beginning his long career with the Knopf firm, still remembers the excitement around the publisher's offices when Kromer's manuscript was being considered.[7] Knopf accepted the book and announced its tentative publication date in the Spring Book Index of *Publishers Weekly* under Kromer's name, but with the added notation "Title not announced."[8] Evidently the Knopf editors had considered the manuscript under its working title, "Three Hots and a Flop." Kromer may have changed the title at the suggestion of someone at Knopf, or an editor there may have made the change independently. Whatever the case, altering the title to *Waiting for Nothing* (a phrase taken from chapter 12 of the book) was a commendable move. The new title captures the essence of Kromer's book in a way that "Three Hots and a Flop" does not.

Waiting for Nothing was published on March 4, 1935, at two dollars a copy. Reviews were attentive and serious though not wholly favorable. Several reviewers mentioned the self-consciousness of Kromer's style, but no one doubted the authenticity of his story. Roland Mulhauser, in the *Saturday Review of Literature*, wrote, "There is a static calm in his point of view suggesting compression and numbness beyond pain.

There is no sentimentalizing pity. There are no emotional outbursts. Nothing but hunger. Still, it is a shocking book: a picture of unmitigated depravity." An anonymous reviewer for the *New York Times* noted the "sheer power of the ghastliness and horror of the narrative"; Dorothy Brewster, in the *Nation,* judged the episodes by turn "grim, repellent, touching, humorous, ribald, tragic." Robert Cantwell, reviewing the book for the *New Republic,* made an obvious connection: Kromer's "fragmentary sketches" were written, "at their best, with something of the sharpness and unblinking acceptance of the horrible that characterize Ernest Hemingway's very early stories of the War." The most favorable review was by Fred T. Marsh in *Books;* he called *Waiting for Nothing* a "little piece of dynamite" but thought it would probably "accomplish nothing in its explosion because people will stuff up their ears with cotton and flee to their bomb-proof cellars."[9] Marsh was right. Despite generally good reviews, *Waiting for Nothing* was a commercial failure and did not even sell out its first printing.[10]

There was, however, one bright spot. Theodore Dreiser read the book in galleys and was so impressed that he agreed to write an introduction for the English edition, which was to be handled by his own British publisher, Constable. The text was freshly typeset for British release, and the edition was published on June 28, 1935. This British edition is a curious literary artifact. Part of the power of Knopf's edition of *Waiting for Nothing* comes from the authorial anonymity of the book. Almost nothing is revealed about Kromer: there are a few details about him on the rear flap of the dust jacket, but essentially the text of the book is a disembodied cry from the void. One turns past the title page and sees the dedication, with its suggestion of a previous attempt at suicide. The text begins on the next recto, and Kromer's story begins to unfold, chapter by chapter, in his mannered, chilling style. The British edition, by contrast, has a table of contents printed on the first recto following the dedication; then one must get through Dreiser's introduction and an autobiographical note by Kromer before reaching the text.

Dreiser undoubtedly contributed this introduction because he thought Kromer's book important and wished to boost its publication in England. During the 1930s Dreiser often championed the cause of the working class, and he had been interested in vagrant life at least since 1899 when he published "Curious Shifts of the Poor" in *Demorest's* and then included parts of that article in *Sister Carrie*, first published in November 1900. Dreiser himself came close to vagrancy in 1903, when he was enduring a lengthy siege of neurasthenia, and he would probably have resorted to begging had he not been rescued and rehabilitated by his brother Paul.[11] Dreiser had retained his interest in bums: several years earlier he had supplied an introduction for a first-person account of life on the stem entitled *Poorhouse Sweeney*.[12] Dreiser undoubtedly meant well when he wrote his introduction to *Waiting for Nothing*, but his prefatory remarks are in his worst style—clumsy, turgid, and in places incoherent. In the entire introduction, only Dreiser's first two sentences really make sense: "This book needs no introduction or foreword," he writes. "It is its own introduction or foreword." Dreiser probably should have left it at that.

Kromer's autobiographical note, prepared specifically for the Constable edition, is also unfortunate. Kromer drops the mask of the narrative persona in the Knopf *Waiting for Nothing* and lets the reader see him as a self-consciously literary young man. His education, he avers, was of little account: "I remember that the Art Appreciation book was pink, and the Biology book was green. Other than that, I do not remember very much about my college education." He records his experiences as a schoolteacher in the West Virginia backwoods and tells of his star pupil, Emil, "who wanted to do nothing in school or in life but catch flies and pull their wings out."

Kromer mentions some of his experiences while on the bum, then writes:

> I had no idea of getting *Waiting for Nothing* published, there-fore, I wrote it just as I felt it, and used the language that stiffs use even when it wasn't always the nicest language in the world.
>
> Parts of the book were scrawled on Bull Durham papers in box cars, margins of religious tracts in a hundred missions, jails, one prison, railroad sand-houses, flop-houses, and on a few memorable occasions actually pecked out with my two index fingers on an honest-to-God typewriter.

Well, perhaps. Whatever the facts of the book's composition, Kromer's autobiographical note identifies him as an individual still living in America; it gives him a past that occurred before the incidents in *Waiting for Nothing*, and it gives him a life that continued after the conclusion of the book. No longer is the narrator a faceless, despairing young man on the edge.

Having progressed through Dreiser's introduction and Kromer's note, the British reader next had to contend with censorship. The first issue of the Constable edition is missing the fourth chapter, a twenty-page section in which the narrator is picked up in a park by a wealthy homosexual known as "Mrs. Carter." "I am a lucky stiff running into this queer," he writes. "For every queer there is a hundred stiffs to make him." Later he explains, "What the hell? A guy has got to eat, and what is more, he has got to flop." For most vagrants this kind of thing is a trade-off, a business proposition. "You can always depend on a stiff having to pay for what he gets," the narrator says at the end of the chapter. "I pull off my clothes and crawl into bed."

Constable originally seems to have seen nothing especially objectionable in this fourth chapter; the text was typeset and printed with the other chapters in the first impression. Bibli-ographical evidence indicates that the sheets of this impression were folded and ready for stitching and binding when Constable decided not to risk publication of chapter 4. Pages 75–94 of the unstitched gatherings (all of chapter 4) were cancelled—that is, were razored out—and in their place the publisher inserted an eight-page gathering, on blue paper no less, on which the following explanation was printed:

Why Chapter IV is missing from
WAITING FOR NOTHING

It is unusual for a publisher to address the reader of one of his books in the middle of that book. But what has happened to *Waiting for Nothing* is, like *Waiting for Nothing* itself, so unusual, that a breach of publishers' custom seems permissible.

Early this year one of Constable's advisers read the first proofs of Tom Kromer's book in New York. He was immediately and deeply impressed by the power and authenticity of the work. Chancing next evening to be in the company of Theodore Dreiser, he found that Dreiser had just read a similar proof and was emphatic that this was the best and most poignant record of the miseries of the down-and-out which the Depression had yet produced.

Dreiser and our reader discussed Kromer and his book for most of the evening; and it was finally agreed that, if Constables bought *Waiting for Nothing* for English production, Dreiser would write a special introduction to appear in the English edition and nowhere else. And so it was settled.

In due course the book was ready for issue in London and an advance copy was sent to a prominent bookseller, known to be interested in books of this kind. He wrote that he had been greatly moved by Kromer's record, but wondered whether possible "objection might be taken" to one chapter. This bookseller is a man whose opinion commands respect, and we at once carefully reconsidered the chapter in question.

Naturally our adviser had taken note that this chapter, which described a particularly terrible experience of Kromer's, was unusually outspoken for an English book. We read the chapter carefully and felt that an obvious narrative of fact like *Waiting for Nothing* was on a totally different basis from a novel; that this thing had happened to the man who said it had happened; and that only if the truth be told about the horrors to which helpless vagrants are exposed, is there any hope of such things being remedied. Now, however, an experienced member of the book trade had sent us a warning; and we must decide whether, under existing conditions in this country, a true incident which could be publicly described in America was one which might not be publicly described in England.

A Publisher faced with this decision has no one to whom he can apply for help, no standard by which he can judge what is fit and proper to print or what, being deemed unfit and improper, will cause him to be prosecuted. He "knows the law," as every citizen is supposed to do. But he has no idea how the law may be interpreted, and no means of finding out. . . .

And so, utterly without guidance or court of appeal, the publisher in the majority of cases leans toward caution, as we have done with *Waiting for Nothing*. We have cut out Chapter IV entirely—cut it out with reluctance and with shame, merely consoling ourselves with the thought that fortunately the continuity of the book is in no way affected. Were we wrong to cut it out? No one can possibly say. Would we have been guilty of corrupting youth had we left it in? Once again, no one—in advance—has the smallest idea. That is how things are in England these days; and that is why *Waiting for Nothing* appears in England in an emasculated form.

CONSTABLE & CO LTD.

Waiting for Nothing was published by Constable in this odd manner—preceded by Dreiser's awkward introduction and Kromer's glib autobiographical note, and interrupted by the blue-paper gathering between chapters 3 and 5. Reviewers mentioned the absence of chapter 4, but apparently nothing else happened. Perhaps emboldened by public indifference, or perhaps simply forgetful, Constable released a later issue of the first impression, this time with pages 75–94 included in the normal collation pattern. Today one can find copies of both issues of the Constable text—with and without chapter 4. This British edition of *Waiting for Nothing* is an authentic case in which the manner of a book's publication, even down to its physical format, interferes with one's apprehension of the text. The prefatory matter and the censoring come between the reader and Kromer's story.[13]

Kromer had left the CCC on September 1, 1934, and had gone back on the road. He had drifted about for a time and had finally landed in Stockton, California, where a husband and wife named Biff and Ruth Gray took him in. Through the Grays, Kromer got a job at the Harvard Bookstore in Stockton and worked there while waiting for the Knopf edition of *Waiting for Nothing* to appear. In midsummer 1935, now a published author, he left Stockton and bummed east, reaching Huntington by August. Already he was beginning to suffer seriously from pulmonary tuberculosis, a condition that would eventually make him an invalid and bring a halt to his writing.

In Huntington, Kromer went to see Thomas Donnelly, who had been a student with him at Marshall. Donnelly had taken his master's and doctoral degrees at New York University and had returned to Marshall to teach government. Arthur S. White, one of the two professors fired from Marshall in 1927, had taken a position on the faculty of the University of New Mexico in Albuquerque and had recently become head of the political science department there. He had offered Donnelly a position at New Mexico, and Donnelly was preparing to travel to Albuquerque for the fall term. New Mexico must have sounded attractive to Kromer—especially its dry climate, good for people with lung ailments. Donnelly promised Kromer that he would attempt to find work for him in Albuquerque, and Kromer left Huntington on September 2, 1935, heading west.

He rode the rails to California, then doubled back to Albuquerque where he enrolled as a part-time student. Donnelly and White had arranged a journalism scholarship to cover his fees. Kromer did well in his studies, but his physical condition soon worsened and in November he began to hemorrhage. He withdrew from the university and entered St. Joseph's Hospital in Albuquerque for treatment. There he met Janet Smith, a young woman from White Plains, New York, who had attended Vassar before coming to New Mexico for treatment of a rheumatic heart condition. Kromer and Janet Smith decided to marry but postponed their plans while Kromer underwent treatment at the Sunnyside Sanitorium in Albuquerque. Eventually the two were wed on December 19, 1936.

Kromer continued to write while in the sanitorium. He published two book reviews in *New Masses,* and Lieber was able to place a revised version of chapters 3 and 4 of "Michael Kohler," Kromer's novel-in-progress, with the *American Spectator,* a journal edited by George Jean Nathan, Ernest Boyd, Eugene O'Neill, and several other prominent literary figures.[14] Kromer's chapters, which concerned a mine explosion, appeared in the September 1936 issue of the *Spectator* under the title "Black Damp."

Through Lincoln Steffens, Kromer had found another outlet for his writing—the *Pacific Weekly.* This periodical, edited by Steffens, W. K. Bassett, Ella Winter (Steffens's wife), and others, was a left-leaning journal issued from Carmel. Nearly all of the writers who published in the *Weekly* were either Communist party members or fellow travelers; most were also members of the Association of Western Writers, which eventually became affiliated with the League of American Writers. Between May 1935 and November 1936, Kromer published ten items in the *Pacific Weekly.* These include an article on a strike in Stockton, California; three sketches called "cameos"; a three-part short story; two other short stories; and a book review. The stories, though bitter in tone, are strong work: they

show Kromer developing a style that is more flexible and evoc-
ative, more dependent on stream-of-consciousness narration,
than the style of *Waiting for Nothing*.

During this period Kromer was also working on a novel entitled "Slumber in the Hills," and in early August 1936 he
submitted skeleton outlines of the first two and last three
chapters of this proposed book to Knopf. The reaction was not
favorable. Knopf editor Bernard Smith, himself a well-known
leftist writer, reported as follows:

> This proposed novel will endeavor to picture the mountain
> people of Carolina—their backwardness, quaintness, humanity,
> humor, love of barter, etc., etc. In the parts submitted these
> qualities are adequately represented, but there is nothing here
> that gives me the feeling that a master is at work, and to me the
> whole idea seems to be an unimportant one. I cannot make my-
> self feel that this will be a book of any genuine value or poten-
> tial saleability. I would therefore discourage Kromer from writ-
> ing this book and suggest that he tell me what his other
> proposed book is—NO PITY FOR THE DEAD.[15]

The "Slumber in the Hills" material was returned to Lieber
on August 13 but has since disappeared. Nothing is known of
Kromer's other proposal, the book his Knopf editor calls "No
Pity for the Dead."[16]

Back in Albuquerque, Kromer was searching for financial
support. By early September he was busy putting together a
proposal for a Guggenheim Fellowship; on September 2, 1936,
he wrote Dreiser to ask if he might use his name as a reference on the application. In his letter to Dreiser, Kromer mentions that he is working on a novel, then adds, "I have been
bedridden with tuberculosis since the publication of my
book, a year of this in a sanitorium." Dreiser responded on
September 22, giving Kromer permission to list him as a reference, but despite support from the famous novelist, Kromer's
application was unsuccessful.[17]

By the spring of 1937, Kromer and his wife were living at 1216 East Central Avenue in Albuquerque. Lieber sent a letter to Kromer at that address on March 15. Apparently Kromer was still in poor health: Lieber writes that he was "shocked to read of your latest illness and the form it assumed. It is truly inconceivable what suffering the human body can endure." Lieber reports on his efforts to market some of the writing Kromer has sent him and encourages his client to continue work on his novel. Lieber wanted to submit the manuscript, once Kromer finished it, to one of the competitions frequently held by trade publishers. "You have a splendid idea there for an outstanding novel," wrote Lieber, "and even if we don't get it into the Houghton Mifflin contest, there is a new Harper contest, as well as a Little Brown contest." Lieber was probably referring to "Michael Kohler," the novel Kromer never completed.[18]

In August 1937, Kromer and his wife acquired a one-acre lot on El Pueblo Road, north of Albuquerque near Alameda. They built an adobe house on the property, and Mrs. Kromer began work for the *Albuquerque Tribune* as a free-lance writer and society editor. Kromer may have continued his efforts to write fiction, but if so, nothing survives from this period. In the early 1940s, the Kromers spent two summers teaching Indian school children at a remote Navajo reservation. Kromer never recovered his health; in the mid-1940s his condition deteriorated to the point that his wife had to give up her newspaper job in order to stay at home with him. In 1945 she began a magazine that she called *Janet Kromer's Shopping Notes*, and she published it until her death in 1960. Thomas Donnelly visited the Kromers occasionally and would sometimes discuss writing projects with Tom, but Donnelly felt that Kromer was no longer interested in writing. Essentially an invalid, he spent most days resting.

Janet Kromer died on November 19, 1960. Kromer continued to live in Albuquerque until April 1961, when his family persuaded him to return to Huntington. Shortly after his wife's death he had suffered a nervous breakdown; in Huntington he underwent shock treatments for the condition. After 1963, Kromer lived with his sister and mother in a house on Brandon Road that he and his sister purchased shortly after he sold his property in Albuquerque. His health was still poor, and he spent much of his time resting and watching television. Kromer died of a heart attack on January 10, 1969, at the age of sixty-two and was buried in Spring Hill Cemetery in Huntington.

"The main facts in human life are five," E. M. Forster tells us: "birth, food, sleep, love and death."[19] If one accepts his list as accurate, then one must ask how most novelists treat these immediate needs in their fiction. How does what Forster calls "homo fictus" compare to homo sapiens? Forster's homo fictus is usually born off stage, is capable of dying on stage, needs very little food or sleep, and is "tirelessly occupied with human relationships" (p. 87). Forster thinks that novelists are concerned more with love (usually sexual) and death than with birth, food, and sleep.

The inversion of this traditional emphasis makes Tom Kromer's Waiting for Nothing a singular book. In the world of Depression-era "skid row" bums, there is little time for human relationships, sexual or otherwise; life on the stem is reduced to an endless daily struggle to find food and sleep, a search for "three hots and a flop." Kromer's universe aligns itself perfectly with what Abraham Maslow calls the "hierarchy of human needs." The economic and social upheaval of the Depression traps Kromer's characters on the lowest rung of Maslow's ladder of self-actualization—the physiological. Their needs—air, water, food, shelter, sleep—are "survival needs: a concern for immediate existence; to be able to eat, breathe, live at this moment."[20] The immediacy of these bodily necessities makes *Waiting for Nothing* disturbing and powerful. Kromer's book forcibly returns the typical reader to a primitive fight for existence.

Kromer does not treat conventional "love" in his book. In both chapter 4, the narrator's meeting with the homosexual "Mrs. Carter," and in chapter 7, his Christmas Eve with the novice prostitute Yvonne, we see the narrator involved in sexual relationships, but as usual, "love" is based on a need for food and shelter. With Mrs. Carter, the narrator prostitutes his body not out of a need for sexual gratification, nor even out of a desire for "affectionate relations with people in general" (Maslow's third level of "love and belongingness"), but only to satisfy his elementary physiological needs. The narrator is repulsed by this homosexual: "These pansies give me the willies, but I have got to get myself a feed. I have not had a decent feed for a week." And though genuine and loving, the relationship with Yvonne is also initially predicated on fundamental survival needs. Food takes precedence over all else. When they first meet, Yvonne, new at the oldest game, makes a clumsy sexual approach to the narrator, who gently rejects her with his own counter-invitation: "Let's eat." We then watch the narrator penny-up on various merchants in order to gather the ingredients of a "beef stew" of baloney butts, stale bread, and onions. Once they have shared food, Yvonne offers the narrator her room and her body. "You can stay here," she says, "until the landlady kicks us out." The sexual invitation is implicit, but even in this moment sexual love is contingent on physical comfort. There is no hope of permanency; these two people will remain lovers only so long as the rent is paid.

Death, Forster's second novelistic preoccupation, is also treated in *Waiting for Nothing*. We hear the death rattle of a gas hound who drinks canned heat, the tubercular croup of an infant who is underfed and underclothed, and the self-inflicted gunshot that signals the end of one stiff's miserable existence. We see the mutilated limbs of a bo who falls beneath the wheels of a drag, the glassy eyes of one stiff who drinks hair tonic, and the frozen body of another who drops dead from exposure in a mission soup-line. Forster believes that most writers find death congenial because, like marriage, it "ends a book neatly, and for the less obvious reason that . . . it [is] easier to work from the known towards the darkness" (p. 82). But in Kromer's world, death is not "darkness," nor is it unfamiliar or mysterious. Rather, it is a concrete fact of life, an almost everyday occurrence that evokes neither fear nor dread but only a sense of relief. About the suicide in the mission flop, the narrator says, "After a guy bumps himself off, he don't have any more troubles. Everything is all right with him." As far as ending his book "neatly," Kromer does in fact focus his last chapter on the death of a stiff, but there is no sense of finality. In the last lines of the book, the narrator is still thinking about the endless futility of his own existence:

> What is a man to do? I know well enough what he can do. All he can do is to try to keep his belly full of enough slop so that he won't rattle when he breathes. All he can do is to try and find himself a lousy flop at night. Day after day, week after week, year after year, always the same—three hots and a flop.

This narrator resembles Sisyphus; his words resonate with the absurdity of *No Exit*. Like the tramps in *Waiting for Godot*, this bum is waiting for nothing.

The narrative stance of Kromer's book is unusual in that he tells his story exclusively in the present tense. He makes the "now" of the reading experience coincide with the "now" of the action of the story. This is literary artifice, of course, yet it gives *Waiting for Nothing* a heightened feeling of immediacy typical of tough-guy novels of the thirties. Kromer's reader finds himself morally implicated through the eerie present-tense narration: because he is asked to experience firsthand the worst of Depression life, he is forced to judge the narrator's behavior as if it were his own.

Like *On the Road*, Kromer's *Waiting for Nothing* is essentially picaresque and therefore episodic. How his chosen sequence of events is more felicitous than any rearrangement of their order might be is difficult to discern. The narrative is circular—it roughly begins and ends in a dismal mission flop—but the order of the intervening episodes seems to have little structural meaning. However episodic it might be, though, *Waiting for Nothing* is no mere naturalistic slice-of-life. Kromer evokes all aspects of the stiff's life while managing the more difficult task of creating a sense of stasis, stagnation, and death. One could easily assign chapter headings such as "In the Mission," "Riding the Blinds," "In the Jungle," or "In the Soup-Line" to Kromer's twelve untitled episodes, but the author's genius lies in his ability to render stultifyingly alike all this diverse experience. He does so in several ways: through the use of the vagrant idiom—words like "dinging," "stemming," and "dummy chunker," with which we become familiar through constant repetition; through the use of simple and repetitious sentence structures that reflect the monotony of "vag" life; and through the reappearance of certain key images, phrases, and sentences that come to function as buzz words of pain and boredom. "You ask for work and they laugh at you for asking for work. There is no work." These lines are a refrain throughout. And the stiffs themselves are always "rats" scurrying for their "holes." Most important, Kromer achieves his static effect through the repetition of certain central events. The entire book is an endless series of "waitings"—waiting for a lice-ridden bed in a mission flop, waiting for stale bread and rancid swill in a soup line, waiting for someone to ding for two bits, waiting for nothing. This sense of arrested motion is even present in the narrator's nightmare of his own death: "Maybe I will be lying in the corner of a box car with the roar of the wheels underneath me. Maybe it will come quick while I am shivering in a soup-line, a soup-line that stretches for a block and never starts moving."

Kromer himself came from a classic proletarian background; his family life is similar to that of Larry Donovan, the proletarian hero of Jack Conroy's *The Disinherited*. Yet Kromer's ideas are essentially apolitical. His narrator has dropped below the worker class to the lumpenproletariat, the horrifying world of stiffs and bos. The book, however, does have its leftist spokesmen—Karl, a writer, and Werner, an artist. Because their work captures the pain and suffering of life on the stem, it is unacceptable to the general public. The cruel irony is that if Karl and Werner would take the "hungry look out of the eyes" of the people in their pictures, they "could buy more hamburger steaks" and take the hungry look out of their own eyes. But both artists agree that this would be sacrilegious, and thus they are reduced to mouthing Marxist rhetoric:

> "Some day there will be an end to all this," says Karl. "Some day we shall have all we want to eat. There is plenty for all. Some day we shall have it."
> "Revolution?" says Werner. . . .
> "Revolution," says Karl. "Not now. There is no leader. But some day there will arise a leader for the masses."

Cut off from any feeling of connection with the masses and relying instead on his individual know-how to survive, the narrator rejects this vision of a better future: "I am tired of such talk as this. You can stop a revolution of stiffs with a sack of toppin's. I have seen one bull kick a hundred stiffs off a drag. When a stiff's gut is empty, he hasn't got the guts to start anything. When his gut is full, he just doesn't see any use in raising hell." Kromer has captured perfectly the whining, whipped-dog tone of the down-and-out vagrant. These stiffs are no threat to property or the social order; they have no politics, no ideology. All they care about is a decent feed and place to sleep.[21]

We must be careful to distinguish between Tom Kromer, the author of *Waiting for Nothing*, and "Kromer," the narrator of the book. In the act of writing this account, author Tom Kromer betrays his hope that the inhuman situation he describes can be corrected. His book functions, on its most obvious level, as an account of life in extremis. Kromer seems to believe that once people are shown degradation and injustice, they will do something to help. It is also important to draw a distinction between "Kromer," the narrator, and the majority of the vagrants he encounters. In *Waiting for Nothing* we see this narrator's strong fellow feeling prevent him from bludgeoning an innocent passerby, from robbing a bank, and even from performing the "dummy chunker," a scam that preys only on people's feelings. The narrator has chosen to show us incidents where he has, in a sense, failed. By emphasizing these failures, Tom Kromer has transformed what could have been a documentary of skid-row life into an artistic creation that traces a personal struggle to preserve human virtues and emotions in the face of a brutal and dehumanizing reality.[22]

Why did Tom Kromer stop writing? Certainly his physical debilitation had much to do with it. He appears to have made a brave struggle against tuberculosis and to have lost. But it may also be that he had nothing more to write about. Having scraped bottom in *Waiting for Nothing*, having depicted life in virtually its most degraded form, Kromer may not have had another story to tell. The few pieces he wrote after *Waiting for Nothing* suggest that he attempted to find subject matter that might have had some meaning. His proposed novel about Appalachia, "Slumber in the Hills," in which he was to depict the "quaintness, humanity, humor" of Carolina mountain people, may have been an effort to move away from the ni-

Tom Kromer in 1935. (Photograph from Emogene Kromer.)

hilism of *Waiting for Nothing*, but his editor at Knopf did not encourage the project. Kromer also attempted to develop a more radical political stance in his fiction. His leftward turn was probably fostered by Lincoln Steffens and his wife Ella Winter and was no doubt helped along by Edward Newhouse's favorable *New Masses* review of *Waiting for Nothing*. Newhouse's assessment was especially friendly, considering the time and the book's lack of an orthodox political message. Newhouse hoped that no one would quibble about Kromer's failure to point "the way out" and instructed readers to ignore the jacket blurb that claimed *Waiting for Nothing* contained no propaganda. "Tom Kromer knows that guys aren't on top because they have brains or because they work hard."[23]

Soon Kromer himself was writing for the *New Masses*. In the issue of June 25, 1935, he reviewed Edward Anderson's *Hungry Men*, an account of vagrant life published by Doubleday, Doran two months after *Waiting for Nothing*. Kromer ridicules Anderson's sunny, romanticized rendering of life on the stem: "When one of Mr. Anderson's puppets gets a gnawing in the pit of his guts, he takes him up to a back door or a restaurant and feeds him. When his hero is mooning on the waterfront over a respectable two-bit whore he is in love with, you will never guess what happens—the Communist in the book hands him fifty bucks and says here take the dough, I'll not be needing it, and make a home for the gal." Kromer knows better. Significantly, in the same review, he revises an image from *Waiting for Nothing* to signal his own political turnabout. "There was a time when you could have stopped a revolution of stiffs with a sack of doughnuts," he writes, "but that time is not now."[24]

Kromer sounds the same note of burgeoning militancy in the sketches he published in the *Pacific Weekly*, Steffens's journal. So angry was Kromer about Anderson's distortions that he revised and republished his *Hungry Men* review there and appropriated Anderson's title for a three-part story of vag life. Kromer's "Hungry Men" covers the years from 1930 to 1935 and depicts the political awakening of the lumpenproletariat. The story ends as a hundred flophouse stiffs join locked-out motormen in turning over streetcars during the 1934 Los Angeles Yellow Car strike:

> The black eyes flashed and the white teeth flashed in the sun and starving men with their rags white from the salt of their own sweat listened in Frisco and L.A. and Detroit and Chi and New York and Mississippi as they stood before the barred windows and the barred doors of their own factories:
> "There is—a way out!
> Our riveting guns built the skyscrapers and bridges,
> Our shovels dug the mines and highways, laid the rails,
> Our muscles and blood went into the ships,
> Went into the fields and all that's here—
> We'll take it now—STAND ASIDE!"

More noteworthy than his revolutionary politics is Kromer's apparent versatility. In his *Pacific Weekly* pieces, he sticks to the subject he knows best but experiments with new voices and styles. "Hungry Men" is written in the manner of the "capsule biographies" of Dos Passos's *U.S.A.* trilogy, while the "cameos" owe much to the irony and understatement of Hemingway's "miniatures" in *In Our Time*. Read together with *Waiting for Nothing*, Kromer's shorter work shows a writer of developing talent and obvious promise.

After *Waiting for Nothing*, Kromer came closest to realizing his potential in "Michael Kohler," a novel fragment based largely on his father's life. Kromer only finished the first six chapters, but we can recover a fuller sense of what he planned to write from a synopsis of the novel that he included with his 1936 Guggenheim application. "Michael Kohler" was to be Kromer's exploration of his own proletarian roots, from his immigrant grandfather's arrival in Chicago in 1885 to his father's death from cancer after working in a West Virginia glass factory. Kromer appears to have been fashioning a narrative with a political theme, a story involving labor unions and the injustices of big management. In his Guggenheim proposal he claims to have studied and researched the historical background of the novel for almost two years; its artistic influences are readily discernible: Zola's *Germinal* (especially the scene in which striking miners burn down a Glen Ellum, Pennsylvania, coal mine) and Conroy's *The Disinherited*, a novel "Michael Kohler" might have rivaled had Kromer completed it.

One must not claim too much for the bits and pieces assembled here with *Waiting for Nothing*. Still, Kromer is surely something more than a "one-book" author. And if his oeuvre is small, he did manage to pass on a literary legacy. Those who have read the stories of the late Breece D'J Pancake, also a native of West Virginia, cannot fail to detect there echoes of Kromer's rhythms and idiom.[25] Bad health eventually caused Kromer to stop writing altogether, but he at least knew that in *Waiting for Nothing* he had come as close to the truth about his subject as anyone would ever come. About life on the stem, there was nothing more to say.

NOTES

1. Some of the biographical details in the Afterword are taken from Frances Gray, "*Waiting for Nothing*: Tom Kromer, 1906–1969," Ph.D. diss., State University of New York at Stony Brook, 1978, 109 pp.

2. See chapter 7 of William Manchester, *Disturber of the Peace: The Life of H. L. Mencken* (New York: Harper and Brothers, 1951).

3. From Kromer's autobiographical note in the British edition of *Waiting for Nothing* (London: Constable, 1935), pp. xxiv–xxv.

4. This information is taken from notes in Kromer's hand that are present among his few surviving papers at the West Virginia University Library, Morgantown.

5. Lincoln Steffens to Marcy Woods, July 5, 1934, Lincoln

Steffens Papers, Rare Book and Manuscript Library, Columbia University. Quoted here with the kind permission of Pete Steffens.

6. Kromer to Steffens, August 28, 1934, Steffens Papers. This letter, and other previously unpublished documents by Kromer that follow in the Afterword, are included with the permission of Kromer's sisters Katherine and Emogene, who are his literary executors.

7. William A. Koshland to James L. W. West III, March 8, 1984.

8. *Publishers Weekly*, January 26, 1935, p. 335.

9. For bibliographical citations to these and other reviews of *Waiting for Nothing*, see the checklist of writings by and about Kromer in this volume.

10. Part of the reason for the poor sales may have been the competition. Also appearing during the spring 1935 publishing season were Wolfe's *Of Time and the River*, Fitzgerald's *Taps at Reveille*, Faulkner's *Pylon*, Steinbeck's *Tortilla Flat*, and, for bestseller purchasers, Enid Bagnold's *National Velvet*. The big Knopf book that spring and summer was Cather's *Lucy Gayheart*, which had sold over fifty thousand copies by August 1935.

11. For Dreiser's autobiographical account of this period, see *An Amateur Laborer* (Philadelphia: University of Pennsylvania Press, 1983).

12. Ed Sweeney, *Poorhouse Sweeney: Life in a County Poorhouse* (New York: Boni and Liveright, 1927).

13. A full hand collation of the Knopf and Constable texts reveals no revision by Kromer for the British typesetting. The accidentals of the Constable text were restyled to British usage, however. In October 1936, *Waiting for Nothing* appeared in a French translation entitled *Les Vagabonds de la faim* (Paris: Calman-Levy). According to a note among Kromer's papers at Morgantown, the translator (Raoul de Roussy de Sales) had difficulty rendering the slang in Kromer's book into French.

14. Dreiser helped found the *American Spectator* and was one of its coeditors for a time, but by 1936 he had long since quarreled with the other editors and had withdrawn from the project.

15. "Readers' Report," August 13, 1936, A. A. Knopf, Inc., Records, Rare Books and Manuscripts Division, New York Public Library, Astor, Lenox and Tilden Foundations. Quoted here with the permission of Alfred A. Knopf, Inc.

16. The reader will recall the earlier reference to the Knopf edition of Michel Malveev's *Weep Not for the Dead*, published two weeks after *Waiting for Nothing*. It would seem likely that Kromer took his tentative title from the Malveev book.

17. These letters are among the Dreiser Papers at the Van Pelt Library, University of Pennsylvania. Portions of Kromer's application for a Guggenheim Fellowship survive in the files of the Guggenheim Foundation. His project was to have been the completion of "Michael Kohler." Kromer's "Plans for Study and Work" from his Guggenheim application are published earlier in this volume together with the six surviving chapters of "Michael Kohler."

18. Maxim Lieber to Kromer, March 15, 1937, West Virginia and Regional History Collection, West Virginia University Library, Morgantown. Quoted here with the permission of Maxim Lieber. In this same letter Lieber writes, "The other day Horace Gregory was in to see me. He is launching a new publication, a bi-annual, I think it may be, to contain a varied assortment of reportage that would give a complete picture of America. He said he was especially interested in your work and his face glowed when he recalled WAITING FOR NOTHING. I gave him a couple of the pieces I have failed to sell and he may perhaps be able to use one of them." Gregory's bi-annual was *New Letters in America* (New York: Norton, 1937), only one volume of which ever appeared. There was no writing by Kromer in that volume.

19. E. M. Forster, *Aspects of the Novel* (New York: Harcourt Brace Jovanovich, 1955), p. 75. Subsequent references are to this edition.

20. See Frank G. Goble, *The Third Force: The Psychology of Abraham Maslow* (New York: Pocket Books, 1970), p. 52.

21. There is a curious Marxist orthodoxy to Kromer's dismissal of the revolutionary potential of "stiffs." In *The Eighteenth Brumaire of Louis Napoleon*, Marx describes the lumpenproletariat as "a disintegrated mass" cut off from its class and particularly susceptible to reactionary ideologies. Kromer's "Marxism," however, seems more experiential than doctrinal. There is no evidence, documentary or otherwise, to suggest that he read Marx at all. In his 1936 Guggenheim application, he claims to have been working in the proletarian literary tradition all along, but it is difficult to give full credence to a grant proposal written after the fact.

22. William Stott classifies *Waiting for Nothing* as an "informant narrative," a subgenre of documentary expression in the 1930s, and criticizes it sharply for what he sees as its literary excesses. Stott, however, finally admits that Kromer's book is "less interesting as a social document than as literature." See *Documentary Expression and Thirties America* (New York: Oxford University Press, 1973), pp. 36–37, 196–98.

23. Edward Newhouse, "Why Wait?" *New Masses*, March 12, 1935, p. 25.

24. For a discussion of the tradition of hobo writing in American literature, see Frederick Feied, *No Pie in the Sky: The Hobo as American Culture Hero in the Works of Jack London, John Dos Passos, and Jack Kerouac* (New York: Citadel Press, 1964).

25. *The Stories of Breece D'J Pancake* (Boston: Little, Brown, 1983).

EDITORIAL NOTE
AND ACKNOWLEDGMENTS

BECAUSE no prepublication version of *Waiting for Nothing* survives, the text published here is that of the 1935 Knopf first edition. And because no manuscript or typescript texts are extant for the other items by Kromer, we have reprinted these writings from their appearances in various periodicals and one newspaper. The emendation policy has been conservative: we have allowed inconsistent orthography to stand and have not imposed formal rules of syntax, punctuation, or hyphenation on Kromer's writings. Obvious typographical errors and incorrect spelling have been emended. The following substantive emendations have been made:

108.19	feet] foot
119.8	tells] tell
160.29	talk] talk for
195.15	to cut] cut
231.27	put it] put
242.15	no] not
242.22	has] have
242.29	attaining] attaining to

Having commented adversely on the arrangement of the British edition of Kromer's book, the editors are conscious of the fact that this volume commits similar sins. Perhaps *Waiting for Nothing* should be published with no scholarly commentary, no additional writings by Kromer, and no checklist of material by and about him. However, we do wish to make Kromer's work available in permanent form, for libraries and scholars as well as for general readers, and we believe that his reputation will benefit from publication of additional material about his life and career. This ancillary matter we have placed at the rear of this volume so that it will interfere as little as possible with a reader's experience of Kromer's writings.

Our greatest debt is to Tom Kromer's two surviving sisters, Emogene and Katherine, for permitting this volume to be published and for assisting us in our research. We also thank Neda M. Westlake, curator of Rare Books, Van Pelt Library, University of Pennsylvania; John D. Stinson, manuscripts specialist, New York Public Library; Kenneth A. Lohf, librarian for Rare Books and Manuscripts at the Butler Library, Columbia University; Harold M. Forbes, associate curator, University Library, West Virginia University; and Donald Farren, head of Special Collections at the University of New Mexico Library.

For various kinds of information we are grateful to the late Alfred A. Knopf; William A. Koshland of Alfred A. Knopf, Inc.; Maxim Lieber; G. Thomas Tanselle, vice-president of the John Simon Guggenheim Memorial Foundation; James L. Thorson, Department of English, University of New Mexico; George S. Baldwin, T. M. Pearce, and Irene Fisher of Albuquerque; and Jim Comstock of Richwood, West Virginia. For research assistance we thank Janet E. Feil of Sacramento, Charles W. Haney and Anita I. Malebranche (Humanities Division) and Glenn McMullen (Special Collections), Newman Library, Virginia Polytechnic Institute and State University.

West wishes to thank the librarians and staff of the National Humanities Center, where he began his portion of the work on this volume. James M. Hutchisson, while working as West's research assistant, found the clue in the Dreiser Papers that pointed the way to Kromer's fugitive publications in the *Pacific Weekly.*

Casciato wishes to thank Charlie Ayer, Jeanne Siraco, Susan Yates, Michele Eayrs, and Rhoda Valentine of the Dodge Library, Northeastern University, and the staff of the McGregor Room, Alderman Library, University of Virginia.

WRITINGS BY AND ABOUT
TOM KROMER

WRITINGS BY KROMER

Waiting for Nothing. New York: Alfred A. Knopf, 1935.

Waiting for Nothing. London: Constable and Company, 1935. Introduction by Theodore Dreiser. Autobiographical note by Kromer.

Waiting for Nothing. American Century Series. New York: Hill and Wang, 1968. Photo-offset reissue of the 1935 Knopf text, with Kromer's autobiographical note from the Constable edition on pp. i–ii. Eight impressions through 1977; now out of print.

Les Vagabonds de la faim. French translation by Raoul de Roussy de Sales. Paris: Calman-Levy, 1936.

"Waiting for Nothing," in Louis Filler, ed., *The Anxious Years: America in the Nineteen Thirties.* New York: Capricorn, 1964. Reprints chapter 1 of Kromer's book.

"Waiting for Nothing," in Harvey Swados, ed., *The American Writer and the Great Depression.* Indianapolis: Bobbs-Merrill, 1966. Reprints chapter 11 of Kromer's book. Note by Swados on Kromer, pp. 351–52.

"From *Waiting for Nothing,*" in Jack Salzman, ed., *Years of Protest: A Collection of American Writings of the 1930's.* New York: Pegasus, 1967. Reprints chapter 8 of Kromer's book.

"Pity the Poor Panhandler; $2 An Hour is All He Gets." *Huntington Herald-Dispatch,* March 1, 1929, pp. 1, 4.

"Murder in Stockton." *Pacific Weekly,* May 10, 1935, pp. 224–25.

"Cameo" ["When the little blonde with the pipestem legs"]. *Pacific Weekly*, May 31, 1935, p. 257.

"Cameo" ["Ruthie had dark hair"]. *Pacific Weekly*, June 7, 1935, p. 273.

"A Very Sad Blurb." Review of Edward Anderson, *Hungry Men*. *Pacific Weekly*, June 21, 1935, pp. 299–300.

"A Very Sad Young Man." *New Masses*, June 25, 1935, pp. 27–28. A variant version of the previous item, likely written originally for *New Masses* and expanded for *Pacific Weekly*.

"Cameo" ["She rented No. 6 on the third floor"]. *Pacific Weekly*, August 26, 1935, p. 88.

"Modern Man." *New Mexico Quarterly* 6 (May 1936): 134–35. Contribution to a symposium on Harvey Fergusson's *Modern Man* (New York: Knopf, 1936).

"Hungry Men," part 1 of a three-part story. *Pacific Weekly*, July 13, 1936, p. 24.

"The Consequences Taken." *Pacific Weekly*, September 7, 1936, pp. 153–54.

"More Hungry Men," part 2 of a three-part story. *Pacific Weekly*, September 28, 1936, pp. 205–6.

"Black Damp: A Story of the Mines." *American Spectator*, September 1936, pp. 8–9. Revised version of chapters 3 and 4 of "Michael Kohler."

" '1934,' " part 3 of a three-part story. *Pacific Weekly*, October 26, 1936, pp. 267–68.

"Too Pretty." Review of William Cunningham, *Pretty Boy*. *New Masses*, November 10, 1936, pp. 25–26.

"A Glass Worker Dies." *Pacific Weekly*, November 16, 1936, pp. 326–27.

"Michael Kohler." *West Virginia Heritage Encyclopedia*, supplementary series, vol. 24 (1974), pp. 320–58.

REVIEWS OF *WAITING FOR NOTHING*

Fred T. Marsh. "Absolutely Down and Out." *Books*, March 3, 1935, p. 2.

Edward Newhouse. "Why Wait?" *New Masses,* March 12, 1935, p. 25.

F. F. K. "A Young Hobo." *New York Times Book Review,* March 17, 1935, p. 12.

Dorothy Brewster. "Men on the Bottom." *Nation,* March 27, 1935, p. 365.

Roland Mulhauser. "Bum and Mission Stiff." *Saturday Review of Literature,* March 30, 1935, p. 584.

Robert Cantwell. "Bound Nowhere." *New Republic,* April 10, 1935, pp. 251–52.

Robin Howe. "Which Arrives." *Pacific Weekly,* April 26, 1935, p. 203.

John Chamberlain. "The World in Books." *Current History* 42 (April 1935): iii.

Derek Verschoyle. "Primitive Societies." *Spectator,* June 28, 1935, p. 1114.

"Waiting for Nothing." *Times Literary Supplement,* July 11, 1935, p. 442.

"An American Down-and-out." *Saturday Review,* July 13, 1935, p. 886.

Peter Quennell. "New Novels." *New Statesman and Nation,* July 13, 1935, pp. 67–68.

R.K.M. Review of *Waiting for Nothing. Boston Transcript,* September 25, 1935, p. 3.

Kenneth Rexroth. "Stiffs on the Road." *New York Times Book Review,* April 21, 1968, pp. 50–51. Review of 1968 Hill and Wang reissue of *Waiting for Nothing.*

OTHER ITEMS

Jim Comstock, "Tom Kromer." *West Virginia Hillbilly,* November 23, 1968, pp. 8, 16.

Jim Comstock. "Tom Kromer and the British." *West Virginia Heritage Encyclopedia,* supplementary series, vol. 14 (1974), pp. 120–22.

Frances Gray. *"Waiting for Nothing:* Tom Kromer, 1906–1969." Ph.D. diss., State University of New York at Stony Brook, 1978.

CPSIA information can be obtained at www.ICGtesting.com
Printed in the USA
LVOW101035181111

255487LV00001B/21/A